A Seller's Market

Market

A Young Jesse McDermitt Novel

Tropical Adventure Series
Volume 1

◆ ◆ ◆ ◆

Wayne Stinnett

 **DOWN ISLAND PRESS**

Copyright © 2023
Published by DOWN ISLAND PRESS, 2023
Beaufort, SC
Copyright © 2023 by Wayne Stinnett

Library of Congress cataloging-in-publication Data
Stinnett, Wayne
A Seller's Market/Wayne Stinnett
p. cm. – (A Young Jesse McDermitt Novel)
ISBN: 978-1-956026-70-2
Edited by Marsha Zinberg, The Write Touch
Final Proofreading by Donna Rich
Graphics and Interior Design by Aurora Publicity

This is a work of fiction. Names, characters, and incidents are either the product of the authors' imagination or are used fictitiously. Any resemblance to actual persons, living or dead, businesses, companies, events, or locales is entirely coincidental. Most of the locations herein are also fictional or are used fictitiously. However, the authors take great pains to depict the location and description of the many well-known islands, locales, beaches, reefs, bars, and restaurants throughout the Florida Keys and the Caribbean to the best of their ability.

If you'd like to receive my newsletter, please sign up on my website.

WWW.WAYNESTINNETT.COM.

Once a month, I'll bring you insights into my private life and writing habits, with updates on what I'm working on, special deals I hear about, and new books by other authors that I'm reading.

Also by Wayne Stinnett

The Jerry Snyder Caribbean Mystery Series

Wayward Sons   Voudoo Child

The Charity Styles Caribbean Thriller Series

Merciless Charity   Vigilant Charity
Ruthless Charity   Lost Charity
Reckless Charity   Elusive Charity
Enduring Charity   Liable Charity

The Jesse McDermitt Caribbean Adventure Series

Fallen Out	Rising Force	Rising Tide
Fallen Palm	Rising Charity	Steady As She Goes
Fallen Hunter	Rising Water	All Ahead Full
Fallen Pride	Rising Spirit	Man Overboard
Fallen Mangrove	Rising Thunder	Cast Off
Fallen King	Rising Warrior	Fish On!
Fallen Honor	Rising Moon	
Fallen Tide	Rising Tide	
Fallen Angel		
Fallen Hero		
Rising Storm		
Rising Fury		

The Young Jesse McDermitt Tropical Adventure Series

A Seller's Market

Non Fiction

Blue Collar to No Collar   No Collar to Tank Top

Chapter One

May 27, 1979
Fort Myers, Florida

The Greyhound bus rolled out of the station and turned right, gray-black diesel smoke belching from its exhaust. It rocked precariously as the rear tires bounced over a curb, which was cracked and disintegrating due to the constant abuse.

A tall young man with short, dark-blond hair sat near the back of the bus and looked out the window at an older couple waving from the front entrance of the bus station.

He knew his grandparents couldn't see him through the bus's tinted windows, but he waved back just the same.

As the Greyhound accelerated away from the station, the young man, fresh out of high school, sat back in his seat and thought about what lay ahead of him.

At barely seventeen, Jesse McDermitt seemed much older than his years—more mature and introspective than most kids. This was due in part to his grandparents' influence. They'd raised him the same way they'd raised his father.

Jesse had not only graduated high school a year early, but had done so with honors, double-lettering in both academics and sports during all three years at Fort Myers High.

Throughout Jesse's senior year, several colleges had sent representatives to talk to the talented runner, receiver, and defensive back, who could play both sides of the ball equally well. But Jesse had other plans for his life. And those plans involved serving others, not himself. So, the college scouts were politely told no.

The bus ride was the *end* of nine years of preparation. What lay at the end of the bus ride was what Jesse considered his destiny, his future.... His beginning.

He'd always known it would be.

Just nine years earlier, when Jesse was in the second grade, he'd come home from school one day to find his grandparents in the living room with his mother. Both women were crying.

Pap had risen from the couch, suddenly looking years older, and very sad. His mom had broken down even more when Pap sat young Jesse down and, in a shaky, halting voice, had explained that Jesse's father, Mam and Pap's only child, had been killed while serving in Vietnam.

The information came as quite a blow to the young man, and he could remember collapsing into his grandfather's arms and sobbing.

The old man had held him tightly, rocking and sobbing with him.

"Be strong, little man," Pap had whispered in his ear. "Your daddy would want you to. If he could, he'd tell you to look after your mama. She's going to need you more than ever now." His voice had gotten really choked up and tears had rolled down the old man's cheeks as he'd muttered, "You're all we have left of my boy."

Jesse remembered looking over at his mother, sitting straight-backed on the edge of the sofa, hands resting on tightly pressed knees, with tears running down her cheeks as she looked at him expectantly.

He'd wiped his nose, rubbing his hand on his jeans, and then went to her and held onto her tightly as she cried. Mam and Pap had then wrapped them both with their arms and their love.

But it wasn't enough for Mom, he thought.

Just a week after that, Jesse came home to find Mam and Pap sitting alone in his living room. His mom had taken an overdose of the tranquilizers the doctor had given her to cope with the grief of losing the only man she'd ever loved.

Jesse McDermitt had become an orphan.

He'd stayed with his grandparents for several weeks after that, keeping to himself mostly, until one day, Pap announced that they all had to go to the courthouse.

There, a judge had decreed, "Since Bowie McDermitt's widow, Helen McDermitt, died with no immediate family, the petition for custody of the minor child, Jesiah Smedley McDermitt, age eight, born March 20, 1962, is hereby granted to his paternal grandparents, Frank and Norma McDermitt." Then he'd banged his gavel. "Next case!"

That'd been just three days after the end of school, and during that summer, Mam and Pap had kept young Jesse busy, doing the "hard chores" that Mam said Pap was getting too old for.

But the old man had been right beside him throughout that long, hot, humid summer. For the most part, they toiled silently—the tasks simple. Their property was large, built way before the neighborhood that grew up nearby, and it needed work.

"Your dad and I did all the two-man jobs whenever he came home," Pap had told Jesse one day. "Think you can do some man-sized work? It'd save me having to hire someone."

They mowed the three-acre yard, trimmed dozens of trees on two adjacent lots, pruned bushes, cleared debris from the wooded areas, then started to work on the fence, replacing every board and post all the way around the property.

"Good fences make good neighbors," the old man had once told him. "Not that you can't trust your neighbor, but family always comes first, and family is what's *inside* the fence. So, a man's got to protect his fence."

After a few weeks, Jesse's skin had darkened like Pap's. They'd finished the fence and all the other work that needed doing, including a few things Jesse had been sure his grandfather had just made up.

They both grieved, and the hard work turned out to be their common way of dealing with it. So, they worked, barely talking, each of them figuring out in their own head how to move forward—how to accept this new relationship.

One morning in July, young Jesse had walked out to the backyard to find his grandfather standing on the edge of the deck, looking out toward the Caloosahatchee, its dark waters flowing slowly, inexorably past the property, as it had for thousands of years.

"How'd you like to help me build a boat, little man?" Pap asked one day, a twinkle in his eye.

Whenever Jesse's father was home, they'd spent a lot of time at Mam and Pap's house, and Jesse remembered how his dad had helped his grandfather with work around the property.

And he remembered how his father had talked about Pap's boatyard and the boat they were building together.

"At your boatyard?" Jesse remembered asking.

"That's right," Pap had replied. "You've never been there."

Throughout the summer, they'd cut boards together—Jesse holding each board in place while Pap cut it, using long, smooth strokes with a handsaw. Pap had demonstrated how to operate the steam box and showed him a book that told how long to steam all kinds of wood to make the boards bendable. He showed Jesse how to drill holes using a hand drill, and they'd hammered hard wooden pegs into place with wooden mallets. They'd spent hours planing and sanding large beams by hand, and stuffing cotton caulking in the narrow gaps in the wood planking.

They'd worked quietly for many weeks, toiling and sweating, and the only words Jesse heard were his grandfather's patient instructions.

"Take your time and do things right," Pap had told him several times as they worked. "Slow is smooth, and smooth is fast. Nothing adds more time to a project than having to do something twice because you rushed it the first time."

Jesse'd barely heard the old man's words in the early days and didn't even know what it was they were working on, except the boards were part of a boat. He was still trying to figure out why things had happened the way they had. None of his friends' parents had ever died before.

He hadn't met any other kids in Mam and Pap's part of the neighborhood; there weren't many, and he hadn't felt like seeking out a playmate, anyway. His old neighborhood was just a short bike ride away, but he didn't feel like answering the questions he was sure his friends would ask him.

His dad's friend, Bill Rainwater, Sr., had called and talked to Pap just a week after Jesse's mother died. His son, Billy, was the same age as Jesse, and they'd met each other many times and were friends, but they lived in the next town over—LaBelle. Pap had told Bill, Sr. that Jesse would call Billy when he was ready.

So, he spent his days with Pap.

Somehow, he had simply known that the hard work was good. The constant drudgery in the stuffy heat of South Florida made him feel better.

He asked himself questions and then sorted out the answers, working through them one at a time, methodically, the only way an eight-year-old boy could.

The old radio in Pap's workshop always played soft, instrumental music. "Cool jazz," Pap had called it. As they worked, the old man would often tell Jesse who the artists were and something about them that he'd found interesting.

He learned the names Chet Baker, Dave Brubeck, Bill Evans, John Coltrane, Gil Evans, Stan Getz, and many more. He learned to recognize the artists' differing styles and often guessed them correctly.

As the summer weeks rolled by, the boy and his grandfather continued their labors, barely noticing the time or day. They spent every day except Sunday at Pap's workshop at the boatyard on the bank of the Peace River, several miles north of where they lived.

Jesse's world of home, neighborhood, and school grew to include two rivers, and over the years he'd learned to love them both, as well as the body of water they flowed into—Pine Island Sound.

It wasn't long before Jesse and his grandfather started talking as they set about their tasks. Jesse had become familiar with each process and didn't need a lot of instruction.

They talked about a lot of things—Pap mostly explaining the ways of the world, and how all people are interconnected and should cooperate. At noon each day, they listened to the news.

Often it was about the fighting in Vietnam.

Jesse didn't like hearing about that and said as much to his grandfather.

Pap had turned Jesse's chin up to look him in the eye. "Don't hide from it, boy. There are mean people in the world, and you can't ever back down from them. If someone hits you, you hit 'em back...

harder. If they go big, you go bigger. Force is the only thing evil understands. You gotta meet them with even greater force and overwhelm them. That means the forces inside *yourself*, too. You should never hide from what frightens you. Not even from yourself. Evil won't hide."

One day while taking a Coke break by the riverbank, Jesse asked his grandfather if it was okay to still feel sad for his mom and dad.

"Your mama, yes," Pap had told him. "Helen was a special woman; she had a way of drawing out whatever pain Bo was feeling. I guess it just all built up in her." He paused, as his eyes moistened. Then he looked down at Jesse. "But don't ever feel sad for Bo. I don't. I feel sad for the pain your mom held in her heart. And I feel sad for you, no longer having two of the finest people in your life that ever existed. I feel sad for your Mam, and I am sad for losing him. But I'm not sad *for* him, Jesse."

He remembered his grandfather's eyes as he gazed out over the river that day. "Bo died protecting others, just as I'd taught him. There's a line good people don't ever cross. When *bad* people cross that line, good people get hurt. If there isn't someone on the other side of that line to stop them, the bad people will surely cross over it."

"You were a Marine too, right, Pap?" he'd asked.

"Still am," the old man had replied with a grin. "Once a Marine, always a Marine. There's no expiration date or limitations on the oaths your father and I both took. If called today, even though I'm an old man, I'd take up the fight again."

He'd paused then, looking out over the dark waters of the river.

"While I might not agree with some of the things you hear people saying on the news," he'd finally said, his voice sounding fierce with conviction, "all these protests and all, I *will* stand and fight to the death for their right to say it. *That* was the oath we took."

7

There was something in his grandfather's tone when he'd spoken those words that had impressed Jesse. He'd begun to see his grandfather a little differently after that.

Sometimes, a friend of the old man would stop by, and they'd talk quietly in a corner, occasionally glancing over at Jesse as he continued to work.

One day in late August, a man in a suit came by. It had been a brutally hot day and Jesse had welcomed it when Pap had told him to take a break, that the two of them had to sit down and talk to the stranger—and that what he had to say involved both of them.

"I only had the one child," Pap had told the man. "Jesse here is *his* only child—my and Norma's only heir. Sell the business. Jackson's offer is a fair one. He needs the work, and I don't. That money goes into a trust for later. Tell the O'Haras I accept their offer for the house, too, and put that into a regular savings account at my bank in the boy's name."

"And the Servicemen's Group Life Insurance?" the man had asked. "It's a quarter million."

His grandfather had looked over at Jesse and asked, "You been paying attention in Bible study, boy?"

Jesse remembered nodding somberly, sure that he was about to learn something very important.

"Is money the root of all evil?" Pap had then asked him in a very serious tone.

"No, sir," Jesse had responded quickly and with great confidence. It was something he and Mam and Pap talked about a lot. "Money can be used to help others get back up and do great things. It's the *love* of money that is evil. It's one of the seven sins—greed."

Pap had given him a rare smile that day. "I'll sign that SGLI policy you were just asking about over to him, too," he'd told the man. "He'll get my Veteran's Group policy one day, also. In sixty years or so, when he retires, he'll be comfortable."

Pap had nodded firmly at him, then turned back to the man. "Same account."

"And you're sure about selling the business?" the man had asked.

Pap had turned to Jesse and studied his face for a moment before replying to the man. "One of these days, everything will be his, but I don't think being an architect is in this boy's future." Then he'd turned back to the stranger. "Yes, sell it all, except the boatyard."

He went on to tell the man that the work they were doing in the shop was a labor of love for him, something he and Jesse's father had done together when Bo had been a boy.

"I don't have a hell of a lot of time left," Pap had explained to the man, then put his arm around Jesse. "I wasn't finished teaching Bo, and I need to give this kid *two* lifetimes of learning before he's ready for the world."

Am I ready for the world? Jesse thought, as the bus lurched away from a traffic light.

It rolled through another little town, and as he watched the pine forest slide past through the window, his mind drifted again.

When that first September living with his grandparents came along, Jesse had asked Pap about school and Pap had told him that he wasn't to worry about that just now; that he was learning far more at the boatyard and in the shop than he ever would in any classroom.

Pap was old school—set in his ways; he preferred hand tools over power saws and drill motors. A handshake was a man's bond—he had no need for lengthy contracts, and most deals were cash.

And Pap declared every penny on his taxes. "Mind your pennies, boy," he'd told him. "And your dollars will take care of themselves."

Pap was a man who didn't finish high school until after he'd come home from the South Pacific in 1945, returning to the classroom as a twenty-three-year-old combat-hardened Marine. He'd gone on to college on the G.I. Bill at University of Florida, way up in Gainesville, where he'd earned a degree in architectural design. He'd built his own business from the ground up, working out of his small garage and shop behind the house.

"Florida's grown a lot since I was your age," Pap had once told him. "I had a hand in that. But I think it's growing too much and too fast these days."

"Slow is smooth," Jesse had replied. "And smooth is fast."

He remembered how Pap had laughed when he'd said that. He liked the old man's laugh.

Chapter
Two

$\bullet$ —— $\bullet$ —— $\bullet$ —— $\bullet$ —— $\bullet$

Jesse had skipped third grade that year, continuing to work in the shop, and when Pap enrolled him the following year, he'd insisted the boy was ready for fifth grade. Indeed, by then Jesse was physically taller than the guidance counselor and he'd scored high enough on the tests to move into junior high if they wanted, thanks mostly to Mam's insistence on three hours of study per day, every day.

On Sunday, there was study, too—Bible study.

Rather than skip another year, Pap had compromised and the following fall, Jesse had started back to school a year ahead of the few friends he'd met, including his closest friend, Billy Rainwater, who lived way out in LaBelle.

Since their fathers were close friends, Jesse and Billy had known each other practically their whole lives. But it wasn't until one day at a local playground, when Jesse came across two bullies picking on Billy because of his skin color and ponytail, that their friendship had been cemented.

Billy was a member of the Calusa people, the original inhabitants of that part of Southwest Florida.

One time when his dad was home, Jesse remembered him suddenly pulling to the curb and running to the aid of a man who was in a brawl with two other men, helping the single man simply because he needed assistance and not even knowing what the altercation was about.

So, Jesse had done the same thing, going at the two older boys with all the fury his nine-year-old body could muster.

He and Billy became best friends after that and soon, they became blood brothers.

Jesse had gone on to excel in middle school, grew even taller and, thanks to the long hours toiling in the hot South Florida sun, he'd packed on a lot of long, sinewy muscle that only got stronger as he grew older.

In his junior year of high school, Pap had taken Jesse to a sort of career fair at his school, with people from many industries talking to all the kids one-on-one about their futures in the job market.

Behind one table stood a man wearing a uniform, one Jesse recognized.

He led Pap past several tables, and then stopped in front of the man in uniform.

Pap had extended a hand to the man. "Semper Fi, Gunny," was all Pap needed to say to get the man's full attention and immediate respect.

He'd responded in kind, and though just a teenager, Jesse could see there was an instantaneous and very strong connection between the two men. A bond that transcended generations.

He and Pap had exchanged several short sentences, Pap mentioning dates and places from his past—Guadalcanal, Cape Gloucester, Peleliu, Iwo Jima, and Okinawa. The gunny's eyes widened more with each place Pap named.

Then the gunny had spoken of places like Da Nang, Khe Sahn, Hue City—all places Jesse remembered his father speaking of when he'd come home on leave.

"My dad was with the Twenty-Sixth Marines in Khe Sahn when he was killed," Jesse had proudly said to the gunny. "He was a staff sergeant."

"What's your name, kid?" the man had asked.

Without even thinking, Jesse gave his full given name. "Jesiah Smedley McDermitt, sir."

The gunny had just stood there and looked at him for a long moment. "Your dad... was Bo McDermitt?"

"Yes, sir."

The decorated Marine's eyes moistened. "I knew your dad, kid," he'd choked out. "He saved my life during a firefight in...." Then he'd turned to Pap. "I was with your son when he died, sir. He spoke highly of you. Toughest man I ever knew."

Pap had never talked much about his time in the Marine Corps, except about all the fun things he and his buddies had gotten away with while on leave. When he was home, his dad had only talked about how beautiful the country was.

Neither had ever talked of war, conflict, or the carnage they both must have witnessed, nor of the personal loss and the pain they felt of that loss.

Pap had also never brought up the idea that Jesse might enlist.

That was the day that had changed young Jesse's life forever and put him on that bus, on a collision course with the Big Green Machine.

The bus slowed and started to lean as it exited the interstate. Then it hit a small bump in the off-ramp, jarring Jesse out of his thoughts. His stomach growled, telling him it was close to dinnertime.

In Jesse's pocket were just four things—a one-way bus ticket to Parris Island, South Carolina, a neatly folded envelope with his orders to report for basic training, his Florida driver's license, and the change from a hundred-dollar bill.

An hour before dawn, he'd had an early breakfast with his grandparents at the new Waffle House near their home in North Fort Myers, and he'd bought a burger and fries when the bus had stopped in Ocala at noon.

The Greyhound turned right, and Jesse saw a sign telling him it was going east on US-90. He sat back in his seat. It was a long way to Parris Island, and Jacksonville was about the halfway point, he guessed.

He'd brought the book that Pap had given him over breakfast. It was just an old mystery by an author Jesse had never heard of. Mam had said she'd picked it up in a yard sale for a quarter to give to Pap, then told him to just drop it in a trash can before getting on the last bus to Parris Island.

"The only thing you'll need to take on the island with you is your license and orders," Pap had explained. "You won't even see those clothes you got on until August, and they probably won't fit by then."

He'd also given Jesse one last word of advice over breakfast.

"Follow your last order first, son," he'd told him. "Your DIs will give you conflicting orders. One'll say do this and when he walks away, another will say do that. And each will seem angry when they come back and see you're not doing what they'd told you to do. Just snap to attention and say in a firm and steady voice, 'Sir, Sergeant So-and-so told the private to do this."

He'd gone on to explain that they'd go back and forth, each demanding to know why their task wasn't being performed, in an attempt to confuse a recruit. Neither could fault him if he simply followed his last order first and when that changed, follow the next one and the next one.

"Jacksonville," the driver's bored voice announced over the speakers. "Next stop, Jacksonville, Florida. *All* passengers will change buses in Jacksonville."

Now standing six-three in his bare feet and tipping the scale at over two hundred pounds, Jesse still had a boyish face. But between the hard physical labor his grandfather had him doing for nearly a decade and which he'd come to dearly love, the workouts for high school football, and the cross-country running he and Billy did, his face was at complete odds with his physique.

Jesse thought back to the previous night and his going-away party at the marina, where Pap kept their latest build—a thirty-foot, cat-rigged ketch that had tons of sail area but could still go under a forty-foot bridge.

Pap was a past commodore of the local yachting club and he and Jesse had built four of the boats docked at the marina, including the one owned by the marina's manager, Ben Kovak, who'd pulled out all the stops to make sure Jesse's party was a success.

When Billy arrived, he'd introduced Jesse to a girl from Labelle, a friend of his girlfriend who'd tagged along.

Cathy was tall and slim, with long, very fine blond hair that the light breeze liked to play with. The two had escaped to Pap's boat, where they sat on the cabin top and watched the sunset.

"I love to watch the sun go down in the evening," she'd told him. "It's so peaceful and beautiful."

"I like to think about what I did that day," he said, watching the sun get closer and closer to the water. "I wonder if something I did might have made the world a little bit better."

"And what mistakes you might have made that day?" Cathy asked, pushing her hair back behind her ear.

Jesse nodded. "I think about what I might have done differently, so I don't make that mistake again."

She'd smiled at him, and Jesse had smiled back, looking deeply into the bluest eyes he'd ever seen.

"Billy told me you were a really old soul," Cathy said. "He was right."

The bus slowed and turned sharply, bouncing over another curb, then angling into a parking spot next to another bus.

"Jacksonville," the driver announced. "Don't leave anything on the bus. Everyone will change buses here for all points north, south, and west."

Jesse rose and moved quickly toward the front, while other passengers wrestled with bags, kids, and pillows.

When he entered the terminal, escaping from the oppressive heat and diesel fumes outside, it was only slightly cooler.

He headed to the board that showed arrivals and departures, checked his ticket, and saw that the next bus he'd be on wasn't leaving for forty minutes.

The ticket agent glanced up at him. "Need help, son?" she asked.

"Is there a place to eat?"

She smiled and pointed toward a bank of doors on the opposite side from where he'd come in. "Out one of those doors and turn right. There's a diner right next door."

He nodded and said thanks, then hurried toward the door. He'd been hoping for a McDonalds or Burger King—something faster than a diner. He didn't want to miss the bus.

When he entered the place, there was only one stool available at the counter. Jesse started to turn around, thinking the wait would be too long, but then the smells forced him to move forward. He sat down between a man in a rumpled suit and a short kid around his own age with red hair.

"What can I get ya?" the waitress behind the counter asked, chewing a wad of gum.

"Cheeseburger with everything, please," Jesse replied. "Medium, with fries and a Coke."

"Be just a minute," she replied, scribbling on her notepad.

"It'll be pretty quick," the red-haired kid said. "I just sat down three minutes ago. Where ya headed?"

"Parris Island, South Carolina," Jesse replied.

"Thought so," he said, sticking out a hand. "Name's Jim. Jim Thurman. I'm headed there, too."

The two shook hands, then Jesse looked out the windows at the tall buildings. He'd been to Miami before, but Jacksonville was a much bigger, industrialized city.

Jesse's burger came quickly, as promised, and Jim waited around till he'd wolfed it down, chugged the Coke, and paid the waitress.

When Jesse stood up, Jim looked up at him in surprise. "Dang, man. How tall are you?"

"Six-three," he replied, realizing the guy was shorter than he'd first thought.

"I just made the height limit," Jim said. "They called guys like me 'tunnel rats' in Vietnam."

"I know," Jesse said, pushing the door open. "My dad died there."

"No shit? Sorry for bringin' it up, bro. Where ya from?"

"You didn't know," Jesse replied. "I'm from Fort Myers. You?"

"Middle Keys," Jim replied, as they reentered the bus terminal. "A little town called Marathon. I'm a fifth-generation Conch. That's what ya call someone born in the Keys."

"Not many of us native Floridians," Jesse replied. "My grandfather was born in Fort Myers, too."

"Tell me about it, man," Jim said, then pointed. "I think that's us over there. More'n half the folks that come into my dad's bar and bait shop are Yankee tourists."

They got in line to board the bus and got their tickets ready, neither carrying anything more than what they had in their pockets.

Jesse slid into a window seat and Jim sat down next to him. "You get a guaranteed contract?"

"Infantry," Jesse replied. "Oh-three-eleven, like my dad and Pap."

"That's your grandpa? Get to see him much?"

Jesse looked over at the guy, now realizing that he was a couple of years older.

"My mom committed suicide after my dad was killed," he said matter-of-factly. "Mam and Pap have raised me since I was eight."

"Ah, shit, man," Jim said. "That's some tough stuff right there."

"It is what it is," Jesse said with a shrug. "What's your contract?"

"Open contract," Jim replied, as the door closed, and the bus's engine started.

Jesse nodded. "You'll be in infantry, too, then."

Jim grinned. "Hell, man, I didn't even think to ask if I could get infantry as a contract."

Chapter Three

———◆———◆———◆———◆———

Big Pine Key, Florida

An attractive, auburn-haired woman in business attire and heels paced back and forth across the tile floor in a large, but entirely empty living room. Her heels clicked on the ceramic tile and the sound echoed throughout the house, seeming to punctuate the woman's impatience.

She wore a navy skirt, just above her knees, with a modest slit that exposed a flash of her right thigh with each step. Her blouse was pale blue, more closely matching her eyes, and her auburn tresses cascaded softly over her shoulders like a lion's mane. Her skin wasn't as pale as most women with her hair color, due to being in the bright, South Florida sun regularly. She wore red lipstick and minimal makeup.

Though she was thirty-eight, Skylar Rizzi was carded almost every time she ordered a drink.

Well, sometimes.

Sky, as her friends called her, was usually a very patient, deliberate woman. In her line of work, she had to be. Homeowners and homebuyers were a skittish bunch, and they needed to be cajoled and gently guided to the ultimate goal—buying or selling a pile of sticks and bricks.

In this case, the hard part was finished; she'd gotten the seller to list with her, and they had agreed not only on the asking price, but also on the renovations needed and a good budget and timetable to work with.

The couple who owned the home lived out of state and the house on Big Pine Key was their winter vacation retreat.

And they wanted to move up.

If all went well with the renovation and sale, she'd not only make a nice commission, but might gain a client if she became the couple's agent when they started shopping for the next vacation home. They didn't want to start looking until their current one was under contract, but the man had made it very clear that if Sky did a good job for him, she'd get that contract, as well.

Damned placating misogynistic Yankee, she thought. *If I did my job well?*

"Times are a-changing, Dr. Snodgrass, sir," she said aloud, her faux subservient voice also echoing.

Sky had been in the real estate business for twenty-one years, ever since the summer before her senior year of high school, when she'd done an internship for a real estate company in Marathon. Her duties mostly consisted of making coffee, filing things, and making copies of listing ads, but she'd kept her eyes and ears open and learned more during that summer than the whole time she'd spent in classes to get her real estate agent's license.

Soon after graduating and getting her agent's license, she became the youngest female real estate agent employed in Monroe County, a field that was still dominated by men.

The firm she'd interned with that summer and eventually landed a job with after graduating was owned by two brothers. They'd inherited the business from their father, who had been one of the biggest real estate magnates in South Florida during the Prohibition years.

Back then, a lot of people living in the Keys became very rich smuggling rum from Cuba. These days, it was marijuana from Mexico and cocaine from South America. But the opportunity was still there.

Sky had always suspected that that was where the brothers' *real* money had come from, because they sucked as Realtors and, even if they'd only listened to half of what their father told them, then he sucked too. Sky and the other agents were all that had kept the firm afloat for more than a decade.

Then, on the same day she'd finally passed the test and received her Realtor's license, the brothers had announced they were retiring and selling the business.

For a very brief moment, Sky had been tempted to ask how much, but then quickly realized it would be too much. Sky had decided right then and there to start her own agency and build it her own way.

By the end of the day, three of her coworkers had agreed to come to work for her as soon as she had an office.

That was taken care of the very next day, but for the first few weeks, they worked sitting on the bare floor or upturned briefcases, until Sky could convince the banker to loan her money to buy furniture.

By then, two of her agents had already closed on pocket listings they had been nurturing but never signed with the brothers. And they had contracts on two more houses and offers in on three as buyer brokers.

The Sky Rizzi Real Estate firm was cash-flow positive right out of the gate.

But Sky had known it wouldn't always be like that. The stars had simply aligned that first week, and the timing on several deals had come to fruition at the same time.

She'd gotten lucky, and she knew it.

But she made sure those starting numbers always stayed in the black, putting some of her own savings into the business early on to keep it afloat. She soon added three more hungry agents, and later, two more. Over the last ten years, her agency had grown and had become one of the premier Realtors in the Florida Keys.

When Sky heard the loud rumble of a motorcycle, she headed to the front door. She opened it and stood in the doorway, feet apart and hands on her hips.

A bearded biker in a leather vest rode slowly up the long, crushed limestone driveway.

The biker stopped, put the kickstand down, and shut off the engine, all without taking his eyes off Sky.

"Where've you been?" she demanded. "You were supposed to be here half an hour ago."

The burly guy smiled, showing perfect teeth. He had deep laugh lines at the corners of his dark brown eyes.

"Sorry, it couldn't be helped," he said. "Ran into a snag on another job. This place all cleared out?"

"Come and see for yourself," Sky said, turning on her fashionable heels and disappearing inside.

The biker trotted up the steps and caught up to her in the middle of the living room. He grabbed her around the waist from behind and lifted her off the ground.

"Where you wanna do it first?" he asked, as she leaned back against him, relishing the man's strength.

Then she remembered her next meeting.

"Cool it, Norbert," she said, and he put her back down. "Your tardiness put *me* behind schedule."

"You know I don't like that," he huffed.

"Oh, yes," she said with a glimmer in her eye. "You prefer Bert, right?"

"That's just as bad," he replied, then grinned. "But you can call me anything you want in bed, baby."

"I'm in a hurry, Bear," she said, patting him on his scruffy cheek. "I have to meet another client up on Long Key in less than an hour."

"Where do we start?"

For the next twenty minutes, Sky showed her boyfriend, who was a licensed building contractor, the work the homeowner wanted done.

He nodded and asked a few pointed questions as she talked, looking around the kitchen with a practiced eye.

"I like it," he said. "It ain't a bearin' wall and it'll really open things up. I remember you sayin' that's a big selling point."

"Without that wall, the kitchen becomes a part of the main living area," Sky said, moving her hands apart as if opening a curtain. "Great for entertaining."

"Yeah, well it ain't gonna be cheap or fast," Bear said. "Those Italian marble countertops and island are what's gonna take a while. Not to mention gettin' *matching* marble floor tile. It won't take me but a few days to make some detailed drawin's and a mockup. Then I'll have to order it from a quarry in Italy." He paused. "The tile's gotta match the countertops?"

Sky nodded. "His wife is emphatic about that."

Bear scratched the side of his face. "Not a lot of quarries do both. Even up in New England."

"Do you know of one in Italy?"

"Well, yeah, but they ain't cheap and it's a fortune to ship."

"The seller has deep pockets," she replied. "And insisted on Italian marble. Can you do it for the budget I gave you?"

"Just openin' up the kitchen and renovatin' it and two bathrooms?"

WAYNE STINNETT

Sky nodded. "The hardwood floors are in good shape but may need some repairs when the wall comes out."

Bear chuckled. "It'll be enough, even if we have to replace the carpet in the bedrooms, should you wanna give my plan a trial run. It sounds like we've got the time. But when it's done, the carpet's gonna stink."

"I don't know, Bear. It sounds risky and I don't know if it's worth it. I have a business and reputation."

"How many bedrooms?"

"Four," she replied. "Plus a three-car garage."

"Whoa!" Bear exclaimed. "Baby, this is the motherlode. It'll be at least three months on the marble anyway. We can harvest right after it gets here. And you're sure the owners won't show up?"

"They're vacationing in Europe," she said, smiling, "and they're not scheduled to return to Boston until just before Christmas. With luck, they won't be coming down here until the first of the year and then they move right into a new vacation home up on Grassy Key."

"More'n enough time," Bear said. "How big are the bedrooms?"

She crooked a finger, and he followed her across the room, where she opened a door. "This is the master. It's almost three hundred square feet."

His eyes fell to the hardwood floor as he tapped a meaty fist against his broad chest. "Be still my heart. Just this and the garage will give us a good five or six hundred pounds, and we won't have to replace no carpet or lug equipment upstairs."

"The other bedrooms are carpeted."

"All the more reason to just stay downstairs," Bear said. "Why be greedy?"

"And you're sure you can grow it in less than four months?"

"It's a weed," he said. "The real trick is controllin' the growth and gettin' it to bud at just the right time. Hell, just this room and

24

the garage, we're looking at a payday of at least a half mil for us.'"

"You're kidding!"

"Good pot's hard to come by, what with all the sprayin' they're doin' down south. Folks are nervous about that shit. Hydroponics is the only way to go. With the right seeds and equipment, I can beat the best in both quality and potency. *And* grow it in almost half the time.'"

"What about the smell?" Sky asked, her doubts slowly succumbing to the numbers Bear was giving her. "You mentioned the carpet. Would it be smelled outside?"

He pointed up to the vents in the ceiling. "Central air. I can plug the vents in this bedroom, seal the door, and put a window air conditioner in and crank it down when it's time for the plants to bud. Any smell will be kept just in this room. It don't permeate finished wood or drywall—not like it does carpet, anyway, and my guys will do a complete cleanup after we harvest."

He nodded toward a window box seat. "Might have to replace that cushion, and the garage will be tricky."

"Why?"

"No insulation in the walls or ceiling; a window shaker won't be enough to cool that much air."

"I can see how that would be trouble."

"And the garage door isn't airtight," he continued. "But I got a way around that."

"What?"

"Ever see a temporary greenhouse?" Bear asked. "I can build one in the garage out of heavy plastic to keep the skunk-weed odor in and put a window AC in there to cool the smaller volume of air around the greenhouse. Since it'll be cooling less air—what's in the greenhouse won't be circulated with it—the AC won't have to work as hard, and the inside of the greenhouse will be cooled by convection."

"I don't even know what you're talking about," Sky said, shaking her head. "But I trust you about these things."

He chuckled. "I never did like botany in school, but I learned a lot, growing pot out on the West Coast."

"How soon can you start?" Sky asked, still a bit unsure. "And are you certain nobody will know?"

"I can bring a crew in tomorrow, get started setting everything up and begin a very slow demolition of the kitchen."

"What if the neighbors come around, asking what's going on?"

He grinned. "You just walk your sexy ass up to all the neighbors' doors with that gorgeous smile and let them know there'll be ongoing construction until Christmas and promise them the workers will be completely wrapped up for the day and gone before happy hour. And don't forget to remind 'em how property value will go up when you flip this place for a big profit."

"Someone still might come by to see what work was being done."

"Not a problem, babe," Bear replied. "I'll put locks on the doors to the garage and bedroom. Any work being done will be in the kitchen or the upstairs bathroom."

"And this bedroom?" she asked. "Why would it be locked?"

He smiled and moved toward her. "This where ya wanna start?"

"You know what I mean."

"We're waiting to start in here," Bear said, obviously making it up as he went. "The homeowner forgot to leave us the key to the bedroom door."

"Who has a lock on a bedroom?"

Bear grinned lecherously down at her. "People with whips and chains hangin' on the walls?"

"You've done this before?"

26

"Whips and chains? No," he replied, grinning. "But I'm game if you are."

"Bear!" she said, punching his shoulder. "Get serious. I'm in a hurry."

"Lotsa people put key locks on bedrooms," he said. "It's not unusual and if someone asks, my guys'll just shrug."

"But you've done the growing thing before?"

"In a house, just once," he said. "But I have a few outdoor gardens growing up north of here on some remote little islands nobody ever goes to, and I've been puttin' together all the equipment to do a project just like this for a long time, hoping to be able to do one on this scale. Ever since we first talked about it last year."

Sky turned and walked over to the padded window seat, the only place in the house to sit unless she were to jump up onto the kitchen counter.

She sat down and crossed her legs, looking back up at Bear. "And you know how to move it?"

"Baby, I been in the pipeline since I was fourteen. I'll have a cash buyer for the whole crop the day we harvest it. My guys'll cut it and start removing the equipment while the buyer takes care of loading, moving, drying, and distribution. None of it any of our concern."

It *was* a brilliant idea, she had to admit that.

Growing marijuana in a vacant house using the latest hydroponics and grow lights kept everything completely out of sight and, as he'd told her several times, vastly cut the amount of time it took to mature.

Sky had grown grass herself, just never on the scale Bear was talking about. She'd always kept a plant or two on her private balcony at the condo.

Five hundred thousand dollars...

Once renovated, the house they were in would sell for a tidy profit for the owner and her commission would be three percent of the purchase price—double that, if she acted as a dual agent and found a buyer herself, which she fully intended to do. She could easily see the deal being very profitable for her bottom line.

Sky only needed a half dozen good sales like this one to make her year, and her agents always over-delivered.

But this deal? This could be more than her and Bear's combined incomes.

Her eyes went to the ceiling and the three bedrooms above. Double the space—double the income?

Maybe even do it again with another house?

They'd have to be ultra-secretive. All her friends knew she partied, but Sky never did it around strangers or in public. Pot was a lot more acceptable in the Keys than most places, but Sky had a professional public image to maintain.

"Five hundred thousand?" she asked, her eyes sparkling at the possibility. "Just using the downstairs?"

"Maybe... six?" Bear replied, his smile bright in his dark, bushy beard.

Then he winked. "Tax free."

Chapter
Four

◆——————◆————◆————◆————◆

Having someone to talk to helped ease the anxiety Jesse felt. He wasn't worried that he might not be good enough—he'd been preparing for this, both mentally and physically, for most of his life. But he felt an eagerness to get started, to meet the challenge head on.

"Where ya goin' after we graduate?" Jim asked when they crossed the South Carolina border. "We get two weeks off with pay!"

"Home, I guess," Jesse replied. "Pap and I were working on a boat when I left, and he said he'd be just about finished with it when I get back. It's a powerboat this time."

"Yeah, you said earlier that you built a few sailboats with him. How big's this powerboat?"

"Twenty-five feet," Jesse replied. "An offshore fishing boat with a small cabin. He said he's even putting a little kitchen in it. Well, a microwave oven, anyway."

"Pop got one of those for the bar," Jim said. "The county said if he didn't serve hot food, the cost of his liquor license was gonna triple."

"And that counts?"

"Sure does," Jim replied. "He keeps a bunch of Cuban sandwiches, frozen French fries, and microwave dinners in the walk-in cooler and can serve a meal in two minutes."

Jesse belched. "Probably better than that diner."

They both laughed, but then the bus slowed, turning off the highway, and their laughter ceased.

"Yemassee, South Carolina," the driver's voice announced. "Passengers changing buses to Parris Island, this is your stop."

As the bus pulled in front of a small station with a single light on outside, Jim and Jesse got up, as did two other young men, and together, they all headed toward the front of the bus.

The driver stood and turned, shaking each boy's hand. "Semper fi, fellas. Keep your heads down."

The four young men got off the bus and joined two others who were waiting on a bench.

"All y'all goin' to P.I.?" a young black man asked, rising to his feet.

"Looks that way," Jim said, sticking his hand out. "Name's Thurman and this here's McDermitt. We're both from South Florida."

The black guy said his name was Jackson and he was from Georgia. The other three were from Alabama and Virginia.

"Guess all the Yankees are on the overnight buses," Jim said. "Any idea how long before our bus to the island will be here?"

"Every hour on the hour," Jesse replied. "They'll take us to the receiving barracks first. We'll be there for a few days, getting uniforms issued and stuff, and then we'll meet our drill instructors."

"How you know this?" Jackson asked.

"My dad was a Marine, and so is my grandfather. I lived here once."

"Then you oughta know it ain't *was*, cuz," Jackson said, exposing big white teeth in a broad smile. "Once a Marine, huh?"

"His dad died in the Nam," Jim said defensively.

"Oh, sorry, my man," Jackson quickly replied.

"No worries," Jesse offered. "You didn't know."

Another bus pulled in, discharging nine more young men, who clustered together at the other corner of the station.

Headlights appeared in the distance, coming out of a light fog on the marsh.

"I think that's our ride," one of the other boys said. "Parris Island, here we come!"

The bus pulled into the station, then backed into a parking area. The door clunked as the driver operated the handle to swing it open.

"This the bus to Parris Island?" Jackson asked the driver when he stepped down.

"Yep," he replied. "Last stop for you boys for a few months. Just give me your tickets and let me see your folders."

They lined up and the driver took their tickets one by one, giving a cursory glance at each manila envelope as the young men filed onto the the bus.

Jim sat across from Jesse as the bus rolled out of the station with fifteen recruits aboard, turning left and accelerating out of the small town.

"This is it, man," Jim said. "We're almost there. Ya nervous?"

Jesse nodded. "A little, I guess. Just wondering where all this will end up taking me. Hey, you never said where you're going when we finish."

"Home, too, I reckon," Jim replied, craning his neck to see the marsh and the water. "I got a girl there. Her name's Juliet, but I call her Jewels—you know, like sparkly things. We're gonna get married as soon as I get to a permanent duty station, and we save up enough money."

Jesse looked out the window. There was no moon, but the marsh out beyond the road was still visible just by the light of the stars. They passed clumps of live oak trees dripping with Spanish moss, then the marsh would come back into view again. It looked peaceful.

Kind of like one of his favorite places down in the Ten Thousand Islands, but older, almost primordial.

After fifteen minutes, in a small town called Burton, the bus turned right. The sign said it was a truck route around the city of Beaufort.

There was almost no traffic on the roads and less than ten minutes later, the bus rolled through a small town called Shell Point, then slowed and turned right.

Jesse saw a large red and gold sign proclaiming *Marine Corps Recruit Depot, Parris Island, South Carolina*, to the right, illuminated by bright spotlights.

Ahead lay a checkpoint, also brightly lit by surrounding security lights. The bus slowed only slightly as the guard waved it through.

"This is it," Jim said.

"Not yet," Jesse replied. "This is just the causeway to the island."

The bus accelerated, and after crossing what seemed like a mile-wide marsh, it began a series of curves through a pine forest.

Jesse craned his neck as the bus passed the entrance to a neighborhood. It looked familiar, but he didn't remember a lot about when he'd lived there with his parents—he was very young then.

Streetlights appeared ahead and the bus slowed, then turned right, once more.

"There they are," one of the other boys in front said.

Jesse and Jim leaned into the aisle. Ahead was a large parking area, well-lit by streetlights casting a yellow-orange glow on everything.

Two drill instructors stood in the middle of it all, hands on their hips, waiting for the bus to stop.

When it did, the door opened and as the inside lights came on, one of the drill instructors exploded onto the bus, shouting, "You have two fuckin' heartbeats to get off my damned bus, recruits! Move! Move! Move!"

Jesse recognized the stripes he wore—a staff sergeant. He hurried off the bus with the others, ready for what lay ahead. The second drill instructor had been joined by a third, both wearing sergeant's chevrons.

Anticipating what he'd find, Jesse rushed toward a spot where four rows of yellow footprints had been painted on the asphalt. He took one of the four at the front, second from right, and assumed the position of attention, as Pap had taught him—heels together, feet at a forty-five- degree angle, fingers curled with the thumb along the seam of his blue jeans, shoulders back, head up, and eyes locked on infinity, straight ahead.

The three drill instructors began yelling orders all at once as they chased and harassed the young men toward the yellow footprints.

"Get on those yellow footprints," the staff sergeant yelled, as the other two continued their verbal onslaught.

"Hurry up! Hurry up!"

"Move! Move!"

"Faster! Move it!

"Put your feet right on 'em, ladies!" the staff sergeant bellowed, as he moved up and down the forming group.

"Move! Move!"

"Faster, recruits! Faster!"

"This is how your feet will be whenever you're standing!"

"Fall in!"

"Move your asses!"

"Put whatever you're carrying by your left foot!"

"Hurry up! Hurry up!"

"Get on those footprints, recruit!"

"Not your orders, recruit!" the staff sergeant yelled at one guy, then turned to another DI. "This fuckwad was going to let his orders blow off into the marsh, Sergeant Davis."

Suddenly, Jesse could hear all three drill instructors descending as one, zeroing in on the kid, yelling insults, orders, and contradicting orders, just as Pap had said they'd do.

The poor kid got a quick lesson, shouting at the top of his lungs, "Sir, yes, sir!"

The air brakes on the bus released with a whoosh, and it began to pull away.

The drill instructors ceased shouting, letting the lonesome sound of the bus leaving be heard by all as it slowly faded into the distance.

He was finally there. It was time. Jesse's destiny had been written years earlier, and he was about to take the very first step in fulfilling it. His chest swelled with pride.

I'm actually here....

The same place his father had been and Pap before him.

"Recruits! Ah-ten-HUH!" a new voice shouted from Jesse's right. He didn't move.

"Stand perfectly still," the staff sergeant said with a menacing growl. "Do not move. Do not speak. Put your eyes on the back of the recruit's head in front of you."

The new man, another drill instructor, moved past Jesse, walking around the mob of recruits, seasoned eyes looking up and down the rows.

Jesse recognized the green chevrons on his khaki blouse and the Vietnam Service Ribbon on his chest.

"My name is Gunnery Sergeant Crane!" he growled, in a voice so low it seemed as if his vocal cords were rattling the ground he walked on. "You are now aboard Marine Corps Recruit Depot, Parris

Island, South Carolina."

Jesse stood perfectly still as the gunnery sergeant turned past the first row. He wasn't sure what time it was, but it was late. He could hear the man's footsteps moving toward the midpoint of the cluster of young men but didn't turn his head. Not even his eyes.

His dad had taught him the position of attention shortly after he'd learned to walk, or so he'd always bragged to friends.

Put your orders in your left hand," Gunnery Sergeant Crane said, "and raise your left hand up in the air. Look around you. Are you all holding up your left hand?"

There was an affirmative mumble, which set the three drill instructors off like rabid pit bulls.

"The first and last words out of your nasty pie holes will be sir!"

"What the fuck? My *grandmother* sounds like she has bigger balls than you girls!"

"Louder! Louder! I can't hear you!"

"The correct response will be 'Sir, yes sir!'" the gunnery sergeant bellowed over all of them. "Do I make myself clear?"

"Sir, yes, sir," Jesse shouted, along with the others.

"I can't hear you!"

"Sir, yes, sir!"

"I asked you shitbirds if you are holding up your left hand?"

"Sir, yes, sir!"

The drill instructors stopped their barking and moved as if called by a silent dog whistle.

"Put your hands back down!" the gunny said. "You are at the position of attention! Understand?"

"Sir, yes, sir!" Jesse shouted, along with the others.

"Your eyes are locked straight ahead. Understand?"

"Sir, yes, sir!"

"Shoulders back, chest out! Understand?"

"Sir, yes, sir!"

"Heels together with your feet at a forty-five-degree angle! Understand?"

"Sir, yes, sir!"

"Your fingers are curled, and your thumb is pressed against the seam of your trousers! Understand?"

"Sir, yes, sir!"

"You are about to take the first step in becoming a member of the world's finest fighting force! The United States Marine Corps!"

Gunnery Sergeant Crane, as it turned out, was one of three senior NCOs who worked around the clock, supervising dozens of receiving drill instructors, and ensuring each recruit had everything they would need to complete basic training.

When he finished, the three drill instructors took over, shouting at individual recruits as they moved up and down the rows while the gunnery sergeant moved to the front of the group.

"This column right here!" he yelled, standing beside the kid next to Jesse. "Stay in line, turn where I am standing, and go through that hatch!"

The kid hesitantly stepped off and when nobody yelled at him, hurried up to the open doors.

Jesse knew this. It was a column of files from the right. Pap had taught him all the drill movements he could remember. Being first in the second row, he instantly snapped his head to the right, watching for the last guy.

That's when Jesse saw the sign over the door for the first time. In blocky gold letters it proclaimed, *Through these portals pass prospects for America's finest fighting force, United States Marines.*

Prospects, he thought. *I won't be a Marine until graduation day.*

When Jesse saw that the last guy in the first row was a few steps away, he called out, "Second squad! Forward march!"

The three junior drill instructors descended on Jesse, all yelling at him at one time.

"This is a diddy bop, recruit!"

"You're not ready to march yet!"

"Get through that hatch, recruit!"

"Move! Move! Move!"

Chapter
Five

Two days after arriving, the new recruits had been issued most of their gear—utility uniforms, boots, sneakers, and PT gear. They'd gotten measured for dress uniforms and had their hair buzzed to the scalp.

One of the drill instructors told Jim that his head was going to rust once all that red hair was cut off, and from that day on, Jim Thurman was called Rusty.

The next two days were a series of physical exams and inoculations for just about any disease in the world.

Hearing and vision were tested and if a recruit wore glasses, they were put in storage along with whatever other personal effects they'd brought, and new glasses with ugly, black frames were issued. The recruits called them BC glasses—a guaranteed birth control device.

The drill instructors were with them day and night, constantly demanding more speed and quicker movement.

They'd all received 782 gear—basically, individual camping equipment, and a pack to put it all in. The pack was called ALICE. The All-Purpose Lightweight Individual Carrying Equipment pack was very similar to the one Pap had given Jesse when he was thirteen and going canoe camping with Billy Rainwater and some friends.

Any free time Jesse and the others had was spent standing at attention with "the little red book" in an outstretched left hand, as they read aloud the eleven general orders for Marine sentries. They did this over and over, any time they were waiting.

On the third day after arriving, one of the drill instructors stepped in front of Jesse and he snapped to attention. His name was Sergeant Wagoner.

"What's your fifth general order, private?"

"Sir," Jesse replied, his voice firm and calm, "the private's fifth general order is to quit my post only when properly relieved, sir!"

Sergeant Wagoner looked him up and down. "You are the platoon guide. When we fall in, you will always be at the right front of the formation. When you pick up your regular drill instructors, and one asks who the guide is, you will immediately report. Do you understand?"

"Sir, yes, sir!"

They had very little free time, and with each passing hour, Jesse knew the time was coming closer when they would finally meet the drill instructors who would be in charge of them and their training for the next three months, shaping them into basically trained Marines.

On the fourth day, after midday chow, the recruits were standing and reciting the general orders for the millionth time, no longer needing the red guidebook.

Suddenly, the door at the back of the room crashed open.

"Attention on deck!" someone yelled, and the monotonous chanting of general orders ceased.

"School circle!" Sergeant Wagoner yelled. "Move!"

Instantly, all the recruits rushed toward where the drill instructor stood, lining up as they'd been instructed, in six columns, shoulder-to- shoulder, with extra room between the middle two.

When all the recruits were seated on the floor, Sergeant Wagoner came to attention and executed an about-face.

For a moment, there was only silence.

Then the door opened and a tall man wearing silver bars on his collar strode into the room, his head bare. Behind him were four drill instructors, all standing at parade rest.

When the lieutenant stepped in front of the sergeant, the enlisted man saluted. "Platoon ten-eighty-one, all present, sir!"

Platoon 1081, Jesse thought. *They've given us a platoon number!*

The lieutenant, a tall, dark-haired man with a square jaw, simply nodded, and Sergeant Wagoner cut his salute, executed an about-face, and marched between the center rows of recruits to the opposite end of the squad bay.

Jesse heard the door open and then close.

This is it, Jesse thought,

He could feel the nervous energy of the group of young men around him. They all knew.

"Recruits, my name is First Lieutenant Holstein," the officer standing before them announced. "And I am your series officer. Assisting me in my duties is your chief drill instructor, Master Sergeant Smedley."

The drill instructors standing in the doorway snapped to attention and the first one strode forward, paused at attention for just a second, then marched over to the side of the squad bay, where he again stood at parade rest.

"Together, he and I will supervise your daily training," Lieutenant Holstein went on, as he strode back and forth in front of the recruits. "Over the next twelve weeks, you will be trained and evaluated on military knowledge, physical fitness, martial arts, marksmanship, water survival, and personal appearance."

He went on to talk about morality and honesty, and about the principle that nobody was permitted to mistreat or threaten anyone else, inviting each recruit to report any abuse directly to him.

"I will now introduce your drill instructors," Lieutenant Holstein said, as he slowly stepped back to the left side.

"Or-word!" the first drill instructor at the door shouted. "Yarch!"

As one, the three men came into the squad bay, a staff sergeant, a sergeant, and a corporal, all angling toward the center. With exacting precision, all three turned and halted facing the recruits, standing at attention and perfectly spaced, with the bespectacled staff sergeant at the front.

"This is your senior drill instructor," the lieutenant said, "Staff Sergeant O'Lowney."

The staff sergeant moved slightly, re-executing the position of attention and clicking his heels together.

The lieutenant moved in front of them, facing the staff sergeant. "Senior drill instructor, take charge of these recruits, and train them to become United States Marines."

The staff sergeant saluted. "Aye aye, sir!" he growled loudly.

When he cut his salute away, the lieutenant did an about-face and walked through the middle of the platoon toward the exterior door.

Staff Sergeant O'Lowney's eyes stayed glued on the retreating form until the door closed again.

"Sit up straight and look at me!" Staff Sergeant O'Lowney bellowed.

Jesse noticed that the senior drill instructor wore a black leather utility belt, while the other two wore green web utility belts.

"My name is Staff Sergeant O'Lowney! And I am *your* senior drill instructor! I'm assisted by drill instructor Sergeant Smith! And drill instructor Corporal Burd!"

As he said each man's name, the two junior drill instructors took one step forward and resumed the position of attention.

When O'Lowney continued, both of the junior drill instructors snapped to parade rest, their faces inscrutable.

"Our mission is to train *you*!" he shouted. "To become!" he continued, as he and the other two drill instructors came to attention. "United States Marines!"

"When I tell you to, you're going to get up on your feet and shake your legs out! Do you understand!

"Sir, yes, sir!"

"Stand up!"

Jesse got quickly to his feet, moving his legs to release the tension he didn't know he'd been holding.

"Move over by your bunks and get on line!" the senior shouted. "Do it now!"

Everyone scrambled to get to their assigned bunks.

"Pick up your seabags!"

"Sir, yes, sir!"

Jesse's seabag held all of his belongings and everything he'd need for the next three months—his uniforms, 782 gear, underwear, socks, stationary for writing home, brass and shoe polish... everything. And it weighed over fifty pounds.

Jesse lifted it by the strap and slung the heavy bag over his head so that it was behind him with the bottom resting under his left arm, with his utility cover in his left hand.

It was time to leave the receiving barracks.

"When I give you the word," O'Lowney began, spit flying from his mouth, "all of you will take two steps forward and face the exit hatch! Do you understand?"

"Sir, yes, sir!"

"Step forward now!"

Jesse took two steps and did a left-face, standing at attention.

The other two drill instructors began striding up and down,

yelling for the recruits to move faster.

"Where's my guide?" Staff Sergeant O'Lowney shouted, standing by the door.

Jesse stepped sideways out of the rank, then hurried toward him and came to attention. "Sir, Private McDermitt reporting as ordered, sir!"

"Right here at the hatch, McDermitt," the senior DI said. "Once I get this mob moving, you're the guide dog. Listen for my instructions."

"Aye aye, sir!"

Jesse and the other recruits were herded out like cattle, with the two junior drill instructors barking orders at them like cattle dogs.

Outside, Staff Sergeant O'Lowney guided Jesse to the left, where two trucks stood waiting. They quickly learned they were actually *called* cattle cars—a Mack truck pulling a semi-trailer designed to carry a lot of people standing up.

The ride was short, just a few blocks, and along the way, Jesse could see other platoons marching on a large parade deck.

As they drove past it, a smaller version of the Iwo Jima statue came into view. Then the trucks turned left, drove another block along the side of the parade deck, then came to a stop next to a three-story brick building that had a central covered entrance and two wings on either side.

The sign out front read, *First Recruit Training Battalion.* It listed the name of the company commanding officer, executive officer, and first sergeant.

The building would be the recruits' home for the next three months; they'd only change which floor they'd be staying on during the three phases of training.

Over the next few weeks, the recruits attended classes on subjects ranging from Marine Corps history and traditions, to CPR, to core values.

They had organized physical training with the other three platoons in their series. It was hard, but Jesse relished it. Getting outside was good, no matter the reason.

They PTed at least three days a week, doing calisthenics, pushups, pullups, and lifting weights, which were made of steel pipes with coffee cans full of cement on the ends.

They ran three miles at least once a week, and then they ran some more.

There were long conditioning marches, following shell roads that meandered for miles around the island, where hand-to-hand combat courses and obstacle courses awaited.

They spent hours on the grinder—the parade deck directly in front of the barracks—learning to march and doing close-order drills. Sergeant Smith was extremely demanding on the parade deck, and his voice when calling cadence was practically lyrical.

Many, many times, a recruit would do something wrong and the whole platoon had to stop and PT. If it happened in the squad bay, the drill instructors would run them all out to the "rose garden," referring to the "We don't promise you a rose garden" recruiting poster.

In the evening, often before the summer sun had even set, the recruits were put to bed for the night. Even this simple act was done with military precision.

"Prepare to mount!"

The recruits dropped what they were doing, closed their footlockers, and moved to either side of their bunks in skivvies, T-shirts, and shower shoes—plain plastic flipflops.

"Mount!"

The bunks were assigned in alphabetical order, with the lower bunk assigned ahead of the upper. Jesse had the bottom, one rack away from the end of the squad bay nearest the exterior hatch. The kid above him was named McDonald, from upstate New York.

Jesse mounted his rack, lying at the position of attention, as McDonald scrambled up on the other side.

"Ahhhd-just!"

That was when the squad bay lights went off and the recruits could get comfortable.

"Seems weird goin' to sleep on a Saturday night when the sun's still up," Malloy whispered from the lower bunk next to Jesse. "Wonder what my buddies back on the block are doin' right now."

"Them and Jodie probably gettin' it on with your girl, Suzie," another recruit remarked a few bunks down.

"Keep the noise down!" the fire watch hissed—a recruit named Flowers.

He wore a silver helmet liner and yellow belt over his shoulder. There were always two recruits on fire watch in the squad bay, all throughout the night.

Jesse thought about Cathy, the girl Billy had introduced him to at his going-away party. He'd had a few girlfriends in high school, but nothing serious had developed, and he was still friends with them. But none were as pretty as Cathy had looked on that night, sitting on Pap's boat's foredeck, watching the sun go down.

She'd given him her address and had asked him to write to her, but so far, he'd only penned a few letters to Mam, one to Pap, and one to Billy.

As he slowly drifted off to sleep, with the sound of the fire watch's footsteps echoing through the squad bay, Jesse resolved to write her a letter the next day and ask her out on a date in the fall, when he went back home as a Marine.

Chapter Six

—————◆———◆———◆———◆—————

Jesse liked the regimented lifestyle. He had no decisions to make—his every waking hour was planned and controlled, enabling him to focus on everything he was supposed to learn.

And he liked most of the guys in his platoon. They were from all over the Eastern United States, from Florida to Maine, and west to the Mississippi. Mostly, they came from large cities.

Rusty's bunk was on the same side of the squad bay as Jesse's, five down from his, but both were normally far too busy to even give a nod to the other.

The two "Florida boys," as Rusty liked to call them, could somehow convey more than just hello with a nod, though. On occasion, they had a few minutes here or there, but they were still essentially strangers. They'd just happened to meet on the bus headed to Parris Island.

Whenever they were marching, Jesse was at the front, carrying the guidon, and Rusty, being one of the shortest guys in the platoon, was at the rear in third squad.

Not that they could talk while marching, but when they stopped for a break or a meal of C-rations, the recruits basically just sat where they were, and talk was minimal.

In the fourth week of training, the platoon moved into Phase Two and were allowed the privilege of blousing their boots for the first time, which consisted of wrapping a tiny bungee cord around the top of the boot and then tucking the bottom of the trousers under it on the inside.

On the very first morning of Phase Two, the platoon was marched to the other side of the small base for Pool Week.

The pool was bigger than any Jesse had ever seen, and it was indoors, with the noise and commands from the swim coaches echoing all through the giant building. One end was about ten feet deep and the other end only waist deep.

By the end of that week, every recruit learned to make a float out of their shirt, how to use the ALICE pack as a float, how to shed their rifle and gear while underwater, and even how to remove their boots, tie the laces together and hang them around their necks.

Jesse had started swimming even before he'd learned to walk. He remembered his dad bragging to a friend that Jesse's first pair of shoes were swim fins. So he had no trouble in the pool, not even weighed down with all the gear.

During one of the exercises for swim qualification, one of the swim coaches stood on a platform yelling down at the recruits trying to tread water.

"If you ever find your landing craft blown up... Believe me, recruits! You're going to want those boots when you reach the coral beachhead to rejoin the fight! Do you understand?"

"Sir, yes, sir!"

The exercise was simple. Jump in the water in boots and utes—or utility uniform—then remove your blouse, button it to the neck, and tie the sleeves tightly around the neck opening, closing off the collar. And do all that while trying not to drown with your boots on. By splashing water under the waist opening, air bubbles got trapped along the back of the shirt and it billowed on the surface.

Once each recruit had made a crude flotation device, they had to remove their boots and swim to the far end of the pool, floating on their inflated blouse.

Jesse slipped underwater with his lungs half full, sinking to the bottom. He knew how much air he needed to take in to be neutrally buoyant. So far, Pool Week had been kind of like a vacation—a little time away from the drill instructors—doing something he enjoyed.

He pulled himself into a ball near the bottom and pulled the laces loose on his boots. Then he removed them one at a time, careful not to drop either one and have to waste precious energy retrieving it.

Twenty feet away, Jesse could make out someone else sitting on the bottom doing the same thing. Without a mask, he couldn't be certain, but he thought he recognized the red scalp of his buddy Rusty. Being from the Keys, he would undoubtedly be a good swimmer, Jesse surmised.

He carefully tied his laces together, hung his boots around his neck, then pushed effortlessly off the bottom. Grabbing his utility blouse from below, he exhaled into the bottom before he surfaced, holding the lower half in one hand and the knotted sleeves and neck with the other.

Looking around, Jesse saw that only he and Rusty were floating, both slowly kicking toward the other end of the pool. Jesse caught up to him with a few long side strokes.

"Hey, this is..." Rusty spat water out. "...kinda fun, ain't it?"

"At least we don't have to worry about gators," Jesse agreed.

"Or sharks, bro. I see one just about every time I dive."

"You're a scuba diver?" Jesse asked, looking over and grinning. "Me too."

"You should definitely come down some time, man. I'll take ya out to Coffin's Patch and Looc Key."

They reached the ladder, where Corporal Burd greeted them, yelling for them to get up the ladder and on line.

They hurried over and stood in their utilities and socks, dripping water. One by one, the other recruits finished the exercise and joined them.

The kid who had the bunk above Jesse's, Jerome McDonald, failed swim qual soon after half the platoon finished the exercise, almost drowning in the process.

He'd been worried about it for over a week. Being from Detroit's inner city, the friendly, black recruit—or "dark green" as they were taught—had never learned to swim.

The Corps didn't differentiate on color—we were all just different shades of green. But it did prefer that its Marines be able to swim.

In Jesse's mind, it was such a foreign concept. He'd never met anyone who didn't enjoy being on or in the water, and he couldn't remember a time when he didn't.

When they got back to their barracks, McDonald and two other guys were ordered to pack their gear.

Not everyone who started with the platoon made it all the way through. Everything was a test, and if a recruit failed a test, they had to do it over. But the training couldn't wait for one or two recruits, so they were simply dropped from the platoon they were in to redo the part they failed with another platoon, then move on with them.

A few were recycled before Pool Week for one reason or another. An overweight kid from Arkansas was recycled to a physical conditioning or PC platoon. The recruits called it the "pork chop" platoon. It was a two-week recycle, where the recruits did nothing but PT and eat reduced, low-fat rations. When they got down to the desired weight, they reentered training with another platoon.

On their first night as a platoon, there had been sixty-three recruits, and they were already down to just fifty-seven, a loss of ten percent in the first four weeks.

Most weren't sent home. They were called retreads because they had to repeat a portion of training. That meant their time on Parris Island went from thirteen weeks to fourteen or fifteen. If they didn't pass the second time around, they were recycled again. Failing a third time meant going home with a terminated contract—not even a discharge.

A couple of new recruits had been picked up by Jesse's platoon, having failed at something in other platoons that were farther ahead in training.

After swim qual, the platoon was broken up into work parties and Jesse was assigned kitchen police duty. KP was basically just cleaning up the mess hall.

All through KP, Jesse was sweating it out in the pot shack—the really nasty, detached, part of the scullery, where he used a large, steam-blasting wand, standing outside the shack, to cut the crud off of large stainless steel pots and pans hung inside.

The scullery was the "dirty" part of the kitchen where the other recruits washed dishes and utensils. By comparison, it was clean. But it was inside and stuffy, while Jesse was outside in the fresh air and sunlight.

While Jesse steam-blasted all day, Rusty got office duty, because he could type.

After KP, the day finally came when they moved out of the three-story brick building and marched out to the rifle range. For the next two weeks, they stayed in the older brick barracks there.

The recruits had been issued M-16 rifles early in training and had learned to drill with them, disassemble them, and clean them. They memorized their serial numbers and the names and functions of all the parts. They'd recited the Rifleman's Creed a million times, and they knew their weapons as well as they knew themselves, just as the creed said they would.

Now they would learn to *fire* their weapons. Accurately.

The range instructors were a lot more patient than the drill instructors—and quieter. This was the *serious* business of the Marine Corps. They wore range helmets, sort of like pith helmets, instead of the drill instructor's campaign cover.

During the first week—Grass Week—the recruits spent hours in large circles around white, fifty-five-gallon barrels that had small black targets painted on them.

They practiced getting into the basic firing positions, "snapping in" and dry firing the weapons for practice as the range coaches moved around them, stopping to adjust a recruit's position or give them calm advice on things like sight alignment or lightly pressing the trigger instead of yanking on it.

A lot of the city kids had never fired a rifle before, but Jesse had bagged his first deer on a hunt with Billy Rainwater when he was thirteen. Billy had taught him how to honor the buck and to thank him.

They spent the second week on the range, firing from the 200-, 300-, and 500-yard lines, going for tight groups, then adjusting the sights to move the group into the center.

With that accomplished on the first day, Jesse spent the next two days, shooting holes in the small white spotters that were used to mark where the previous bullet had hit the black center ring.

Jesse excelled at the rifle range, drawing the attention of the range coaches. On qualification day, he was not only the high shooter in the platoon but was dubbed the deadliest recruit on Parris Island by Staff Sergeant Tankersley, the range chief. Like most over the rank of sergeant, he was a Vietnam vet. But unlike the others, he always wore a dress uniform instead of utilities. Once, when he was close by, watching Jesse shoot, Jesse stole a glance back and noted a pale blue ribbon with silver stars on the top of his ribbon rack.

The Medal of Honor?

After the rifle range, Platoon 1081 entered the third and final phase of training, which built on everything they'd learned up to that point. They fired their weapons on full-automatic, firing short three- or four-round bursts over a parapet wall. They threw live grenades from "fighting holes." They maneuvered through an urban battlefield setting. They got to fire the venerable M-1911, Colt .45 caliber semi-automatic handgun. Pap had one identical to the ones they had on the pistol range.

Jesse also qualified as expert there.

During the ninth week of training, the platoon took on the massive Confidence Course for the last time. By then, they'd become used to some of the obstacle's dizzying heights. There were fifteen obstacles, some thirty feet tall, and the recruits gained more confidence, not just in themselves but in one another.

By then, unit cohesion was nearly complete, and the individual recruits had melded into a single entity—their platoon.

Jesse had made it through all the obstacles during their first encounter in their second week of training, but it had taxed him both physically and mentally.

Many in his platoon had failed to negotiate some of the tougher obstacles, many succumbing to gravity on the Slide For Life, and finishing the course in dripping wet cammies after plummeting twenty feet into a pond.

Unlike everything else they did, the Confidence Course wasn't a pass or fail part of boot camp. It was just what the name implied—a series of very difficult obstacles that instilled confidence in the young men who encountered them, and in many cases, forced them to work together.

This time Jesse and the others in his platoon weren't raw Phase

One recruits. They'd become stronger, tougher, and more confident.

Getting across some of the obstacles required teamwork, and every recruit made sure that every other recruit not only conquered the course but *dominated* it.

No man left behind.

Chapter Seven

———◆———◆———◆———◆———

Finally, the day before graduation came. The recruits who had family attending were given base liberty on Thursday—a few free hours to spend with loved ones before the graduation ceremony the next morning.

The drill instructors behaved differently in the last couple of weeks of training. Their constant demand for more speed and greater excellence had lightened. The recruits didn't need repeated haranguing to do what they had to do with speed and precision. The drill instructors became almost like mentors or big brothers.

Except Sergeant Smith. His demands for perfection on the drill field never diminished, and in final drill competition with the three other platoons in their series, Platoon 1081 came out on top.

Jesse spotted Mam and Pap coming through the hatch and quickly rose from his footlocker and approached Sergeant Smith.

"Sir, the private's family has arrived. Permission to be excused?"

Sergeant Smith looked up at him and one corner of his mouth twitched a fraction of an inch. "You mean to tell me there are more McDermitts?"

Jesse had found that his Virginia drawl was a bit more pronounced when he wasn't yelling. But he wanted to get away. He didn't want Mam and Pap to be exposed to these rough men.

Smith glanced around Jesse's shoulder, then stepped aside and faced his grandparents.

Jesse executed an about-face, then marched backward one step to be next to his drill instructor.

Mam looked Jesse right in the eye. He wanted desperately to take her arm and escort her out of the squad bay. She only smiled at him.

"Sergeant Smith?" Pap said, extending a hand as if greeting an old friend he hadn't seen in a while. "Staff Sergeant Frank McDermitt, USMC, retired. This is my wife, Norma. We are Private McDermitt's grandparents."

Uncomfortably, Jesse kept his eyes locked on infinity beyond the far wall.

Out of the corner of his eye, Jesse saw Smith look up at him and he actually grinned—something Jesse had never seen.

"I knew it," Smith said, shaking Pap's hand and smiling openly. "His middle name—Smedley."

"Our son's insistence," Mam said. "He was killed in action in 1968. Our daughter-in-law chose Jesiah."

Jesse cringed as Smith turned toward his grandmother and removed his cover. "Ma'am, it's a pleasure."

"How did our boy do, Sergeant?" Mam asked, speaking in a tone Jesse had never heard before—clipped and to the point—as if she were interrogating an underling.

Smith glanced at Jesse once more, then put his cover back on before responding.

"You are to be commended, Mr. and Mrs. McDermitt," Sergeant Smith said. "You've raised a fine young man, and tomorrow he will be a fine Marine. He'll be recognized during the ceremony as company high shooter *and* honor grad."

Staff Sergeant O'Lowney approached and stood on Jesse's left.

Sergeant Smith waved a hand toward the older couple. "May I present Staff Sergeant and Mrs. McDermitt," he said to O'Lowney.

Then he turned to Mam. "This is Staff Sergeant O'Lowney, the senior drill instructor."

"South Pacific?" O'Lowney asked, shaking Pap's hand.

Pap's eyes cut to O'Lowney's ribbon rack, tracing the man's military history in a single glance. Jesse had already recognized O'Lowney's Vietnam Service ribbon, as well as a Bronze Star ribbon with Combat V for valor.

"Three years," Pap replied. "Guadalcanal, Cape Gloucester, Peleliu, Iwo Jima, and Okinawa. Field promoted to staff NCO and medically retired."

Jesse's eyes shifted for a microsecond to his grandfather. *Did he say* medically *retired?*

Jesse had heard Pap mention those islands and during his Marine Corps history classes, he'd learned more about each one.

He realized that Pap always recited them in that order, the same order in which he'd landed on each island. And now he knew that his grandfather had apparently been wounded in action and mustered out.

Pap had never talked about his experiences during the war, only about the things that he did between campaigns.

O'Lowney nodded solemnly. "Semper Fi, sir."

"Semper Fi," Pap replied. "Do you mind if we take this young recruit off your hands for a while? I haven't been here in nearly forty years, and Norma's never been here at all. I'd like Jesse to show us around."

"Just have him back by sixteen hundred," O'Lowney said, then both drill instructors turned and left.

"Can we get outta here?" Jesse asked, uncomfortable about his grandparents being in that place.

Pap chuckled. "Car's parked to the west of the grinder."

Jesse led the way to the hatch, then held it open for his

grandparents. As Mam started down the steps, Pap stopped to admire the expert badge hanging on Jesse's starched khaki blouse.

"High shooter, huh?"

"Yes, sir," Jesse replied.

"What was your score?"

"Two-fifty, sir."

Pap arched an eyebrow. "Not too shabby."

Jesse grinned and followed the old man outside, putting his piss cutter on his head and adjusting the fit.

For rifle qualification, each recruit had been issued fifty rounds of ammunition. Twenty were to be fired at the 200-yard line, where Jesse had hit all twenty in the center ring, firing from standing and kneeling positions. Then they'd moved back to the 300, where they'd fired another twenty rounds in the kneeling and sitting positions.

When they'd moved back to the 500-yard line, over a quarter mile from the targets, they had to fire ten more rounds from the prone position.

Staff Sergeant Tankersley, the range chief, had come down to where Jesse and two other recruits were setting up, having heard that he'd reached the 500-yard line with a perfect score—forty straight bullseyes.

Two-fifty was the maximum score, and after Jesse had calmly hammered ten more bullseyes using iron sights, the range coach shook his hand and congratulated him.

Stepping out into the bright sunlight, Jesse spotted Rusty at the edge of the barracks access road. He was standing with who Jesse guessed were his parents and a pretty girl who couldn't have been more than five feet tall—obviously his girlfriend, Juliet. Rusty had talked about her for most of the bus ride through Georgia.

"Jesse!" he called, seeing them come outside.

He waved. "Hey, Rusty!"

"This here's my best buddy, Jesse McDermitt," Rusty said to the girl. "He's from up Fort Myers way. Jesse, this here's my girl, Juliet, and my folks, Shorty and Dreama."

Jesse felt absolutely immense standing next to Rusty and his family. Rusty was the tallest and he was only five-six.

Jesse shook hands with all three, then turned to Mam and Pap. "These are my grandparents, Frank and Norma McDermitt," he said.

Everyone else shook hands and Juliet looked up at her boyfriend. "Rusty?"

"It's just what the guys call me," he said, blushing slightly.

She smiled. "I like it."

Shorty chuckled. "Maybe you can change the name of the bait shop one day... Rusty's Place. Got a nice ring."

"You own a bait shop?" Pap asked. "That explains why these two gravitated toward one another. Jesse and I are devout anglers."

"Shorty's Bar and Bait Shop," the man replied. "In Marathon on the ocean side, at mile marker forty-eight."

"We were gonna head over to the PX," Rusty said to Jesse. "There's a McDonald's there. Remember?"

"McDonald's?" Pap asked.

"I been dreamin' of a big ole cheeseburger for months," Rusty replied.

"Then I'd suggest the NCO Club if there is one," Pap offered.

"We can't go in there," Rusty said. "We ain't even Marines yet, let alone NCOs."

"Good thing I am," Pap replied. "Do you know where it is? I guarantee they'll have bigger burgers than any fast-food joint."

Rusty grinned and pointed across the parking lot. "Just over there."

The seven of them walked the few blocks through Mainside, stopping to take pictures at the Iron Mike statue.

When they reached the NCO club, they went inside, and Pap showed the hostess his old Marine Corps ID, she smiled brightly, looking right at Jesse before turning back to Pap. "How many are in your party, Staff Sergeant McDermitt?"

Another uncomfortable moment came as they were seated— three couples and one single guy, Jesse. The hostess, who was likely in her mid-twenties, smiled at him again.

That added to his discomfort.

It wasn't that he was nervous around girls, it was just that he didn't understand them much, and always got mixed signals.

He'd written several letters to Cathy, and she'd written back to each one. He'd told her that his grandparents were driving up and asked if she'd come with them. In her last letter, she'd said that she would.

"Cathy stopped by Wednesday night," Mam said, as Jesse sat between her and Rusty. "She felt terrible that she couldn't come."

"I don't know if she told you," Pap said. "But her mother is a single lady and not in very good health."

"She was in the hospital for several days last week," Mam added. "And she only came home on Monday."

"Is Cathy your girl?" Juliet asked.

Jesse shrugged. "We only met the night before I left to come here. I think I'd... like her to be."

"Then she will be," Juliet said with finality. She smiled and turned to Rusty. "Hard for a girl to resist a man in uniform." Then she looked back at Jesse. "Besides, she'd have to be blind *and* stupid not to want to be your girl."

"If not," Rusty said, nudging him in the side, "that hostess chick seemed like she'd like to get to know you, bro."

Pap was right. The burgers were huge and grilled perfectly.

Several times when the back door opened, Jesse could see a

large charcoal grill out back with smoke billowing from the chimney.

"We should get together and do some fishin' and divin'," Rusty suggested, as they walked back toward the parking lot after lunch. "We got two weeks' leave startin' on Monday, if ya wanna come down for a few days."

"That could be fun," Jesse said, stopping and taking a little red book out of his trouser pocket. "What's your number?"

Rusty pulled his guidebook out and, after they'd exchanged numbers, looked at his pocket watch and said, "We better get goin', Pop."

Shorty noticed the watch and nodded at it. "You still carryin' that old thing?"

"It keeps good time," Rusty said. "And ya told me your pop gave it to you."

Rusty had carried the watch all through boot camp, smuggling it from his civilian belongings when the receiving drill instructors weren't looking. How he'd managed to keep their own drill instructors from finding it for three months, Jesse had no idea.

"What did you need a watch for in boot camp?" Pap asked.

"To check the tides," Rusty replied, then turned to his father. "We spent a coupla days out on Ellis Island a few weeks back. The tide here rises and falls more'n seven feet!"

"I wonder what they catch around here," Jesse said, as they walked down the third row of vehicles.

"Lots of reedy marshes," Rusty observed. "Prolly some trout and redfish back in there."

"What's your favorite fighting fish?" Shorty asked Pap.

"Hmm, tough to say," Jesse's grandfather replied. "Offshore, I've fought blue *and* black marlin for over an hour."

"Oh, yeah!" Shorty exclaimed. "I don't get out to the Stream very much. But along the reef, you can't beat an amberjack. Pound for pound, the strongest fish in the ocean. We call 'em reef donkeys."

"Apt name," Pap agreed, as they walked slowly through the parking lot. "Jesse and I fish mostly near-shore for trout and snook. And for fun... bonefish."

"Now you're talkin'," Shorty said. "Takes a lot of skill to get the gray ghost alongside the boat."

When they reached Pap's 1973 Thunderbird, they said goodbye and split up, both young men promising to keep in touch.

"Hey," Jesse said, as Rusty and his family turned to leave, "I forgot to ask. What are your orders?"

"Gonna be a grunt, just like ya said," Rusty replied. "I report to SOI at Camp Geiger two weeks from Monday."

"Same here!" Jesse said. "If we're too busy tomorrow, I'll see you then, if I can't come down for some diving."

They split up and Mam got in the backseat of Pap's huge, two-door highway cruiser. The hood was so long, Jesse remembered he could lay his head at the top of it and his sneakers still didn't hang over the front end.

Pap started the car and pushed the buttons to make all the windows go down to let the heat out. Then he switched the air conditioner on high.

"Your buddy got away with the watch, did he?" Pap asked, looking back and winking at Mam. "Every recruit tries to pull something over on their DIs." Then he looked over at Jesse. "What did you get away with?"

Jesse's head jerked and his mouth opened a little.

Mam started laughing in the backseat. "You should never play poker, sweetie," she said. "Your face *can't* tell a lie."

"Give it," Pap said, grinning.

Pap's a Marine, Jesse thought instantaneously. *A Marine staff*

NCO. He just gave me an order.

The oath echoed in Jesse's head in the next millisecond.

...I will obey the orders of the President of the United States and the orders of the officers appointed over me, according to regulations and the Uniform Code of Military Justice. So help me God.

"Sir! I impersonated a first lieutenant and PTed the recruits in another part of our barracks, sir!"

Pap stared at him, dumbfounded. Finally, he shook his head. "You *what?*"

Jesse looked over at the old man. "It was Rusty's idea, on account of me and the series commander being the same height and build. He and I, along with a recruit named Couch, made silver bars out of the inside wrapper of a pack of cigarettes."

Pap burst out laughing. "That's a whole lot better than what I did," he finally said, chuckling.

"Huh?"

Pap put the car in gear then grinned at Jesse. "I walked on the grass any chance I got."

"Oh, Frank," Mam said, pretending she was swooning. She leaned forward and patted Jesse's shoulder. "Why, Jesse, you probably didn't know your grandfather was such a *rebel!*"

The following morning, right after chow, Platoon 1081 formed up for the last time. The other three platoons in their series were formed up one ahead of them and two behind, and another series in a different battalion formed up behind them.

The drill instructors went up and down the ranks, adjusting uniforms and talking quietly to the soon-to-be Marines. There was very little for them to pick at, but they had to.

Sergeant Smith stepped in front of Jesse, flicked imaginary lint from his shoulder and looked up at him.

"I've been around this man's Corps for fifteen years," he said, his Virginia drawl as calm and smooth as stones in a stream. "You're gonna do great things in our ranks, McDermitt."

Not recruit, not maggot, not rock, Jesse thought. *He called me by name, breaking protocol.*

Seeming the appropriate thing to do, Jesse also broke protocol by glancing down at the shorter man and using the Y-word for the first time in months. "Thank you, sir. I won't let you down."

Sergeant Smith smiled for a moment, his eyes drifting as though thinking of something from long ago.

"Bravo Zulu, maggot," he said, then executed a facing movement and marched away.

Fifteen years, he thought. *How was he only a sergeant?*

There was little other fanfare from the three drill instructors, who'd been with them every hour of every day for the last thirteen weeks. But the "well done" comment from Sergeant Smith made Jesse's chest swell a little.

The drill instructors' jobs were finished. The platoon was now made up of basically trained Marines, ready to move on to further, more specialized training.

Across the grinder, it was an odd sight. After thirteen weeks of seeing little besides the green camouflage utilities, the gray interior walls of the squad bay, and the red brick of many of the buildings, Jesse's eyes weren't used to so much color.

There were men and women, boys and girls, a few uniforms mixed in, but mostly it was a cacophony of color.

"Company!" the chief drill instructor bellowed from the far side of the access road as he came to attention.

Staff Sergeant O'Lowney snapped to, turned his head, and

shouted over his shoulder, "Plah-toon Ten-Eighty-One!"

Jesse waited for the command of execution from the chief drill instructor.

"Ah-ten-HUH!"

As one, nearly five hundred recruits' heels, plus those of about thirty drill instructors and company staff, came together with a single click.

"Right... Face!"

The band, which was ahead of Platoon 1080, stepped off, playing the familiar rat-a-tat drum march.

Lifting the guidon slightly with his fingertips, Jesse executed another right face, then stepped off four paces to the head of the starboard column. There, he stopped, made a left face, and lowered the guidon beside his right foot.

"Fo-ward! HUH!"

In perfect precision, all four platoons stepped off to march around the grinder one last time.

Another series of four platoons from Second Battalion marched behind their four platoons, making eight platoons of fifty to sixty recruits marching together—over four hundred individuals—yet the sound of their footfalls seemed as if it was but one pair of heels striking the deck, as the Parris Island Marine Corps Band opened with Sousa's *Semper Fidelis*.

After all their time on the grinder, Jesse's platoon of individual recruits had become one. With the band playing, there was no need for the drill instructors to call cadence.

They all marched to the beat of the same drum now. City kids, country kids, whatever race, religion, or background, they had all come together as a single unit.

They passed in review of the base commander and other dignitaries, where, on the "eyes right" command, Jesse dipped the guidon level as Staff Sergeant O'Lowney, marching at the head of first squad, executed a salute with his sword, and all but fourth squad turned their heads toward the dignitaries.

After two more turns, the eight platoons formed in the middle and awaited the command to be dismissed for the very last time.

The late August sun was blistering, and Jesse could feel the heat of the asphalt parade deck through the soles of his highly spit-shined dress shoes. The dark blue of his dress uniform absorbed the heat, and a line of sweat ran down the middle of his back, as well as down both sides of his face.

The guidons were retired, the high shooters and honor grads were recognized, and the company CO said a few words, then turned the platoons over to their drill instructors.

The dismissal command came from Platoon 1080's senior drill instructor first, followed quickly by each consecutive senior of each platoon.

"Plah-toon! One thousand eighty-one!" Staff Sergeant O'Lowney barked. "Dee-us... missed!"

"Aye, aye, sir!"

As one, the platoon stepped back, executed an about-face, and then it was over.

They were Marines.

Chapter Eight

—————◆————◆————◆————◆—————

The T-bird started across the long, two-lane causeway as Jesse stared out the passenger window at the vast salt marsh that surrounded most of Parris Island. They were in a line of evenly spaced cars, and only slowed a little as they reached the main gate.

Two MPs stood at the intersection, stopping traffic so several cars with new Marines and their families could turn north or south.

One of them stopped Pap and then they both allowed the traffic on the highway to continue.

"What are those people doing?" Mam asked, leaning between the seats.

Across the highway, a small crowd was gathered on the side of the road—men in some kind of uniform, women, even a few kids and young teens.

"Legionnaires," Pap said.

The people just stood there, as if waiting for something. Then the two MPs started blowing whistles and waving their arms as they stepped out onto the highway. Once they had both directions of traffic stopped, the one closest did a facing movement and moved his arm up and down, directing Pap to proceed, then he turned back to face the lead car and stood at parade rest.

Pap rolled through the intersection, turning left, and the crowd on the side of the road began waving American and Marine Corps flags, yelling and cheering.

Jesse pushed the button to make his window go down and turned to look as Pap steered the T-Bird around the corner. There were two girls, probably no more than six and eight, both with curly blond hair, and two slightly older boys, maybe fifteen or so, along with the men in uniform and several older women.

"That was for you, Jesse," Mam squealed. "Good to see there are still people who appreciate the military."

"Parris Island is between two towns," Pap said. "Port Royal and Beaufort. There's a large Navy hospital in Port Royal, and a Marine air station on the other side of Beaufort. Military towns are different than others in rural America. Always have been and always will be."

Not far out of Port Royal, as Pap headed south on US-17, they encountered a slower moving car, and Pap was about to pull out and pass on the two-lane road.

Jesse glanced over. The speedometer was at seventy-five. When he looked back up, seeing that there was nothing coming in the opposite direction, his eyes cut to the car ahead, instantly noting the black star on the left side of the tag.

"That's a cop, Pap," Jesse said quietly, but making sure the old man could hear him.

Pap let up on the gas, letting the big, 429-cubic-inch engine wind down. "Are you sure?"

"Look at the tag," Jesse said. "It's an unmarked county deputy."

Throughout the long, five-hundred-mile drive, Jesse talked about all the things that he'd learned and been through in the last three months.

Mam asked tons of questions, and Pap interjected a few times, but mostly it was Jesse talking.

After spending three months only speaking when spoken to, and then at a yell, it was nice to just talk.

Mam caught him up on what was going on with all the

neighbors along the river and mentioned all the people she'd run into who'd wished Jesse luck.

"The O'Hara girl moved back in to take care of Nancy," Mam said. "I don't know if you ever met her. She was in high school when you came to live with us."

Mam rarely mentioned the deaths of her only child and his wife, always referring to that tragic change in Jesse's life as "when you came to live with us" rather than to the catalyst that caused it.

"I vaguely remember meeting Mr. and Mrs. O'Hara," Jesse replied. "Is she sick?"

"She's not doing too well," Mam told him.

The O'Haras had bought the house Jesse had lived in for eight years with his mom and dad. His dad would come home after deployments or transfers, but whenever he was stationed close by, up in North Carolina, or at Parris Island, Jesse and his mom would move there and live in base housing for the summer until he transferred again. They'd spent two summers at Parris Island, but it was when Jesse was just three or four.

They could have gone with him to California, but Jesse's father had wanted him to have as stable a home life as possible.

In Jesse's first eight years of life, his father was only physically with his family for two years, eight months, and twelve days. He'd been deployed to Vietnam three times before he was killed.

Jesse felt great pride that his father was able to devote even that much time away from his duties. It had to have been very difficult for both his parents.

He imagined his drill instructors acting as his dad had when he was home on leave, or even more to the point, during the summers they'd spent with him in base housing at Parris Island and Camp Lejeune.

He knew by their wedding bands that two of his drill instructors,

O'Lowney and Smith, were married.

Did they play catch with their sons like his own father had? Did they toss their covers and utility blouses on a porch chair and pick up a football?

A radio station would fade out and Pap would turn the knob and search for a new one, always managing to find a jazz station. He kept the volume low, and the big Ford ate up the miles with ease, heading south on US-17 toward Florida in air-conditioned comfort.

For the rest of the afternoon, they drove steadily south, stopping only three times for gas and head calls. They covered the distance in about half the time it had taken the bus to get to Parris Island.

That day seemed like a lifetime earlier to Jesse, rather than just thirteen weeks ago.

When Pap finally pulled into the driveway, Billy's dad's pickup was parked on the far-left side. The sun had already disappeared from the sky and for a moment, the headlights shone on Billy and his girlfriend, Penny, who were sitting on the front porch swing. And on Cathy, who was sitting on the steps petting Molly, the family black Lab.

They all got up and came running out as Jesse unfolded himself from the front seat.

"Whoa-ho!" Billy exclaimed, coming to a stop.

Molly fell onto the tops of Jesse's shoes, rubbing her back against his leg. It didn't matter if it'd been thirteen weeks or thirteen minutes, her joy at seeing him was always the same.

"I don't know whether to salute you or grab your arm, brother."

Jesse pulled his cover onto his head, then extended his right hand.

Billy took Jesse's wrist, and Jesse locked onto his, shaking hands the Calusa way.

Then he knelt down and began rubbing Molly's chest vigorously. "Did ya miss me, girl? Huh?"

Rising, he turned to face Cathy. "How's your mom? Mam and Pap told me she'd been in the hospital."

Cathy smiled and let out a breath. "She's doing better. I'm so sorry I couldn't—"

"Don't even think about it," Jesse said. "Family always comes first."

She smiled and stepped into his arms, hers going around his waist and up his back.

"You've gotten bigger."

"Probably," Jesse agreed, a bit embarrassed. "I, uh, haven't seen a scale since the first week's medical exam, though."

"Why don't you young folks come on inside," Mam said. "The mosquitoes must have been eating you alive out here."

"Thanks, Mam," Billy said. "But we can't stay, and I know you must be pretty tired. We just stopped by to let Molly out and we wanted to welcome Jesse home."

Billy's hair was longer, past his collar again. He'd cut it at the beginning of his junior year, after some inbred swamp denizen had taken a Buck knife to it, while he and Penny were sitting in a movie theater. The guy had paid a serious physical price for his transgression, and it had shamed Billy considerably.

After not seeing hair on anyone's head in three months, it looked totally foreign, though before that incident, Billy's hair had been down to the middle of his back.

"I hope I can see you while you're home," Cathy said.

Jesse let out a sigh of relief. "How about tomorrow?"

"The beach!" Billy suggested.

"Yeah," Jesse agreed. "I need a saltwater fix. I'll bring the rods."

"And I'll bring the grill."

"Is this just a guy thing?" Cathy asked.

"Oh, no!" he replied quickly, then saw her smile. He smiled back. "That is, unless you don't like cobia."

"Trust me, Cat," Penny said. "With these two around, you will *never* die of hunger or boredom."

They said their goodbyes, and as Billy and the two girls drove away, Jesse followed Molly and his grandparents up the familiar steps to the porch. Pap had built the home himself, shortly after returning from the war in the Pacific—every plank, stud, rafter, and nail.

"You should have gone with them," Mam said. "After the past three months, you must be wound tighter than a watch spring."

"Not really," Jesse replied, walking into the familiar foyer and removing his cover. "The first ten days or so were really challenging, but after that, it just... I don't know... I, uh..."

"Felt like you were where you were meant to be?" Pap asked.

"Yes, sir," he replied, following them into Mam's big kitchen. "Exactly like that. Did you feel that way, too?"

Pap opened a cupboard and turned around with a pair of shot glasses and a bottle.

"No, not me," he said. "But your daddy... Well, let's just say the apple didn't fall real far from the tree with you. Bo told me those very words when he reenlisted. 'Dad,' he'd said, 'I love Florida, but the Corps is where I am meant to be.'"

"You boys go into the den with that," Mam ordered. "I'll heat up dinner." She hugged Jesse again. "Leftover pot roast from Wednesday."

"Mmm," Jesse hummed. "The flavors mix better after a day or two."

After Pap tapped his thigh lightly with the glasses, Molly got up from her rug, and she and Jesse followed him into his inner sanctum.

72

As a kid, Jesse wasn't allowed to play in Pap's den. It was only in the last two years that his grandfather had ever invited him in to talk about serious things—man things.

He paused and looked around. The room, just like the house, was deeply familiar. He knew the grain and knots in every floor plank of the house.

The wood paneling of the den's walls was dark hardwood, not cheap laminated stuff. The matching wood and leather recliners were deep and comfortable, with a reading light between them, which gave off a soft, tan glow that was easy on the eyes.

Pap's civic awards, certificates, licenses, and diplomas were displayed on one wall, with a trophy-sized bull dolphin opposite, resplendent in its iridescent, neon-blue and chartreuse-green head and back. The sides were gold, sprinkled with a mixture of bright blue and black spots, and the belly was yellow, fading to a silvery-white.

He'd always thought the fish was magnificent. Nothing he and Pap had ever caught even came close. Pap had caught the dolphin in the late 1940s, while on a friend's boat down in the Gulf Stream. They'd caught marlins there, as well. Probably close to where his new friend Rusty lived.

There was only one small space in the room dedicated to Pap's military service—a small table in the corner, sort of a shrine box, displaying his rank insignia, his ribbons, and a gold eagle, globe, and anchor, the emblem of the Marine Corps.

Knowing what he now knew about Pap's service, he could understand why he rarely talked about it.

Pap had walked through Hell carrying jerry cans full of gas, and he'd survived. At least that's what it had seemed like to Jesse, from what he'd learned in his Marine Corps History classes.

He looked around again, his eyes settling on the brick fireplace.

Why Pap had wanted a fireplace in South Florida, he'd never explained. But on the occasional chilly night, Pap would light it, even though it meant kicking on the AC sometimes.

"Better to have it and not need it, than need it and not have it," Pap had told him years earlier.

All around him were familiar things, memories of growing up in that house.

At the same time, everything in the room—the great fish, the chairs, the reading light between them, even Pap and Molly—seemed almost unfamiliar in a way.

He was expecting Sergeant Smith to come storming through the door any minute.

"Unblouse," Pap said, placing the bottle and glasses on the small table in front of the recliners.

Jesse placed his cover on the edge of the table, removed his white utility belt, and placed it beside the barracks cap. Then he unbuttoned his dark blue tunic and shrugged out of it.

"That young lady was right," Pap said, uncorking the bottle. "You've filled out a lot in just three months."

Jesse hung his blouse on Pap's coat rack, then returned to where his grandfather stood. Suddenly, he saw him in a new light. He knew the man standing before him was sixty-three years old, but Jesse suddenly saw a man in his twenties, charging up some beach with his Marine buddies, a carbine and bayonet in his hands, while mortar shells rained down on their landing craft.

Guadalcanal, Cape Gloucester, Peleliu, Iwo Jima, Okinawa...

Every Marine knew those places, and suddenly Jesse was filled with immense pride at following in his grandfather's and father's footsteps.

Pap handed Jesse a shot glass with a half-inch of dark brown liquid in it.

74

Jesse looked at it. "What's this?"

"Pusser's," Pap replied. "A Royal Marine first introduced me to the Royal Navy's grog when we were evacuated from Okinawa for R and R in Australia. This new rum company now owns the rights to the recipe the Royal Navy abandoned."

"Pap, I'm not even eighteen yet."

"Fuck it," Pap said and raised his glass. "I'm old and this is *my* house."

Jesse rarely heard Pap curse, and that word had never escaped his lips that he could remember.

"And you're a Marine," Jesse said, accepting the glass.

He'd drunk beer and rum before, even bourbon. But he'd never drunk any kind of alcohol in his grandparents' house or anywhere around them.

"*We...* are Marines, Jesse," Pap said, his tone serious. "To God, Country, and Corps!"

"Semper fi!" Jesse said and lifted the glass to his lips.

Pap placed his glass upright on the table and reached for the bottle, arching an eyebrow. Jesse placed his glass upright beside Pap's.

He poured another shot for each of them and extended his glass again.

Jesse raised his. "To Gunnery Sergeant Bo McDermitt."

Pap's eyes moistened as he lifted his glass just another inch higher, his chest swelling. "And to *all* Marines who fell before us."

Once more, the dark amber liquid burned down Jesse's throat, which seemed to tighten at the old man's words.

Guadalcanal, Cape Gloucester, Peleliu, Iwo Jima, Okinawa...

Pap had lost more than a son to armed conflict, Jesse knew that now. He'd never mentioned buddies he'd lost, but after what he'd just gone through, he knew that he'd been close with many who didn't come home.

At Parris Island, they'd studied those five battles among others. They were spoken of with reverence, as some of the deadliest fighting in Marine Corps history had taken place on those islands.

And Pap had been there.

Jesse no longer wondered if his grandfather had seen men die in combat. He'd never asked that question and Pap had never volunteered the information. But now, standing before him, Jesse knew he'd not only seen men die, but he'd lost friends, brothers-in-arms, and had likely watched them, perhaps even held them, as they took their last breaths.

Just as Jesse's recruiter had been with his father when he'd died.

As one, they placed their glasses on the table, inverted.

"Sit down, Jesse," Pap said, waving a hand toward the chair on the left.

Pap's chair was on the right. Always had been. There was a familiar, yet strange whoosh of air as he sat down.

And Molly's bed was beside Pap's chair, as always. She took two turns around the bed before settling into it.

Jesse sat down, and out of habit, took the sitting position of attention, heels together, hands on his knees.

"You're officially on *leave*," Pap said, relaxing into his recliner as he shook his head and chuckled. "At ease."

"Sorry," Jesse said. "Kind of a—"

"A habit that you have to learn to fall in and out of in the snap of a finger," Pap said. "You'll be living two lives from now on, son."

"I'm not sure I know what you mean."

"Your dad told me once how he sometimes only had a few minutes to transition," Pap said. "Part of you will forever be a Marine, son. But you have to be a civilian, also. One day, you'll be a husband and a dad. The Corps doesn't issue wives and kids, so they

76

don't have a manual or guidebook for them. When you're not on duty, you assume those roles, and you'll have to learn to change from one to the other."

"Did you have to do that?" Jesse asked.

"No. I left once and came home once. When the job was finished, it was over, and I picked up where I'd left off."

"I don't think I'll be doing any of that any time soon."

Pap grinned. "You have a little over twelve hours to make your first transition back to the lazy ways of the Lee Island Coast. When you go out with young Cathy tomorrow, you can't be marching around and shouting everything."

"I feel like one of my drill instructors is gonna barge in any second," Jesse said, relaxing his posture.

"You had a longer and more intense experience than I had. Even Bo's boot camp was shorter. We were being rushed into war. If you and those Marines you graduated with this morning were to go into battle tomorrow, you'd be way better prepared than we were. God willing, you won't ever have to find out."

"But you survived it," Jesse said, his voice low as he repeated the names. "Guadalcanal, Cape Gloucester, Peleliu, Iwo Jima, and Okinawa."

"I was lucky, son. A lot of my buddies didn't come home."

Jesse could see both pain and pride in Pap's eyes.

"Ever thought of going back there?" he asked without thinking.

"What on earth for?"

"I don't know," Jesse said, finding his eyes wandering to the big dolphinfish. "Closure, maybe."

"Don't tell me they teach all that feel-good crap now, like they do in the Navy."

They both laughed.

"Yeah," Pap said, breathing out softly. "I think about it a lot, actually. More so, now that I'm getting older. Some of the best men I've ever known are still there on those rocks."

"If I get stationed at Okinawa," Jesse said, turning back to face his grandfather, "maybe you and Mam could come and visit."

Pap looked at him and nodded firmly. "If you do. I definitely *will* come. Can't speak for your grandmother, though."

"You boys come and eat," Mam called from the kitchen.

"Coming," Pap yelled back, as they both rose.

Molly beat them both to the door.

Pap winked at Jesse and whispered, "Whenever you *do* find that one girl, don't ever make her wait. Call that Pap's rule number one. A happy wife means a happier life."

Chapter Nine

———◆——◆——◆——◆——◆———

The next morning, Jesse was up with the sun. Wearing just shorts, a loose-fitting USMC tank top, and running shoes, he went for a jog through the neighborhood with Molly.

He carried her leash, but it wasn't clipped to her collar. The two had made this same run for years, and all the sights, scents, and sounds were deeply engrained in her mind. So, she trotted alongside him, matching his pace with ease.

The houses along the river were older than the ones closer to the highway. Pap had been the first to build in the area, considered at the time to be way outside the Fort Myers city limit. It was now a suburb and within the city limits.

They jogged up each street, rounding a block to the next avenue, hitting every road in the twenty-block neighborhood. Jesse knew that it was just a little over three miles, following his familiar route.

He couldn't put a finger on just what it was, but everything seemed different. Yet, he'd run through the neighborhood at least twice a week for several years.

Have I changed? he wondered, rounding the corner onto the street he'd once lived on with his mom.

When they'd married, Bo had insisted on buying a house in the same area where he and Helen had grown up. He felt it doubly important when Jesse was born. He'd believed it necessary to have solid roots, though the Corps moved him around a lot.

Though it'd been only nine years earlier, Jesse paused for a moment to look at the neighborhood more closely, but he had a hard time remembering which house he'd spent the majority of his first eight years of life in.

"Can I help you?" a woman asked as she paused in her leaf raking under a large live oak.

Jesse looked up at the branches, belatedly recognizing it was his old yard, and his initials were carved in a branch way up there.

Jesse hadn't even realized he'd stopped running.

"I'm sorry, ma'am," he stammered. "I used to live here. I think."

She smiled. "Yes, I know." She laid the rake down and stepped toward them, petting Molly, and then extending a hand to Jesse. "We only met once," she said, smiling. "It was nine years ago. I'm Susie O'Hara. Welcome home, Jesse."

The O'Haras! he thought. They were the older couple who'd bought the house. They'd had a pretty teenage daughter in high school then.

"Sorry," Jesse said, shaking her hand. "How's your mom?"

"Not very well ever since Dad passed away a few years ago," she replied. "So I moved in to help take care of things after my divorce. Your grandmother brings Molly by every Tuesday to see Mom. It seems to be the only joy she gets anymore."

Jesse's face fell. "I'm so sorry. Mam mentioned she wasn't feeling very well."

She smiled. "Thanks. I was born late in my parents' lives. They were almost forty when I came along. Mom's sixty-five now."

She held onto his hand for a moment longer than was comfortable. Then she released it and studied him, her hip cocked and one hand resting on it.

"How long are you home for?" she asked.

"I have to report for infantry training on the tenth."

She smiled again. She was still pretty but was much older than Jesse. Probably twenty-five, at least.

"Maybe I'll see you again before you have to leave," she said. "My door's always open."

He just nodded. "Good to see you again."

He almost executed a facing movement before just turning and jogging away at a slightly faster pace than he and Molly had been running before.

When they got back to the house, Mam was in her familiar big blue housecoat at the stove, and though he couldn't see it, he could smell the bacon and hear it sizzling.

"Go get showered," she said, when he kissed her cheek. "Breakfast will be on in ten minutes."

"At Parris Island, I showered and dressed in seven."

"Then get hopping, before I find a three-minute chore for you."

Jesse showered quickly, put on a pair of cutoff blue jeans and a plain white T-shirt—one that was issued to him. His other T-shirts were a little too tight.

As he was about to leave the bathroom, he noticed the scale by the sink and stepped on it.

"What the...?" he muttered, looking down.

He stepped off the device and double-checked that it was zeroed out.

"Must be something wrong with it."

He went into the kitchen and found Pap sitting at the table, reading the newspaper.

"Went for a run this morning?" he asked, folding the paper and setting it aside.

"Yes, sir," Jesse replied absently. "Three miles."

"Something troubling you, son?" Pap asked.

"Do you have a scale in your bathroom too?"

Mam turned around and placed a platter of bacon on the table, smacking Pap's hand as he reached for a piece.

"Yes, we do," she said. "Is something wrong with the one in your bathroom?"

"It says I weigh two hundred and fifteen pounds," Jesse replied. "That can't be right."

Mam looked him up and down. "No, I'd say that's about right. Your dad was the same height and weighed more than that. You just filled out, that's all."

"Mind if I check?"

"Eggs will be on the table in two minutes," she replied, turning back to the stove.

Jesse hurried into his grandparents' bedroom. He'd jumped and played on their big bed when he was little, but now it too seemed to be from another place or time.

In the bathroom, he stepped on the scale. It read 214 pounds.

Jesse had always been athletic and tall for his age. In high school football, he'd played running back and receiver, and had even played defensive linebacker for a season in JV. He'd also played center for the basketball team, was on the swim team, dabbled in baseball, and was a high jumper and long-distance runner on the track and field team.

A lot of guys *lost* weight in boot camp, but Jesse had no fat to lose. So the three months of intense physical training had done nothing but add muscle.

After breakfast, Jesse moved to the sink to wash the dishes, as he'd always done.

"I'll get that," Pap said. "I need you to go out back to the garage and get that book on engineering conversions for me. You know, the one you thought you'd *memorize* before graduating high school?"

"What do you need to convert?" Jesse asked, accepting the challenge.

Pap laughed. "A whole bunch of things, son. I'm working on a little side project with a German engineer and he's going to call later this morning."

Jesse shrugged and ducked out the back door, Molly on his heels.

It was very rare that Pap helped with what he considered to be "woman's work." But it was a trek out to the garage and Pap was getting old. Maybe washing dishes was the lesser of two evils for him.

Molly trotted alongside him across what should have been a very familiar yard. He'd thrown tennis balls across it for the dog to fetch for hours on end. Later, he'd built a target where the center went into a pipe and the ball dropped out below. Molly fetched, while he perfected his pitching. His and Billy's first campout had been right down by the river, where Billy had shown him how to cook fish on a large flat rock by building a campfire on the rock and slowly cooking the fish next to the fire instead of over it.

When he reached the big garage, he opened the side door and stepped inside, his hand easily finding the light switch.

The buzzing and crackling of the fluorescent bulbs as the lights flickered to life revealed something that froze Jesse's feet to the ground.

The lights in the open rafters blazed forth, and bathed in their glow was a beautiful 1965 Mustang. It was painted a dark maroon color that seemed to absorb the light like a black hole in space.

Jesse's mouth fell open.

His eyes took it all in at once, then focused on a number of things that had obviously been customized. The chrome strip on the leading edge of the hood was gone, as were the big, blocky letters, F.O.R.D., just behind it.

Jesse blinked in disbelief.

He and Billy had talked about this exact model many times, and Jesse had often said that putting the manufacturer's name on the front of a Mustang was like painting the word HOUSE on all four walls. Anyone who knew anything at all knew that the Mustang was a Ford product.

And there it was, the unadorned hood filled and fared to perfection.

A pair of six-inch chrome rally lights were mounted above the bumper close together in the middle—something else he'd mentioned to his friend.

The chrome rally wheels had a matching maroon stripe just inside the bead, and the tires were Goodrich T/A radials, wider than stock on the front and even more substantial in the rear.

The radio antenna was gone.

Jesse's eyes traced along the roof line.

Twin antennas on the rear fenders, angled back.

Again, exactly like he'd talked about with Billy. All of it. As if it had been built straight from Jesse's own mind.

A white pinpoint of a stripe started at the side of the headlight cowl and stretched all the way back to the scoop on the rear fender, widening as it went to a full two inches, then following the contour of the side scoop down and around it before running forward again to the front wheel well, getting thinner to another point. The effect he'd imagined, and was now looking at, was exhilarating.

The car looked like it was going fast, just sitting there under fluorescent lights. And the stripe was an idea Jesse had only just mentioned in a letter to Billy during the first phase of boot camp.

There was a clicking sound and the catch on the big garage doors released.

Jesse tore his eyes away from the car, staring toward the

widening opening as the heavy doors slowly started to swing open, driven by giant, spring-loaded hinges.

Pap stood outside with Mam, the remote control for the door in his hand. Another click would activate a hydraulic pump that would pull the doors closed until they latched again. Pap had come up with the idea of using one of those rollup garage door remotes to activate the two things. Clicking one turned off the power to the electromagnet to release the catch and at the same time, released an electromagnetic valve on the pump to allow hydraulic fluid to flow freely. Pressing the other button engaged the electromagnets, closing the valve and turning on the pump. When the catch latched, it turned the pump off.

The true test of Pap's device over others was when there was a power outage. Without power, the electromagnets released the catch and opened the valve, allowing the doors to swing open without power, while everybody else's cars were trapped in their garages.

"Surprise, son," Pap said, as Mam broke away from him and came bustling toward Jesse.

"I could barely keep my mouth shut," she said, squeezing him tightly.

A horn honked, and Jesse looked past his grandfather as Billy's dad's truck pulled in. He and the girls got out, then ran toward the garage.

Jesse gaped at his grandfather. "Pap... Mam... I, um, I don't know what to say. You bought me a *car?*"

"Built it, Kemosabe," Billy said. "At my dad's shop. It was Mam's idea."

Jesse looked at his grandmother. "Your idea?"

"You boys would go on and on about this kind of car. All the things you'd do to fix it up. I just told your grandfather what you liked." She paused and looked the car over. "It's little and looks a bit gaudy, if you ask me."

"Billy did most of the work," Pap said, as they all came into the garage. "Under Bill's watchful eye, of course. But Billy did most of the grunt work."

"And everything was all laid out in detailed drawings and schematics by Pap," Billy added. "He even came out on weekends and helped turn some wrenches. It's cool, huh?"

Jesse peered inside at the white upholstery. The backseat had the Mustang horse in full gallop stitched into the upholstery. The pile carpeting was the same color as the exterior and looked brand new.

There was a full instrument package that surrounded a round speedometer and tach, the speedo winding all the way around to 140.

Jesse released Mam and hugged his grandfather. "I don't know what to say," he repeated.

"Yeah, we got that part," Billy said.

He turned and hugged his best friend. "I owe you and Leaping Panther a steak dinner."

Billy took Jesse by the arms and stepped back. "You owe nothing, brother. The work was a gift from my people to yours. Mam and Pap provided everything."

Jesse turned to his grandfather. "You shouldn't have, Pap."

"You don't want to ride a *bus* to Camp Lejeune, do you?" Pap asked with a crooked grin. "Every warrior *needs* a chariot."

Chapter Ten

━━━━◆━━━━◆━━━━◆━━━━◆━━━━

Cathy got in with Jesse and he started the Mustang's engine. It had a mellow, throaty exhaust sound and he didn't hear anything unusual from the engine compartment.

The gauges flickered, then steadied as Jesse looked at each one. The tach showed the engine was idling at 625 rpm. The water temperature was low, but Jesse knew that once the engine warmed up a minute, it would rise. The oil pressure was higher than normal, but he knew that would drop slightly as the heat thinned the oil. The ammeter was pegging the C—the charging side. The gas gauge said he had a full tank, and the odometer at the bottom of the speedometer showed that the car had just over 32,000 miles, which was either extremely low for a fourteen-year-old car, or normal mileage. The odometer only had five digits and could have rolled back over to zero after it reached 99,999 miles. Ten thousand miles a year was normal driving.

He desperately wanted to open the hood, but in front of his grandparents and Billy, it seemed akin to looking a gift horse in the mouth to see how old it was.

It had a four-speed, manual transmission with a Hurst shifter, which fit Jesse's hand like it was molded from it.

He backed carefully out of the garage into the sunlight, marveling at the deep paint of the hood. With Mam and Pap waving goodbye, Jesse followed Billy out to the highway.

Billy turned left and Jesse pulled out behind him, shifting through the gears with a light touch. He felt no hesitancy when he pushed on the gas pedal.

"Billy actually *built* this car?" Cathy asked.

Jesse glanced over. With the windows down, she was trying to corral her hair, but wispy strands floated around in the wind.

"Billy's a wizard with a wrench or welder," Jesse said. "His dad, too. They build mostly trucks, though."

"I've never met his parents," she said.

"His dad, Bill Senior, is known by their people as Leaping Panther. He's the chieftain of the Calusa. Three out of four of Billy's grandparents are Calusa and the fourth, Seminole. One day, Billy will become the Calusa chieftain."

"You've known each other a long time?"

Jesse nodded. "Since playground days. My folks and his were friends."

"Penny told me your parents died," Cathy said. "I'm so sorry. How did it happen?"

It always bothered Jesse when people said they were sorry. They didn't cause it. Remorse should be shown by the Vietnamese soldier who pulled the trigger, but perhaps, like Jesse's father, he might have been fighting for what *he* believed in.

Jesse knew that if his mother could somehow undo what she'd done, she would be sorry for it.

"My dad was a Marine," Jesse replied. "He was killed in the line of duty in Vietnam and in her grief, my mother overdosed on sleeping pills."

Cathy's eyes grew wider. "I'm so sorry, Jesse. I just can't imagine."

Four miles down the road, Billy pulled into his neighborhood and parked his dad's truck in the driveway. Jesse stopped at the side of the dirt road in front of the gate.

"That 289 sounds radical!" Jesse said, getting out to allow Billy to get in the backseat from his side.

"No man," Billy said, tumbling in next to Penny. "The badges on the *outside* say it's a 289, but that's just so nobody knows what's *really* under the hood."

Jesse got in and turned around in his seat, putting an arm over the back. "What'd you do?"

"Physically, it's only a little bigger," he replied. "So it didn't require a *whole* lot of cutting to stuff it in. But the mods we did have to make look way better than stock and are stronger than original. They had to be."

Jesse started the engine again. "What is it, man?"

"A 351 small-block, made in Windsor, Ontario," he replied, still grinning like a showman. "Same 'basic' block as the 289, but this one's been factory-bored and stroked to, get this... *four hundred and twenty-seven cubes, man!*"

Jesse's head jerked around in disbelief. "There's no way *that* fit in *this* car!"

"It's not the big-block like the 429 in Pap's T-bird or the 460 in my dad's pickup," Billy said. "It's called a Boss 427—a crate small-block."

"But even a 351—"

"Again, you're thinking of the big-block 351 *Cleveland*," Billy said, shaking his head as Jesse turned and put the car in first gear.

"What do you mean by crate?" Cathy asked, looking back at Billy.

"A factory-built engine comes in a wooden crate," Billy explained. "'Crate motor' is just garage slang." Billy pulled himself forward using the seat back, to be heard over the wind and exhaust noise, as Jesse shifted up through the gears. "And I never said it was an *easy* fit, Kemosabe. It's still *officially* a small-block Mustang, The Boss 427 is the same Windsor block as the 289 and 351, but needs bigger valves, which meant bigger heads, and bigger, long-tube headers, which made it four inches wider."

Jesse shifted to fourth and eased up on the gas, keeping the car at a nice cruising speed for a sunny summer day.

He caught Billy's eye in the mirror. "That's kind of a lot in a small car like this."

Cathy laughed. "It's not perfect for someone as tall as you," she said. "But it's a really cool car."

"The width and height were the easy parts—there's plenty of space between the shock towers. We just replaced the inside fender wells with custom-welded pieces to fit around everything. We made them beefier than stock, so we could mount things on them, like cable and hose brackets. And being three inches taller only meant a low-rise manifold and a narrower air cleaner than that big blue bucket thing on the stock engine. Finished it with a Holley 750 four-barrel. To look at it side-by-side with a stock 289 Mustang, most wouldn't know the difference."

Cathy turned around in her seat. "If that was the easy part, what was the hard part?"

"The hard part was the extra five inches of length that would have put the shifter under Jesse's elbow."

Jesse eased the clutch out as a light changed and he turned toward town, shifting smoothly through the gears again.

He looked at Billy in the mirror again, expecting him to continue, but he just grinned. He was enjoying himself.

"Why's it longer if it's the same block?" Jesse asked, rolling his eyes.

"From there back, nothing else is original either," Billy said. "Bigger bellhousing, longer tranny, custom shaft and a narrowed nine-inch."

"How'd you do it?"

"Part of it's in your hand," Billy replied. "The Hurst shifter had to be modified with a custom linkage. Pap designed and machined the whole fabrication in our shop."

"Pap did?" Jesse asked.

"We put the car on a lift and Pap used a micrometer to measure everything up, then he drew the linkage up on paper, cut and machined every part, and when we put it together, the movement of the shifter felt even better."

Jesse slowed for another light, looking in the mirror at Billy. "What's the transmission out of."

"It's a rebuilt Borg-Warner top loader out of a fifty-eight pickup," Billy replied. "Dad's been hanging onto it for years waiting for the right project. Thing's bulletproof and geared perfect for this car. The tranny's two inches longer than stock, and we made up the rest by moving the motor mounts two inches forward and getting rid of the clutch fan and cowling. Then we put a pair of electric pusher fans in front of the radiator."

Billy sat back and crossed his arms. "They come on sequentially as needed. Should keep the coolant at around two hundred degrees, even if you wanted to run the road course at Le Mans."

"Mam said she overheard us talking," Jesse said, glancing up in the mirror again. "But you and I never talked about anything like this."

Billy shrugged. "That was Pap's idea. He asked me what was the most powerful engine that could be put in the car without twisting the body like a pretzel, so I told him, and he agreed. There's no replacement for displacement."

"It's beautiful," Cathy said, turning and leaning against the door. "How fast does it go?"

"That's something I'd be afraid to find out," Jesse admitted, then glanced in the mirror. "What's your guess, Billy?"

"Know that long stretch of nothing, just the other side of dad's four-by-four shop? I buried the speedometer yesterday before getting half a mile."

Jesse grinned.

Knowing that he had that kind of power at his beck and call was comforting in a way. He doubted he'd ever need to drive at over 140 miles per hour, but it was good to know that if he ever did need to, he could. Pap's reasoning for the fireplace came instantly to his mind.

Better to have it and not need it, than need it and not have it.

Jesse smiled contentedly.

And better still, not to flaunt it, he thought. Keeping the 289 badges was a good idea.

But he had more than just himself to think about now, so it was unlikely he'd ever check Billy's reported top-end speed.

"Go ahead," Billy urged. "Open her up."

Jesse shook his head. "Can't do it, brother. This isn't my body anymore. It belongs to the Corps."

In that instant, Jesse knew why everything seemed both familiar and foreign to him at the same time.

He was a part of something bigger than himself now—something special.

At just seventeen, he now had obligations and commitments, not to mention some big boots to fill. Marines of the past *and* future counted on him. He had to live up to the legacy left by Marines like his father and grandfather, and countless men and women before them. And one day, he would lead other Marines. He would *not* let them down either.

It gave him a momentary nostalgic feeling, realizing that part of his life was ending, and a new chapter was opening up before him.

You'll be living two lives from now on, son.

A part of his mind was looking forward to the coming challenges of infantry school. He knew he would be tested under even more grueling conditions there, learning advanced unit tactics and about different weapons and how to employ them.

But right then, he was a seventeen-year-old kid having fun. He looked over at Cathy and grinned. He was on leave! He had a beautiful girl beside him! His best buddy had his six, and he now had one incredible hot rod!

Ten minutes later, they crossed the bridge to Fort Myers Beach and Jesse downshifted, preparing to turn into a small parking area at a stretch of beach he preferred and where it was usually not crowded.

"We're not going to Lovers Key?"

Jesse glanced over. She looked disappointed.

He'd spent a good bit of his childhood on Lovers before they built the bridge and bulldozed most of it. Whenever his dad was home, they'd take his boat there for overnight campouts. When he was away, his mom took him there in Dad's boat for walks along the shoreline and a picnic lunch. Sometimes, they had the whole island to themselves.

But once the bridge was built, the sleepy little island of his childhood was overrun by developers and Jesse hated it.

He smiled at Cathy and slowly pressed on the gas. "Sure, we can go to Lovers Key."

The day at the beach turned into two, then two became three. At first, Jesse felt as if that was what he wanted, after being away from his Gulf waters for too long.

And in most ways, it was.

The sun and salt air seemed to revive him. After three months of weekly haircuts and having a cover on his grape any time he was outside, he had a tan line around his head, just above his ears, and he was determined to make that disappear.

But the crowds, and eventually the company, were a distraction from his thoughts about what lay ahead. And Cathy seemed different from the pretty, introspective girl he'd met months earlier.

On the morning of his fourth day home, after his morning run, Jesse drove to Leaping Panther Garage, to thank Billy's dad for the work he'd done.

Later, he and Billy sat on stacks of mud tires in the second garage bay, drinking bottles of Coke. As kids, they'd ridden their bikes to the old gas station Billy's dad had turned into a 4x4 truck repair and customizing shop. It sat alone on the north side of State Road 80, almost exactly halfway between where the two boys lived, and the property included almost a quarter mile of riverfront on the Caloosahatchee, which also flowed past Jesse's grandparents' house.

There was little that Bill Rainwater, Sr. couldn't do with metal, a welding machine, and his big red toolboxes. Since before either Billy or Jesse was born, Leaping Panther had built big, beefy four-wheel-drive vehicles for hundreds of ranchers and farmers from Flamingo, at the south end of the Everglades, all the way up to Kissimmee.

He'd made a name for himself when Walt Disney started building his theme park near Orlando, and the developer needed robust, reliable trucks to move people and equipment around on the sprawling 25,000-acre complex.

As chieftain of the Calusa, a tribe that was once spread all over Southwest Florida, Leaping Panther had some notoriety as a woodsman and was the only bidder for the Disney project who'd actually visited the property. And he'd ridden all over it with the lead engineer, who was also a hunter, driving Leaping Panther's own International Travelall, custom-built for exactly the terrain they encountered.

He'd pointed out low wetlands, where feral hogs often congregated, and showed the engineer several "rubs" on the sides of low-hanging live oak branches where large bucks had scraped their antlers.

Though he was nowhere near the lowest bidder on the project, the engineer had gone to the project manager and pointed out the cost of downtime and vehicle repairs if they used inferior equipment.

Leaping Panther Garage built and equipped a dozen 4x4s that summer, and while Jesse's dad was home on leave, he'd pitched in to help his friend, with Jesse and Billy fetching parts and tools.

No two were alike—there were Chevys, Fords, and Dodges; some were pickups, and some wagons. It didn't matter, because they all had the same Cummins diesel engines, heavy-duty Allison transmissions, and solid front and rear axles. They relied on oversized wheels and tires to get the heavy-duty axles over the saw palmetto trunks, which grew horizontally on the ground, often overlapping each other.

The trucks weren't meant to be driven on roads, nor were they all meant for the high pines and palmettos—two were built specifically to go through the lowland bogs with minimal damage to the environment and had to be trailered to the sites. The others were built for specific jobs in an area that was mostly high, dense pine forest and they rarely needed to ford deep water.

The competitor's trucks were modified street machines that could go offroad. A little.

That was one of Jesse's favorite summers. They'd worked and

hung out with their dads in that very garage, fishing for largemouth in the evening, and their moms would arrive with dinner and a big blanket for them all to sit on and eat fried chicken. Friends, white, black, and red, came to help, and the order was delivered on time.

"What's bugging you, Kemosabe?" Billy asked, wresting Jesse's mind from the past.

Leaping Panther was on a short stepladder, bent over, with his torso and shoulders under the hood of an old Dodge Power Wagon. "He is right, Jesse," he said, turning to look over at the two young men. "You seem like you're somewhere else."

"Sorry," Jesse said. "It's... I don't know... weird sometimes, being back home again."

He liked Billy's dad. He never came off as being superior just because he was older. Some of their friends' fathers talked arrogantly about their jobs or positions. Pap had mostly just ignored them, telling Jesse later that he was too old to play manhood measuring games. But Leaping Panther wasn't like that. He listened and would only offer advice if he was asked for it, or felt it was needed. He often referenced a legend or talked of someone he knew of who had experienced the same thing and what happened to them in their situation.

When he talked, it was always man-to-man, either with his son, or his son's friends. Maybe it was just that he was closer to them in age, at thirty-five, than Pap was at sixty-three—a whole generation.

After Jesse's parents died, Leaping Panther had stepped in as a surrogate of sorts, taking valuable time off work for several years, so that he could spend time with his son and with Jesse, playing ball, throwing Frisbees, fishing, or just observing the world they lived in.

Leaping Panther stepped down from the ladder and got a Coke from the machine, popping the top off with an opener built into the front. Then he moved a couple of tools on the work bench and hopped up on it.

"I noticed it the first time I saw you after you came home," he said, then took a drink. "Ahh, that is good.... You have changed, Night Crawler. You might not even have noticed it. But I see it in your eyes, and I hear it in your words, spoken straight from your heart. You have begun a transformation, just as the caterpillar becomes the butterfly."

Billy's dad had received a vision on the night Jesse was born. He and Jesse's father had been close friends as *they* were growing up. In his vision, he saw a night crawler—a type of large earthworm that is great bait for large-mouth bass. He'd only revealed Jesse's Indian name to him when he and Billy became blood brothers, a year after Jesse's father and mother died.

The soft-spoken leader of the Calusa people still called him that from time to time.

Jesse hoped he wasn't about to change his name from Night Crawler to Butterfly.

"Everything and everyone seems different to *me*," Jesse tried to explain. "Things like my front porch, my bedroom, even my dog, unchanged for most of my life, seem like they now belong to someone else."

"Does the butterfly know it was once a caterpillar?" the older man asked.

Leaping Panther wore his hair long, as was the custom of his people. He wasn't a tall man, but he was powerfully built, with broad shoulders and a thick chest. There was little the man couldn't put his shoulder against that wouldn't move. But with people and animals, he had a way of speaking that was completely open and non-confrontational. Even his dark eyes seemed like those of a gentle deer or puppy.

He never asked a question unless he already knew the answer.

"I think... in some way," Jesse said, struggling to put his thoughts into words, "the butterfly knows that it was once *different.*"

"The butterfly cannot understand just what that difference *is*," Leaping Panther added, then looked Jesse in the eye. "I saw the same change in your father almost twenty years ago."

He was talking about when Jesse's dad had enlisted.

"I can't put my finger on it," Jesse said. "But it feels like a part of me is... I don't know... like it's drifting away on the tide or something."

"I do not think the change is complete," Leaping Panther said, then chugged more of his Coke. "Change is a confusing time for any man. I think you have much to do in this world." His gaze went back and forth between Jesse and Billy. "Both of you will change the world. *Your* individual paths, and those of your friends and family, are at a divergence. A man must forge his own path at some point. Yet, these separate paths will cross back upon one another many times as you move along yours and they upon theirs. Just as it has these past four days that you have been home. But this is only your path *temporarily* reconnecting, before bearing away again.

"You must learn to be fluid, like the tide you mentioned. You must move with the ebb and flow between two worlds if you are to stay afloat in either."

Leaping Panther paused, his soft eyes fixed on Jesse's. "I think you need more time among your *own* people, and I do not mean the whites."

He drained his bottle and dropped it into a red barrel that had *Glass* stenciled on the side, and then went back to work on the Dodge.

Jesse followed Billy outside to the Mustang.

"Your dad's cool," Jesse said, stopping beside his car. "And you are too, my friend. Thank you for this."

"It is what we do," Billy said, passing the thanks off like the gift was nothing. "It was Mam and Pap mostly. While we worked on it together, Pap spoke very proudly of you. Pop and I just cut and welded shit and turned some wrenches."

"Hey, how come you don't have a car?"

"What for?" Billy replied, glancing over at a row of 4x4s inside the fence, waiting on parts. "I can drive one of any number of trucks we're building any time I need to go somewhere."

"I mean your own, dork."

Billy grinned. "I have my own dork—you."

"You know what the hell I mean."

Billy leaned against the Mustang and patted the fender. "This is just a thing, brother. It is beautiful, no doubt." He paused and grinned. "You could even say a work of art. But this car, just like the tall grass in the Glades, the trees in the cypress heads, and each one of us, will one day return to the ground from which all things come. You cannot own the ground when you are a part of it."

"Deep thoughts for an Injun," Jesse quipped, paraphrasing a line from Matt Dillon on *Gunsmoke*, one of their favorite TV shows.

Billy grinned. "I'm a deep Injun."

He pushed some stones around with his foot, and then squinted up at Jesse in the bright sunlight. "Hey, uh, how hard was it? I mean, physically. For real."

"Boot camp?" Jesse asked.

Billy nodded.

"It was hard," he said, "but the physical part wasn't as tough as the mental. Imagine all day, every day, football practice. With classes in between, and it lasts all summer long."

"Under Coach Kennedy?" Billy asked, grinning. "The guy who never sweats."

"Sergeant Smith never sweated either," Jesse said. "Long

conditioning marches with full packs, like we did that summer in tenth grade around Corkscrew Swamp."

"A lot of weightlifting?" he asked. "I mean... you came back even bigger."

"Just a few pounds," Jesse replied. "There was a little weightlifting, but it was more just the constant PT—sometimes the drill instructors would PT everyone for one guy's mistake. A lot of running, almost always in formation. I told you about the battalion obstacle course and the confidence course. We only ran the C-course twice, but the O-course was at least once a week. Why are you asking?"

"I was talking to the recruiter."

"No way!" Jesse exclaimed. Then he grinned. "You know they don't make allowances for the hair on account of tribal culture."

Billy looked up and grinned again. "Even if it looks like yours, it's no worse than it is now."

Billy had felt ashamed after the redneck had quickly cut his ponytail off the previous year. In his eyes, whether it was shoulder-length or buzz cut, it was all the same.

Jesse opened the door and got in his car, then looked up at Billy. "Oh, it can *definitely* be worse. I actually need a haircut right now, and in the first month, yours'll be way shorter. Thanks again for the work you did, Kemosabe."

Chapter Eleven

━━━◆━━━◆━━━◆━━━◆━━━◆━━━

Molly hadn't wanted to run with him the next morning, so Jesse went alone. Maintaining himself to the best of his physical ability was now a priority to him, and that meant morning PT and watching what he ate.

Molly was almost six, and in dog years that meant she was already middle-aged and starting to lose that spirited inclination to run just for fun.

Though it was early when he stepped out the front door and stretched on the porch, the temperature hadn't dropped very much overnight, and was climbing toward ninety at sunrise. The humidity already had beads of perspiration rolling down his face, although he was just warming up.

High heat and humidity had never bothered Jesse. He'd spent the bulk of his free time outside for as long as he could remember. As a kid, it was where his friends were. Outside was a place, just like school, home, or the old fort he and Billy had built on the bank of the river behind Leaping Panther Garage.

"Where are you going?" Mam often asked him when Jesse was headed toward the door.

"Outside."

"Where, outside?"

"I won't know until I get there," had always been his standard reply, which was the truth.

The exchange had played out hundreds of times over the years and, if it was still daylight, that's where Jesse would be—outside.

The heat and humidity of Parris Island was comparable, so it'd never been uncomfortable for Jesse. Some of the city kids from up north had a hard time with it, though. Most adapted. Some went to the pork chop platoon.

He started running toward the end of the west end of the road, the sound of his footfalls the only noise he could hear. At least with his ears.

In his head, Jesse could hear Sergeant Smith singing a double-time cadence. *Lo, righta, lo, righta, lo, righta, lay-o... Lefoot, righta, layo. .. Lo, right, layo... Lefty, righta, layo... Loveta double time!*

As his "go-fasters" slapped the pavement in time with Sergeant Smith's internalized cadence, Jesse let his mind drift.

After spending four days with Cathy—sunrise to after sunset, except for one day when she had to go home early to be with her mom, and another day when she had to work four hours at the mall—Jesse was beginning to think she was a bit shallow.

She was nice and sweet, and there weren't many girls who were prettier, but a lot of her energy seemed to be focused on being noticed by others. And on being noticed *with* Jesse.

He preferred quiet, out-of-the-way places where there wasn't anyone else around to intrude on conversation. But Cathy liked to be around other people—lots of other people—and go to the more popular places, where lots of people gathered.

They'd gone to the beach three times—all three to Lovers Key. They'd hung out at a popular pizza place in Cape Coral, but in all that time they hadn't had much in the way of meaningful conversation. Nothing like that first night on Pap's boat.

Had his absence from all the normalcy he'd come to know blown that short time they had into something more than it was?

They'd kissed the night they'd met at his going-away party, and they'd made out a few times since he'd returned, parked at the beach after sunset, but that's as far as they'd gone.

Not that it had to be all about the physical, Jesse thought, as he rounded the last block.

Jesse spotted Suzie O'Hara, once more raking leaves. She stopped and watched him as he approached the house that he'd once lived in.

"Good morning," she called out, waving. "Do you run every day?"

Jesse recognized it as an invitation to stop and chat.

She wore short shorts, popularized by the TV show featuring a scantily clad Catherine Bach as Daisy Duke. Her blouse was tied under her breasts and open enough to expose ample cleavage.

"I have to stay in shape," he replied, stopping on the side of the street. "And running or swimming has always been a part of that."

She took a step toward him, dropping the rake where she'd been working.

Jesse noticed that there really weren't that many leaves in the yard.

He also noticed that her hair was teased, creating a large halo of streaked blond locks, framing a face that was made up with eyeliner and red lipstick.

"How are Frank and Norma?" she asked, looking him up and down and then smiling.

All of Jesse's friends called his grandparents Mam and Pap, just as he did. Jesse was unused to the familiarity.

"They're fine," he replied, then, for no reason added, "Pap's working on a design project with a German architect."

Still smiling, Suzie cocked her head slightly. "What's a woman gotta do to get you to ask her out?"

"Uh, what?"

She came closer, stopping well within arm's length. "I'm a single woman, Jesse. You're a single man, right?"

"Um, yeah," he replied awkwardly, not really sure of his status.

Unlike Cathy, this woman didn't beat around the bush when it came to what she wanted.

"No strings, Jesse," she said, toying with a strand of hair hanging in front of her shoulder. "I'm not looking for a relationship. I have to stay home with Mother every night, and a girl gets lonely for company."

"You know I'm only seventeen," he said, unable to come up with anything else.

Her eyes strayed to his chest, which was almost at her eye level, before looking back up into his eyes with a sultry gaze. "And I'm only twenty-six, a woman in her prime. Women don't peak, sexually, until their late thirties."

Jesse felt his face flush.

"It's called being friends... 'with benefits,'" she said, taking another small step and placing her fingertips against his chest. "A friend who has a certain... *need*, that only someone like you can fill."

Her touch felt like a lightning bolt, and he was paralyzed by it.

"You're only here a few more nights anyway," she whispered softly. "We could have a lot of fun when the sun, um... goes down. No ties, no relationship, nobody even needs to know. When you leave, it's over."

Since he was tall, most of the girls he'd dated in high school were also tall, like Cathy. But Suzie was tiny, almost impish, but curvy everywhere a woman should be. His chin was above the top of her head, even with her hair piled up on top. He doubted that she could even weigh half what he did.

"I... um..."

She moved her fingers to his lips. "Mother goes to bed by nine, and she could sleep through a hurricane. Tonight at nine?"

She gently moved her hand up and down on his lips, and Jesse found himself nodding.

Suzie smiled. "I hear Salty Dog's has fresh oysters. You should try them."

"Oysters," Jesse mumbled absently.

"Nature's *aphrodisiac*," she replied, then turned and walked slowly across the lawn, putting way more motion into her hips than was normal for walking. She paused to bend at the waist and pick up the rake.

Jesse's mouth was agape when she glanced back and saw him staring.

"You did what?" Billy asked, as he and Jesse sat on Mam and Pap's front porch later that morning.

"I have two dates," Jesse replied, struggling to comprehend why he hadn't just told Suzie no. "I'm picking up Cathy in two hours and we're going to—"

"Lovers Key," Billy finished. "I don't get it. Way too many people there."

"Yeah," Jesse agreed, nodding. "But she likes it."

"And what about doing things *you* like to do?"

Jesse shrugged. "I don't think it ever entered her mind."

"So you decided to go out with someone else?"

"She's older," Jesse said, noncommittally.

"How old?"

Jesse shrugged one shoulder. "Twenty-six."

Billy slowly shook his head. "What prompted you to ask a

twenty-six-year-old out on a date? And more importantly, where'd you get the balls?"

"Yuck, yuck," Jesse said in mock laughter. "I didn't ask her out."

Billy's eyes went wide. "Man, I *gotta* go to Parris Island now! Where are you taking her?"

Jesse's face flushed again. "Nowhere."

"Nowhere?" Billy asked. "Doesn't sound like a date at all."

"She wants me to come over after her mother goes to bed."

"Do I know this chick?"

"Remember the people who bought my house after Mom and Dad died?"

"The O'Haras?"

"They had a daughter," Jesse said. "She was in high school then."

Billy snapped his fingers. "Suzie O'Hara! I heard she was back in town. Holy crap, man!"

"I'm not going," Jesse said. "It doesn't seem right. Especially in my old house."

"Yeah, I see what you mean," Billy said. "Shoot, she's probably staying in your old room."

"And I don't see things going anywhere with Cathy, either."

Billy nodded. "I never realized how self-centered she was. I'd only met her a couple of times when Penny suggested we match you two up at the party. So, what are you going to do?"

The screen door opened, and Mam stepped out with the cordless phone in her hand. "Jesse, you have a phone call."

Jesse's face fell. *Cathy.*

He took the handset and held it to his ear. "Hello?"

"Jesse, you ole barracuda!" a familiar voice said. "It's Rusty Thurman."

Jesse's face lit up. "Hey, *hey*, Rusty! Good to hear from you! How are things down in the Keys?"

"Another shitty day in paradise," Rusty replied. There was a pause. "To be honest, bro, I feel like a fish outta water. It's like all my friends are stuck in a time warp, still in high school."

"Like everything you knew seems foreign to you now?"

"Yeah!" Rusty exclaimed. "Weird, ain't it? Hey look, I just picked up a new boat. Wanna go divin'?"

Jesse looked over at Billy, who nodded, having heard the exchange. "School starts Monday, Kemosabe. You should go. Be with *your* people, like Dad said."

My people, Jesse thought. *Other Marines.*

"Can your folks put me up?" he asked Rusty. "I don't want to impose."

"Impose, my ass," Rusty said. "But then again, I have seen you eat, so you'll have to put at least twenty pounds of fish in the ice box for your stay."

"It's a deal," Jesse said, not sure how he would explain it to Mam and Pap.

Or Cathy.

"How soon can ya get down here?" Rusty asked. "My new boat is super cool. Wait'll ya see it. There's a Greyhound stop a block from our driveway."

Jesse grinned at Billy. "I'll be driving," he said. "A '65 Mustang."

"Cool! All I have is my dad's wheels. Can ya get here by the weekend? There's a lot of reefs to dive and it being the last weekend of summer, should be lots of tourist chicks."

"How do I get there?"

"Go south on Useless-One," Rusty replied with a chuckle. "That's what we call US-1 down here. There's only one traffic light in Marathon, so when you get to it, make a U-turn, and then pull down the first driveway you come to after the K-Mart, headed back north.

There's a mailbox on a leaning post there; it ain't got no numbers on it, though. If ya get lost, ask anyone ya see where Shorty's Bait Shop is. Everyone knows Pop."

"I'll be there tomorrow," Jesse said, making up his mind. "Before sunset."

Pap would understand and maybe the two of them could explain it to Mam. But he'd still have to tell Cathy.

"That was your friend from boot camp, right?" Billy asked.

"Yeah. He invited me down to the Keys to do some scuba diving."

"Gas tank's full," Billy said. "We just stopped at Floyd's last night, but that won't be enough to get you there."

"How much gas does it hold?"

"The gas tank is OEM—original equipment from the manufacturer," Billy replied. "But it's new and holds sixteen gallons, so you can probably get about a hundred and fifty miles on a tank."

"Less than ten miles per gallon?"

"Around town, yeah," Billy answered. "Maybe eleven or twelve going across Alligator Alley, but you better fill up down in Copeland.

There aren't any gas stations after that until you get to the outskirts of Miami. Wish I could go with you."

"That'd be cool," Jesse agreed. "Remember how clear the water was two summers ago when we went down there?"

"Yeah, we could see fish on the bottom, thirty feet below the boat," Billy replied, a wistful look on his face.

Then his features became serious. "You're part of another tribe now," he said somberly. "I think that's what dad meant. How do you plan to tell Cathy?"

"I don't know," Jesse replied, honestly. "I don't want to hurt her feelings. But I just don't see a relationship, man. Who knows where I'll be this time next year?"

Billy turned to face him. "You've been home over half a week, my brother. Have you taken her down to Ten Thousand Islands? Or out in the Corkscrew? No. You've been too busy doing what *she* wanted. Has she given any thought to *your* feelings?"

"Yeah, but still."

Billy winked. "But I wouldn't blame you for seeing Suzie before you left. She's a fox."

Jesse looked at his friend. "A fox? She's not a piece of meat."

But a side of beef was exactly what he'd felt like, talking to Suzie a few hours earlier.

"Look," Billy said. "Cathy's not right for you. I see it, and you *know* it. She doesn't like any of the things you do. So the sooner you end it, the better for both of you. But in the meantime..."

Jesse shook his head. "I'll tell Cathy today that I'm leaving in the morning, but I don't think I'll be spending any time with Suzie."

Later, when Jesse and Cathy were at Lovers Key, he'd told her about the phone call from his Marine buddy, and his plan to drive down to the Keys the next morning to do some scuba diving.

"I can't just drop everything and go down there, Jesse," she'd replied. "I have Mom to worry about, and I have a *job*, remember? Besides, I don't even know how to dive."

There was something in the way she said the word "job" that struck a nerve. As if being a Marine was akin to being jobless.

"Yeah, um..." Jesse stuttered. "About that. It's kind of a, uh... guy trip."

She'd stared at him for a long moment before jumping to her feet and snatching up her towel from the sand.

"Fine! Go then!" she shouted at him, then turned and stormed away, angling toward some girls she knew from Cape Coral.

Of course, Jesse had gone after her, but she was quickly swallowed up by a group of friends, who all took her side. So he'd left her with her friends and driven home alone.

When he arrived, he'd found that Mam had already laid out a suitcase on his bed, along with a stack of clean skivvies and socks, and had even pulled his dive bag out of the closet. Jesse spent the rest of the afternoon packing and playing with Molly in the backyard.

Later that evening, after supper, as Jesse was loading his things into the Mustang's trunk, Pap came out.

"Are you sure you have everything?"

The sun had already dropped below the trees and the frogs had begun singing—high-pitched trills from the little green treefrogs in the oleanders, along with the deep resonance of the bullfrogs along the riverbank were like music in the still night air. Jesse had always found the sounds of a late summer evening peaceful to his ears.

"I won't need much," he replied as he lifted the small suitcase, packed with a bunch of his civilian clothes, and put it in on top of the dive bag. "This will get me through next week and hold me over through infantry school. We probably won't have a lot of free time, and I don't think it's a good idea to take a bunch of stuff I'll just have to pack and move again when I finish school and get orders to my next duty station."

"It won't be a far move," Pap said. "Odds are, you'll be assigned to one of the infantry units at Lejeune."

Jesse cocked his head slightly. Pap had always pronounced the name of the base that way, as if it had an R in it—La-Jurn.

"Why do you say it like that?" he asked, genuinely curious. "I've only heard it pronounced La-June."

"It's named after the thirteenth commandant," Pap explained.

"I had some classes in college with his grandson and met General Lejeune once. It was before the war and long after he'd retired. It was his foresight that prepared the Corps for what was to come in the Pacific Campaign. He was already in his seventies when I met him, but just two years earlier, he'd volunteered to return to duty after Hitler invaded Poland. He was one tough old gyrene, that's for sure.

"Anyway, he was from southern Louisiana," Pap continued, "and his father had been an officer in the Confederate Army. He spoke like the well-educated Southern gentleman he was, and that's how *he* pronounced his name."

"La-Jurn?"

"More of a softer J," Pap said. "Like Zsa Zsa Gabor—Le... *Zhurn.* It's French."

"Le-zhurn," Jesse parroted, letting the sound roll off his tongue.

A light blue Camaro with a black landau top pulled over to the curb in front of the house.

"I wonder what she wants?" Pap asked rhetorically, as he turned toward the end of the driveway.

Jesse closed the trunk and looked over the Mustang's roof to see Suzie O'Hara coming up the driveway. She'd ditched the short shorts and halter in favor of a more conservative bright yellow, sleeveless summer dress.

She'd also cleaned the makeup off her face, which actually made her look better, in Jesse's opinion.

"Hello, Mr. McDermitt," she said, smiling at Pap.

"How are you, Suzie?" Pap asked, smiling politely. "How's your mother?"

"Oh, I'm fine," she replied. "And mom is doing well; she just went to bed a little while ago, so I've been doing some work around the house. Thank you for asking."

"What can I do for you?" Pap asked.

Her eyes cut to Jesse for a moment, then back to Pap. "I have a bunch of things that need to be moved out to the garage," she replied. "But they're heavy. I was wondering if I could borrow your grandson for an hour or two. I'll be glad to pay him."

"Nonsense," Pap said, beaming, and patting Jesse on the shoulder. "Neither he nor I would ever accept payment for helping a lady in need."

A lady in need..., Jesse thought. *A need that only he could fill, she'd told him.*

Jesse turned quickly toward his grandfather. "I really have to—"

"Go and help a neighbor," Pap said slowly, giving him a look of admonishment. "You're not leaving until morning."

"Oh?" Suzie's eyes cut to Jesse's and sparkled. "I thought you were home for *two* weeks."

"I'm, uh... going down to the Keys to visit someone."

She smiled, demurely clasping her hands together in front. "Well, if this is your last night, you probably have plans."

"He doesn't," Pap said. "We were just going to watch a movie and turn in after the news, like always."

Suzie turned and faced Jesse, still smiling like a pageant queen, her waist-length hair falling over her shoulder. "Well, that makes me about the luckiest girl around... that I caught you before you left, I mean."

Chapter Twelve

◆　◆　◆　◆

Jesse got an early start the following morning, hitting the road just after breakfast, with a lot of things on his mind, not the least of which was the adventure he imagined lay ahead.

He'd done some weekend outings with Billy and some other friends, canoeing deep into Corkscrew Swamp to camp for the night, but this was the first time he was going off for a whole week by himself. Well, except for the three months at PI.

He'd been to the Keys quite a few times, the first trip being with his parents—a Christmas sailing cruise in Dad's new boat, that he and Pap had built. And the old man had taken him down there three times, once in a seaplane.

It felt right. He was a man—a Marine. He was making adult decisions now based on what he was beginning to realize was a whole change in his perception. He felt good about this. The Mustang felt good. The call from Rusty and this trip felt good.

But little else did.

Jesse took that as it was. He would learn to cope with the feeling of being different. To do as Pap had said, shift into and out of the two lives.

But what if he didn't want to shift? What if he liked the strict, regimented life better than the civilian world?

He pushed a bit harder on the gas pedal, then, noting that he was already going eighty, let up again. He wanted to get there by the afternoon, and it would be at least a five-hour drive.

Longer, he realized, if he got pulled over by the Highway Patrol for speeding.

Heading east on State Road 82, he reached Immokalee in less than an hour, then turned south on US 29, which took him to Copeland, another hour and change later.

Jesse wasn't watching the time.

He stopped for gas before getting on State Road 48, the long, lonely stretch of highway that ran through the Everglades—Alligator Alley.

What Jesse didn't feel good about was what had happened the previous day with Cathy, but it was done and there was nothing he could do to change any of it. Besides, he'd probably be gone until spring, anyway.

If we started a relationship, he told himself, *we might not see each other again for months.*

In a week, he'd be in infantry school, which would take two months. Then he'd be assigned to a unit after that, probably in early November.

While he might be able to get a week's leave after SOI and before reporting to his unit, he didn't want to miss his first Marine Corps birthday, and that would be the week after he finished infantry school.

The Marine Corps had a long-standing tradition that the oldest and youngest Marines in attendance cut the birthday cake. He was seventeen and wanted to be part of that tradition. Next year, there might be another seventeen-year-old.

Being a new guy, he figured getting leave at Christmas wasn't likely, so he'd already resigned himself to not being able to come home for several months, until he could take leave in the spring—and that was a long time for either of them to wait.

Billy was right: it turned out that they just didn't have much in common, so it was probably best to end it early. But it still bothered him that he'd left with her being angry at him.

Billy had been wrong about one thing, though.

Suzie wasn't staying in Jesse's old room. When he'd arrived to help her move boxes, she'd had him follow her into what had been a guest bedroom when he lived there. It was larger than his room and had a private bathroom. His mom had promised it would be his when he was older, but until then, they wanted to keep it available for her parents to visit. He only barely remembered them. They'd died when Jesse was five.

Once inside, Suzie had closed and locked the bedroom door.

There hadn't been anything that needed moving or even lifting, except her, as he'd found out later that she was quite a gymnast. What there had been an abundance of were low lights, soft music, and candles.

He'd been very reluctant at first, especially since she'd lied to him and Pap to get him to come over. But in the end, he and Suzie had at least satisfied one another's *physical* needs. But it left Jesse feeling empty when he walked home, exhausted, two hours later.

The drive across Alligator Alley was uneventful, and Jesse stopped for gas again when he reached the outskirts of Miami.

The Mustang was running perfectly, and he found that he'd actually gotten a little over twelve miles per gallon since leaving Copeland. And that was running at sixty-five most of the way. He also found that Billy had been right on the money with the temperature gauge. It would creep up if he accelerated, but then he could hear the second fan click on and the temperature gauge would drop back to just below two hundred degrees.

He paid the tolls and took the bypass south around the edge of the city, and was soon on US 1 in Homestead, or "Useless One," as

Rusty had called it.

After crossing a long causeway and then a bridge, he slowed as he entered Key Largo, where US 1 got a name—the Overseas Highway.

It was well past lunchtime when Jesse passed a sign welcoming him to Marathon. A quarter mile from the first traffic light he'd seen in several miles, he glanced over and saw a leaning mailbox next to a gravel road that disappeared into the gloom of dense foliage.

There was a convenience store and gas station at the light and the Mustang's gauge was just above a quarter, so rather than make a U-turn, he pulled in to fill up.

As he was pumping the gas, a big, bearded man, his graying hair pulled back in a ponytail, came out of the store, and strode toward a motorcycle parked on the other side of the gas pump. He wore jeans and a T-shirt, with a leather vest covered in patches. One at the top of his left chest read *Bear*.

The man saw him looking and Jesse nodded.

"Nice ride, kid," he said, then put a six-pack of beer in a saddlebag, and slung a leg over the bike. "Sixty-six?"

"Sixty-five," Jesse replied, admiring the custom paint and chrome of the Harley.

"Here for the weekend to do some diving?"

"A week," Jesse found himself saying. "Staying with a friend."

The man started the Harley, which was loud and throaty, nodded his head, then roared away.

Jesse went inside to get his change, then got back in the car and pulled out of the station, headed north. He slowed as he approached the leaning mailbox, then turned onto the gravel driveway, which crunched under his tires. It was narrow, barely wide enough for two cars, and on either side were dense mangroves and casuarinas—a natural wetland. Everything was carefully trimmed along the edge

116

of the narrow road, or driveway, or whatever it was, which turned left, then right, apparently for no reason at all, except to give someone coming in a feeling of calmness. The road was raised above the wetland around it, so its path had been intentionally set.

After several hundred yards, the road emerged into a small sand and grass clearing, large enough for maybe ten cars. An old pickup was parked under one side of a big live oak, so Jesse turned and parked under the other side. He'd already learned just how hot it got inside the dark- maroon Mustang when it was parked in the hot Florida summer sun.

Shutting off the engine, Jesse heard a screen door slam, and looked ahead to see Rusty coming out of a two-story house. To Jesse's right was a large, metal-roofed building with many windows, which Jesse assumed was the bait shop. It was close to a narrow channel and there were a couple of boats tied up there.

"Whoa-ho!" Rusty exclaimed, running up to meet Jesse, who was climbing out of the car. "This is one badass ride, bro!"

"Thanks, Rusty," Jesse said, shaking the shorter man's hand. "How's it going?"

The first thing Jesse noticed about his new friend was that his hair looked normal, as did his mannerisms, and the way he talked. Rusty sounded like a yokel, but Jesse could tell he was both intelligent and insightful.

Rusty cocked his head a little and squinted. "Better, now that I see your ugly mug, jarhead."

"Ha! You looked in a mirror lately?"

"You and this hot rod are about the only things that ain't *unusual* in some way. You got bags?"

"My seabag's in the trunk," Jesse said. "I figured you and I could *drive* up to Camp Geiger. If we split the gas, it won't be much more than our bus tickets, faster, and way more fun. What'd you mean by 'unusual'?"

Rusty walked around the front of the Mustang, admiring the wheels and paint job. "What's under the hood?" he asked, seeming a bit anxious.

Jesse walked around the front of the Mustang and used the small key on his keyring to release two recessed locks on either side of the hood. Then he reached under the grill and pulled the release, opening the hood to Rusty's astonished eyes.

His friend's mouth hung open for a moment, then he leaned over and checked the badge on the fender.

Rusty pointed at the engine. "That ain't no 289, bro. That's a 351 Windsor. I know my Ford motors."

"Kind of," Jesse replied, grinning. "It's a Windsor small block, alright, but it's a Boss 427."

"Holy shit, man!" Rusty exclaimed. "A stroked small block?"

"Pap paid for the restoration while I was at PI, and my friend Billy Rainwater and his dad built it. Billy says 'There's no replacement—'"

"For displacement!" Rusty finished. "I'd like to meet this friend of yours one day. Bring your dive gear?"

"In the trunk, along with my seabag and suitcase."

"Well, let's get to divin'!"

"Right now?"

"Well, grab your gear and we'll stash it first. You got your choice of the spare room in the house..." He pointed toward the structure he'd come out of. "Or ya can bunk with me in the rum shack."

"Rum shack?" Jesse asked, closing the hood, and locking it. "Don't know what that is, but I like the name."

"Grab your bags. It ain't big, but I like it. Moved out there the second night I was home. Kinda like campin', like when we went out to Ellis Island."

Rusty took the suitcase as Jesse hefted the seabag and dive bag out of the trunk, slinging one on each shoulder.

Rusty led the way, walking past the bait shop, then headed down a slightly sloped lawn toward the water's edge a hundred yards away. There was a seawall made of tumbled boulders there that rose several feet above the ground and a good eight feet above the water.

Beyond the seawall, Jesse could see broken limestone shallows for hundreds of yards out, with some ledges rising above the surface.

"That's Vaca Key Bight," Rusty said. "Those shallows and them boulders have protected this property from a dozen hurricanes."

A small, tin-roofed shack stood next to the seawall. It was painted white and had only a door visible on the left side.

"That there was my great-grandpa's distillery," Rusty proclaimed, as they walked down the slope, falling into step by rote. "Tolliver Thurman built the still before Prohibition started, shipping sugar cane up from Havana, 'cause it was easier and cheaper than going to the cane fields on the mainland. He made *legal* rum when he started."

"He made rum?" Jesse asked. "Right here?"

"Ole Tolliver was already in his forties then," Rusty replied, reaching the door to the small shack. "He figured the closer to the water he put his still, the less distance he'd have to lug stuff. This old shack has been underwater almost to the roof seven times and lost its roof four of those."

"And he made legal rum out of Cuban sugar cane?"

Rusty nodded. "He used a few Caribbean spices in his. That didn't last long, though. Two years later, the railroad reached Marathon in a sprint from the mainland and that's how the town got its name."

He pulled the door open and stepped inside. Jesse followed and found a fairly clean and dry room about twelve feet wide and twenty long with two large windows facing the sea. He immediately felt his anxiety level drop looking out at the water.

"Nice," Jesse said, nodding, and looking around.

"Anyway," Rusty continued, as he put Jesse's suitcase inside the door, "with the coming of the railroad, it made gettin' sugar by rail faster, cheaper, and a lot safer than crossin' the Gulf Stream. And he shipped his legal rum by rail, too. Until Prohibition, that is. Then he went back to Cuba and started shippin' his bootleg rum by boat."

Jesse looked up. There was no ceiling, just exposed beams about nine feet off the wood floor. The metal roof had a full-length ridge vent for ventilation, and the beams were thick and dark in color.

"Those beams are solid mahogany," Rusty said. "The walls are solid concrete, a foot thick."

"You sound like one of those tour guides," Jesse said.

Rusty chuckled. "Sorry 'bout that. Goes with bein' a bartender. Folks are always askin' about the history here."

A pair of well-worn recliners dominated the right wall across from a small TV sitting on a milk crate below the windows. Beyond, Jesse could see turquoise water to the horizon.

"The wind's always off the water," Rusty said. "Open 'em just a crack, and it stays pretty cool in here, even on a hot day."

At the far end of the room was a set of wooden bunk beds and two large chests.

"I got the bottom," Rusty said. "There's more sittin'-up headroom up there on the top."

"So, your great-grandfather made rum right here in this building?" Jesse asked again, noting a part of the metal roof that had a round hole and a patch over it. "And now you sleep here."

"The chimney ran right up through there, where you're lookin'. My grandpa made rum here, too. And Pop helped him. All the way up until I came along. Gramps passed the year before that and Pop thought it was too risky by then, what with the highway going by so close."

"Close?" Jesse said, dropping his seabag beside his suitcase. "This place is a quarter mile through a jungle. How much land is it?"

"Proximity is a relative thing, bro. My family was here way before the railroad. Then, after the Labor Day Hurricane of 1935, we were cut off again. Then they built the Overseas Highway."

"Useless One," Jesse said.

"Folks around here, at least the Conchs like us, mostly get around by boat. What with all the tourist cars now, it's faster. And there ain't never no traffic jams. The ocean's big and the island's small. We own fifty-two acres, depending on the tide," Rusty replied. "We only own a two-hundred-foot easement for highway frontage, though, which keeps the taxes down. My third great-grandpa bought it and donated the wetlands on either side of the road to the state—a natural, untouchable buffer. But we got two thousand feet of waterfront here on the east side; just this five hundred of it cleared."

Jesse looked around the single room. "Where's the head?"

"Back of the bait shop," Rusty replied. "Even has a freshwater shower. C'mon. I gotta get the keys to the boat, anyway, and we can tell Pop we're headin' out."

"Is there somewhere we can get some chow?" Jesse asked. "I haven't eaten since breakfast."

Rusty laughed. "Already scroungin' food and you ain't even caught your first fish to pay for it yet. Better hope you're as good with a speargun as you are with an M-16."

Chapter Thirteen

◆ ◆ ◆ ◆

Bear Bering waited until the woman with the whiny kid paid for her purchase and headed to the door, then he walked toward the counter with a six-pack of Bud.

The clerk nodded and looked outside. The woman was getting in her car and a Mustang was pulling up to the gas pumps.

"Make it quick," Bear said, reaching into his pocket and sliding a rolled-up plastic bag across the counter, covering it with his big hand.

The kid reached into his pocket and slid a twenty-dollar bill across, snatching the bag when Bear uncovered it. Then he rang up the beer, told him the price, and Bear slid the twenty back.

He took his change and picked up the beer, then headed back outside. The kid with the Mustang looked over at him and nodded his head.

"Nice ride, kid," Bear said, as he stashed his beer in the right saddlebag.

He slung a leg over the bike and asked, "Sixty-six?"

"Sixty-five," he replied.

He looked like one of those uptight Ivy League punks, well over six feet tall, with close-cropped hair and the shoulders of a defensive linebacker.

"Here for the weekend to do some diving?" he asked.

"A week," the kid replied. "Staying with a friend."

Bear started the Harley, revved it a couple times, then nodded at the kid and took off, crossing the northbound lane and heading south toward the Seven Mile Bridge.

With his deliveries completed for the day, it was time to check on the plants in the grow house, and maybe have a little fun with Sky who was going to meet him there.

When he got to the house, her car wasn't there, so he parked the bike near the steps, shut it off, and went inside to check on the work his guys had done that week.

Because he was the contractor for the remodel, the neighbors knew him on sight by now and they knew that the sound of his bike heralded the end of the workday, so they paid him no mind.

They'd been working on the house for three months, using the job as cover to grow pot in the garage and master bedroom while the owners were in Europe until the end of the year.

The renovations in the kitchen were nearing completion and they'd be starting on the bathrooms next, which would take a lot less time, mostly because they'd been stalling with the kitchen remodel until the plants matured. That way the workmen didn't have to go traipsing through the bedroom to get to the bathroom. The master bedroom was full of nearly mature plants.

The kitchen's island and countertops were finished, and he had to admit, the matching Italian marble looked damned fine. The sinks were installed, and he checked the cabinet beneath them.

Good, the plumbing's all done, too, he thought, as he heard a car coming up the driveway.

He continued his inspection of the large, stainless steel, vented hood over the gas stove and oven. It was wired up, and when he flipped the switches on the front, the lights and fan came on.

"Everything okay?" Sky asked, as she came through the front door.

Bear turned and smiled. She was dressed as usual, professional, but with a bit of a wild side. The tight-fitting skirt really accentuated the narrowness of her waist.

"The kitchen is all but finished," he announced, spreading his arms wide. "I got my tile guy coming back tomorrow to re-caulk the backsplash—he left a one-eighth-inch imperfection behind the stove."

"Leave it to you to find the punch-out items nobody would ever see," she said, reaching up on her fashionable heels to kiss him. "How are the plants? Ready to move?"

She'd asked that question at least twice a week for the last month and it was starting to get on his nerves. He'd told her from the start that the plants would reach maximum maturity in fifteen to sixteen weeks. Saturday would only be fourteen.

"Haven't looked," he replied, a bit gruffly. "But I'd say no, not for another ten to seventeen days. Just like I been tellin' ya for a month now."

"It's just that I'm nervous," she said. "It's been three months and every day, I expect a cop to walk into my office."

"Just play it cool for a little bit longer," he said, trying to keep his voice in check. "C'mon, let's have a look in the garage."

He unlocked the door from the kitchen and was hit by a blast of cold air. He'd dropped the humidity setting on the big window AC unit to force the plants to bud.

"Oh, my God!" Sky said, stepping through the door. "It's frigid in here."

"That's what makes them bud," he said, as she joined him in the narrow, three-foot-wide perimeter of the garage that surrounded the greenhouse.

As she passed, he got a noseful of her seductive perfume, which never failed to get him excited. He caressed her ass, then closed and relocked the door.

Moving to the center of the walkway, he pulled back the first flap of heavy plastic and stepped through, then pushed on past the next one and into the growing area.

The pungent aroma of top-shelf weed easily overpowered Sky's perfume.

He inspected a few plants as he moved along the center row toward the pump, which was located in the middle of the garage, distributing nutrient-rich water to the rows of healthy plants. The buds were getting close, but he knew at least another ten days would be needed until they could get top dollar for the whole crop.

"I'd give it another week, at least," he said, pulling a large bud toward her. "See the little hairs starting to grow? That means it's almost there."

"I just wish it'd grow faster," she said, wrapping her arms around herself. "How cold is it in here?"

"It's runnin' on a humidistat," Bear replied. "Gotta keep the humidity at forty percent or less. I'd guess it's about sixty degrees. Your nipples are pokin' through your shirt *and* bra. Why don't we get it on here in the pot field?"

"In this cold?" she protested. "Not on your life. I just want this all out of here before we get caught."

He backhanded her without warning.

"I told you it'd be ready when it's ready!" he shouted as she cowered away from him. "Now get your fuckin' skirt off, or just hike it up and turn around."

Chapter Fourteen

◆━━━━◆━━━━◆━━━━◆

They went back outside and headed up the lawn to the bait shop. Jesse figured it was probably fifteen feet above the ground level the rum shack was built on. He looked along the shoreline in both directions, where it turned to rocky shoals and mangroves all the way to the highway in one direction, and around the end of the island in the other.

"It's almost like a fortress," Jesse said.

"It's been that a time or two," Rusty replied, pausing a moment at the door. "During the Second and Third Seminole Wars, Captain Augustus—he was my third great-grandpa—he traded with the Indians and provided them with guns from Cuba. We've been outlaws ever since, choosing what side to be on based on our own moral compass."

Rusty pulled the door open, and they entered as Jesse digested the information Rusty had given him. Now and then, he let the fun-loving local yokel façade slip and Jesse got a glimpse of the real Rusty.

"Hey, Jesse," Shorty Thurman called out when they walked into the bait shop. "Welcome to Key Vaca. How was the drive?"

"Hey, Mr. Thurman," Jesse replied. "It was relaxing after I got out of Homestead."

"Just call me Shorty, son," he replied. "Everyone else does. Yeah, that drive never fails to turn back the clock to island time for romantics and lovers of the sea. Hope you like fish."

"Yes, sir," Jesse replied. "I love seafood."

It smelled like a bait shop but to Jesse, that wasn't an unpleasant odor, just one that he associated with one of his favorite things to do—go fishing.

It was smaller than it seemed from the outside, and when Jesse heard music through a closed door, he remembered Rusty saying it was a bait shop and *bar*.

"Thought I'd take Jesse out to Coffin's Patch," Rusty said, pulling a small cooler from behind the counter and putting a six-pack of Cokes in it, along with some ice and two large, wrapped bundles. "Maybe spear some hogs."

"Hogfish?" Jesse asked.

Shorty grinned at him. "Ever eat one?"

"Plenty," Jesse replied. "Best fish in the sea, if you ask me."

"There's four full tanks in the compressor room," Shorty said. "But weather's comin' in about sunset. I wouldn't count on any evening dives if I were you."

Rusty grabbed a set of keys that were hanging on a post by the register. "Wasn't anything on the weather report this morning."

"It'll come," Shorty said. "Mark my word, son."

"Be back in a few hours, then," Rusty said, seeming to accept what his dad had told him without question.

The two went out a side door and Rusty pointed. "The head's right there." Then he opened a door next to it and grabbed a scuba tank.

Jesse quickly relieved his bladder, then helped his friend carry the four tanks and his dive gear down to a small dock area.

"I got us a coupla Cubans," Rusty said, carrying two tanks, lifted way up to keep them from dragging. "Should hold us over till supper."

Jesse only had to raise his tanks slightly, but the combined weight of the tanks and dive bag were causing beads of sweat to pop out on his forehead.

It felt good.

"How's your dad know it's going to rain?" Jesse asked.

"Dad's only been up to the mainland a handful of times his whole life," Rusty replied. "When ya spend a lifetime on an island, ya learn things they don't teach in meteorology school."

They reached the dock and Rusty stopped next to a boat with a center helm and bimini top. "Whatta ya think?" he said, putting his two tanks down on the dock. "It's a Bertram. Twenty feet long, and you can walk circles around the center console while fightin' a big fish. She's got a hunnert-and-sixty-five-horse Mercruiser inboard/ outboard."

"It's yours?" Jesse asked.

"*All* mine," he replied. "No financin'. Saved up all through winter crawfish season."

"That was your job? You caught and sold lobsters?"

Rusty looked at him with an expression that seemed to convey he was schooling a child. "There ain't no *jobs* in the Keys, bro. Here, we hustle. I fished sometimes, fixed boats at other times, did some trading for this or that, but always made a buck, and I been tendin' bar since I was fourteen. My first Marine Corps paycheck put me over the top to get the boat. It felt like we belonged together from the start, ya know."

Jesse glanced toward the parking lot, where the Mustang sat in the shade of the big oak tree. "I don't know which of us is luckier."

"Well, me, o' course, ya dumb ground-pounder. I got a girl to share it with. I take it since you double-timed down here on a whim, there ain't no 'Suzie' back home?"

Suzie and Jodie were the fictional girlfriend and best friend of every recruit, who were imagined to be cheating together while the recruit was away. Still, Jesse winced slightly at the name.

"Not really," he replied. "I thought there might be, but it just wasn't in the cards."

"Ha! *Cards*," Rusty said, as if the word left a bad taste in his mouth. "Play the joker, bro. Try on a bunch of suits till ya find that one queen of hearts that fills out your straight. Jewels knows a bunch of local gals and there's hot- and cold-runnin' tourist women here every day."

"I don't really—"

"We'll have ya sittin' by a beach fire, gettin' lucky with someone fun by end of tomorrow—that's a *gar-own-tee*."

Rusty stepped down into the boat and Jesse handed him his dive bag, then the tanks, which Rusty stored in a tank rack bolted to the back of the helm seat.

"You know boats?" Rusty asked.

"Fine time to ask," Jesse quipped. "But yeah, you can't grow up in coastal Florida and not. Pap and I built five over the last ten years."

"How big?" Rusty asked, opening the cooler and tossing Jesse one of the bundles.

"Two thirty-two-foot sailboats and a couple of small powerboats about this size. We were almost done with a thirty-eight-foot sportfisher when I shipped to PI."

Jesse tore open the paper and took a large bite of the sandwich.

"He a boat builder, is he?"

Jesse shook his head and stepped aboard while chewing. "He was an architect. But he sold his business and retired when my folks died."

Rusty stuck the key in the ignition and looked over at Jesse. "I've heard ya say that in just that way a few times, bro." His tone turned serious. "Like it ain't no big deal. I wouldn't know what to do without Mom and Pop."

Jesse wolfed down another bite. The sandwich was filled with several kinds of spiced meats and cheeses and was plenty hefty.

"I was lucky to have grandparents who could take me," Jesse said, also serious. "The two of them did all four jobs—mom, dad, grandmother, and grandfather. And never once acted as if I was a burden." He shrugged. "I'm not the only orphan kid and I've now lived longer without my parents than with them."

"For real, man? Half your life? How old are you?"

Jesse didn't need to calculate how old he was on the day his mother died. He'd done that many times, until it was memorized. He'd only needed to double that. He'd marked that date with a silent prayer to his parents before going to bed that night.

"I turned seventeen last March," he said. "Just before we met. The day I'd been longer without my parents than with them was during our first week with our drill instructors."

"And ya spent that day alone?" Rusty asked, a tinge of sadness in his voice.

Jesse grinned. "I wasn't alone. Hell, there wasn't a single second during that whole three months *any* of us was ever alone."

Rusty visibly shivered. "I can't imagine losin' my folks."

"We *all* will one day," Jesse said. "And it's likely that Mam and Pap won't live to see me make sergeant major."

"You're plannin' to be a lifer then, huh?" Rusty grinned. "I keep expectin' Sergeant Smith to get up in my face every time I turn around."

Jesse burst into laughter, harder than he had since before he shipped out for boot camp. "Me too!"

Jesse suddenly froze, realizing that Rusty's boat, though he'd never seen it before, seemed more familiar than his own bedroom back home.

He looked around the dock area, taking in the beauty of a place he'd never been before. Somehow, this little island felt more like home to him than his own hometown on the Caloosahatchee.

Jesse came to the sudden realization that he'd probably not be spending more than a Christmas or two with his grandparents for at least the next four years, maybe forever.

With that realization came another, one that he'd felt earlier while gassing up in Copeland.

Pap had been preparing Jesse for years to be independent and to think on his own. Many kids never knew their grandparents and fewer had an adult relationship with them. Pap knew there'd come a day when he and Mam weren't going to be around and had prepared Jesse for when that happened. Pap told him the night before he got on the bus that it was satisfying for him, knowing that Jesse would have a Marine family when he and Mam were gone. It struck Jesse then that Pap had been getting him ready for that eventuality since he was eight years old, working in the hot sun with him.

"What's wrong, bro?" Rusty asked, looking up at him with a worried expression. "You look a million miles away."

"I don't know," Jesse replied. "You mentioned feeling out of place a couple of times—once on the phone and again when I first got here. You used the word 'unusual.'"

"I ain't figured it out," Rusty said, looking back toward the bait shop and his family home.

"I get that feeling too, sometimes," Jesse said, looking around again at the small dock area and the shallow cut leading out to the ocean. "Is it all the time for you? When you feel like that, I mean. Or are there places or times where you feel like everything's cool?"

Rusty turned and looked toward the other end of the small canal, where it opened into the bright turquoise water. "No, not all the time," he replied. "When I'm with Jewels, everything seems normal. And out there. So far, just when I'm with her, or on this boat, out there on the reef—the only places I've felt... I don't know. Normal, I guess."

He turned the key and the engine started instantly.

"Been the same for me," Jesse said. "But here, I get sort of like a *déjà vu* feeling. Not like I'd been here before, but more like this is where I'm supposed to be. I felt the same at PI."

"I stuck out a lot there," Rusty said. "It ain't fun always bein' the shortest. Hard for the DIs to miss ya."

"Trust me," Jesse said. "Being tall makes you an even *bigger* target."

Rusty laughed. "I didn't see Sergeant Smith gettin' up in your face."

Jesse chuckled with him. "You were the *only one* in the platoon he *could* get face-to-face with."

Rusty grinned, then his expression turned serious. "See that red, white, and blue ribbon at the top of his rack?"

Jesse nodded somberly. "Silver star. He had a purple heart too."

Rusty put the boat in gear. "Seen some heavy shit."

The water was flat calm on the way out, and the heavy boat stuck to the surface like it was on a trailer. Once out of sight of land, Jesse could tell where the reef was. The turquoise water ended a mile ahead, where he could see ocean rollers making whitewater swirls and eddies over the shallow reef. Beyond that, the ocean was cobalt blue.

Rusty turned slightly, angling toward two other boats that seemed to be anchored very close together, just inside the reef.

"That's a coupla buddies of mine," he shouted over the wind and engine. "Ansil and Gregor. One's a burnout hippy and the other ain't got both oars in the water half the time, but they always find fish."

Still a quarter mile away, Rusty slowed to a little over idle speed as they approached the other boats, which were both flying the red and white "diver down" flag. Jesse looked over the side and could see the bottom quite clearly, about thirty feet below.

"That you, Thurman?" a voice came over the water as a man jumped onto the gunwale of the nearest boat. He hung onto the bimini top with one hand, waving with the other.

The guy was rail-thin, tanned, with wet hair way past his shoulders and a thin beard. He wore tattered jean cutoffs and had some sort of gold necklace just below his chin.

Rusty stepped out of the shadow of the bimini top and waved. "Hey, Ans. Y'all find anything?"

"Good hog!" the man called back as they came closer. "A few snapper and grouper, too. No bugs, though. Haven't seen ya around in a few weeks. Pull up and tie off. We're about done for the day, anyway."

By bugs, Jesse assumed the man meant lobster. The season had just opened a few weeks earlier, and at least around Fort Myers, he'd heard from Billy and a couple of others that a week later, they were scarce.

"We'll be over in a jiff," Rusty said, then under his breath added, "Jesse, put them fenders back out. It'd be rude not to catch up on the coconut telegraph."

"Coconut what?"

"Local gossip," he replied. "These islands are small, and most folks know one another if they're Conchs like me."

As they tied off, two divers surfaced at the stern of the second boat, "Yo, Thurman!" one of them yelled, as Ansil climbed over to the other boat to help them aboard.

Rusty waved. "Hey, Gregor. Good to see y'all."

"That's Gregor," Rusty said under his breath, then grinned up at Jesse. "And his sister, Rachel."

"Hi, Jim," the woman called out, handing a pair of fins up. "I

134

haven't seen you in a month. Where've you been?"

"Weeks?" Jesse asked. "A month?"

"Yeah," Rusty replied under his breath. "It's island time." Then he shouted over to the woman. "More like three months, Rach. I went to boot camp at Parris Island, remember?"

"Oh, yeah," Rachel said, handing Ansil her tank and buoyancy compensator. "So, are you back home to stay now?"

Gregor handed Ansil a large orange bag, blood dripping from the mesh at the bottom.

"Just another week," Rusty explained. "Then me and Jesse here have to report to Camp Geiger up in North Carolina."

Rachel climbed up a small ladder bolted to a platform next to the outboard. She was also thin, like Ansil, but not in the same way. The body-hugging wetsuit she wore didn't hide the fact that she was a woman.

She vaulted the two boats' gunwales and was standing right in front of Jesse in only a second, surprising him.

Her eyes sparkled with mischief as she unzipped and peeled the dive suit down off her shoulders and arms. She was dark tanned and wore a light blue bikini under the thin dive suit.

"And Jesse is?" she asked, looking him up and down.

"Rusty and I went through boot camp together," Jesse said. "Jesse McDermitt. From Fort Myers."

"Well, welcome to Coffin's Patch, Jesse McMyers!" she exclaimed, then leaned across the gunwale and kissed him deeply, hands grasping the back of his head.

She stepped back, leaning on the helm seat, pulled a tie loose from her hair, and shook it out. "I like you, Jesse McMyers." Then she turned to Rusty. "Bring him out to Party Island tonight. Tie off to my sloop and we'll swim up together. But right now, we have to skedaddle. You know how it is."

Chapter Fifteen

———◆———◆———◆———◆———

Rusty hurried forward to drop an anchor to the sandy bottom as the two men started to untie the boats. That done, they both went over to the other one and untied it.

Rachel went to the helm and started the engine, then tossed her wet hair over one shoulder, looked back, and smiled at Jesse. "See you tonight, Jesse McMyers."

As soon as the boats had drifted apart, Rachel took off, bringing her boat up on plane and turning toward shore. The second boat took off after her with both men aboard.

"I think she likes ya," Rusty said, opening his own dive bag and pulling a regulator out and setting it aside.

"How old is she?"

"Rach?" Rusty paused and looked up while attaching his BC to a tank. "Lessee, she was a senior when I was in eighth grade, I think. So four years older'n me—twenty-five."

"You're twenty-one?"

"Will be in November."

"How do you know them?" Jesse asked, setting up his own gear.

"Rachel and Gregor from school," he replied. "He's two years older'n her. There's only about two hunnert kids in the school, seventh through twelfth."

"Wow!" Jesse said. "We graduated more than two hundred."

"Ansil, well, he just dropped anchor in Boot Key Harbor one

day," Rusty continued. "I guess it was about ten years ago. Then his engine died, and he never got around to fixing it. He's married to his third dock queen now. That's what ya call a liveaboard boat that don't run and never leaves the dock."

Rusty looked up and grinned. "That's what I meant about the coconut telegraph. There's only two hunnert people in this town between any six years of age. Some kids leave after high school and some tourists stay on after vacation to balance it out. Age eighteen to thirty? Twice that—about four hunnert people." He shrugged. "Small town; everyone's up in everyone else's business here. Can't avoid it. Word of mouth is how we've communicated for generations—the coconut telegraph."

"But your friends didn't stay around to talk very long."

Rusty looked down fidgeting with his gear. "Yeah, well, I guess they were in a hurry."

There was something else, Jesse thought but let it go. "You said your family's been here a long time. How long?"

"The house was built in 1838 by my third great-grandpa, Captain Augustus Thurman, a sailing ship captain out of Boston. Think I mentioned him before. It's built out of Dade County pine, same as the bait shop. Can't find wood like that no more. I'm the fifth Conch born in that house, and God willin' there'll be some more. Jewels wants a big family."

Jesse connected the low-pressure hose to the auto-inflator of his BC, then opened the tank's valve to check the air pressure. "What's the plan?"

"I put out two hunnert feet of anchor rode," he replied, strapping his BC around his chest. "The current flows right along the inside of the reef here, at only 'bout a knot on the surface, practically still at the bottom. The boat'll end up a couple hundred feet down the reef from the anchor.

"When you're ready, sit up there on the gunwale behind ya—mind the teak and fiberglass—then just roll off backwards. We'll follow the anchor line down and start right where they left off. If anyone else comes along, they'll drop anchor where our boat is and do the same. This whole reef's usually pretty productive. Take your time, and don't shoot nothin' you don't know for certain is legal. The Marine Patrol likes to harass us."

Rusty opened a deck hatch, removed a triple-banded spear gun, and handed it to Jesse. "On the bottom, we'll spread out and drift back to the boat. Should take twenty minutes with almost no effort. Let's see if you're as good a marksman in the underwater world as you are on land."

The water was startlingly clear, Jesse noted, as he righted himself next to the boat. He could see Rusty on the other side, just below the hull, holding up the okay sign.

He signaled back and the two started swimming toward the front of the boat. Jesse could see the anchor line stretching way into the distance, angling downward. Beyond that, it stretched across the sandy bottom, mostly visible. There was a slight current, but it was easy to overcome.

When they reached the anchor line, Rusty led the way, swimming against the current with short but powerful kicks. He followed the line downward without holding onto it, and they soon reached the bottom, where they followed the line all the way to the anchor.

Leap-frogging his friends was smart, and if someone else arrived and did the same, it ensured no part of the reef was overfished and gave each boats' divers a spot on the reef that hadn't been covered by previous divers.

When they reached the anchor, Rusty extended his own spear gun to Jesse, holding up his index finger—one minute.

Jesse took the speargun, then Rusty moved over to the anchor, pushing the spades deeper into the sandy bottom. Rusty took his gun back and pointed toward the reef.

They spread out as they approached the reef, which looked unbroken as far as Jesse could see in either direction.

Jesse had done some drift diving before, but usually it was with someone on the boat, following the divers' flag or bubbles. Anchored drift diving was something new, but the current was light and the reef barely drifted past Jesse's mask as he held himself motionless in the water.

Exhaling, Jesse dropped closer to the sandy bottom, looking over at Rusty, who had turned and was slowly swimming with the current, about ten feet away from the reef.

Jesse did the same, turning eastward, according to his wrist-mounted compass. Under a ledge, he spotted a fairly large parrotfish, foraging on coral polyps. He remembered someone telling him once that most of the sand on beaches in the tropics was from parrotfish eating coral and pooping sand.

Jesse paused and checked the speargun. He'd used a few before and easily found that the spear was in the locked position, so he stretched the shortest band first, latching the steel hook into the first notch of the spear. He repeated the process for the other two bands, then resumed the hunt.

A moment later, a large black grouper emerged from a crevice just ahead, turning toward Rusty, who was swimming away.

Jesse's speargun came up, gripped in both hands, the spear tip leading the way, as he held his breath and stalked what looked like at least a thirty-incher.

The fish was unaware of his presence, but the angle wasn't good enough. Jesse inhaled very little, and he began to rise slightly, still not making any bubble sounds.

Finally, he was above and just behind the big fish, his body angled downward. When he released the trigger, the spear found its mark in the back of the grouper's head and it twitched only once before dropping to the bottom, still.

Within seconds, Jesse had the fish in his bag and reached in to unscrew the spear tip and slide the shaft out of the fish's body. He'd lost more than one injured fish trying to do it while wrestling the fish outside the bag.

He screwed the tip back onto the spear shaft, loaded and locked it, then stretched the three bands once more. Ahead, Rusty was just putting what looked like a large brownish-gray snapper into his bag.

Jesse continued swimming slowly along the reef, letting the current do most of the work, and turning into it if he got too close to Rusty. He wasn't just hunting, he was also admiring the beauty of the reef and the thousands of colorful fish that darted in and out of crevices in the coral.

He looked ahead and saw Rusty also moving and peering under ledges. Beyond him, Jesse could see the boat and looking back, he realized they'd only covered a third of the distance.

By the time they reached the boat and headed to the surface, Jesse had added two medium-sized hogfish to his bag. He glanced at his pressure gauge as he and Rusty neared the surface and was surprised to see that he still had over 1,800 psi left.

"How's your air?" Rusty asked, when they reached the back of the boat. "Got enough for another pass?"

"A little over eighteen hundred," Jesse replied. "What kind of snapper was that you got? The first one."

"Cubera snapper," Rusty replied. "Great eatin'. You get anything?"

"Two hogs and a big black grouper."

"How big?"

"Well over the limit," Jesse replied.

Rusty tossed his fins over the transom, then unclipped a short line from his BC and connected the carabiner to one of the boats hold-down eye-rings, then he inflated the BC and shrugged out of it, letting it drift back on its short tether.

"Clip yours to the carabiner on my BC," he instructed, as he climbed the ladder with his bag.

Jesse did as he was told and both young men were soon aboard with their goodie bags. Rusty opened the cubera's mouth, showing Jesse the long, almost canine-like teeth. It was a monster—easily thirty pounds, but it was dwarfed by the giant black grouper from Jesse's bag.

"Dang!" Jesse gasped as the fish were laid out. "That's bigger than it looked in the water."

Rusty looked up at him and grinned. "That's what *she* said."

They both laughed at the crude joke, sitting on opposite gunwales.

"Should we move the boat for another dive?" Jesse asked.

Rusty opened the cooler and took out two cans of Coke, handing one to Jesse. "No need," he replied. "We can rest here a minute and do the same thing again."

Jesse looked over the roiling water above the reef. "What's on the other side?"

"The bottom drops away pretty quick," Rusty said. "Sometimes you can see big gamefish over there, but nothing you could likely spear. Too fast and they don't get close enough."

"Like what?"

"Permit, wahoo, tuna, and dolphin sometimes... I even saw a big black marlin over there once." He looked down at the five fish they already had. "I can't believe you outdid me in my own waters, bro. You're a natural."

"Naw, I was lucky," Jesse replied. "The grouper came out to see what you were doing and never even saw me coming up behind him." He paused and looked across the reef toward deeper water. "Let's try the other side. How close can you get to these big gamefish?"

"Current's a lot stronger over there," Rusty said. "If we overshoot the boat on this side, it's a bitch of a swim against it."

"We could take turns drift diving," Jesse suggested. "The boat might even attract something."

"Not a bad idea," Rusty said. "I once caught two dolphin by trollin' past a sheet of plywood floatin' in the Gulf Stream. Likely to see sharks, too. You okay with that?"

"I've dived with sharks before," Jesse assured him. "I want to check it out."

"Get the anchor, then," Rusty said. "I'll get our gear. There's a cut in the reef just east of here and the relief is steeper." He looked up at the sun, then at a cloud bank to the southeast. "But we can't spend a lot of time. Gotta get these fish on ice, and don't forget that storm Pop mentioned."

Jesse hauled on the anchor line, pulling the boat against the current as Rusty got ready to get underway. He got the engine started and eased the boat forward, making Jesse's job much easier.

Twenty minutes later, as if following some invisible trail, Rusty turned south toward the reef.

"This cut's a lot bigger'n most," he said, craning his neck to see ahead. "About fifty feet wide here. Can't hardly miss it."

Jesse could only barely make out the difference in the water.

Once outside the reef, the boat rode differently, as it was lifted by the long rollers that passed under the hull to spend their energy on the reef. The bottom fell away quickly, until nothing could be seen but clear, blue water.

Rusty turned again and began paralleling the reef, heading back the way they'd come.

"So, how come you're not with Juliet today?" Jesse shouted over the engine and wind noise.

"She's at work," he replied. "She takes shifts as a waitress at different places whenever someone needs help. Today, she's workin' over at the 7 Mile Grill. She'll be at the bait shop once the storm passes, then we'll head out to Party Island."

"Is that the real name?"

"'Course not," Rusty said, pulling back on the throttle. "It's just what the kids call it. Like a lot of smaller keys 'round here, it don't have a real name." He shifted to neutral and killed the engine. "This here's as good a spot as any. How do you wanna do this? I just bought this boat. Be a shame to wreck it on the reef."

"I promise I won't break your boat if you wanna go first."

"Naw, you go first," Rusty replied. "I'll just drift and keep an eye on ya. Like ya said, somethin' might be attracted to the shadow and come up for a look-see."

"Okay, I'll go first," Jesse said. "Will you be able to follow my bubbles, or should I do a flag drag?"

"Vis is at least sixty feet here, bro," Rusty said. "You won't ever be out of my sight. Just drift with the current, twenty or thirty feet down, and I'll do the same on the surface. If ya hear the engine start, we're gettin' too close to the reef. But I won't move off too far, I can't still see your bubbles."

Rusty kept an eye on the roiling water as Jesse got back into his BC with his fins on, then pulled his mask on. Rusty started to hand the spear gun to him and stopped.

"You sure you wanna do this?" he asked. "You spear somethin' big and don't kill it, ya might get dragged to Cuba."

"I'm touched that you're so concerned," Jesse said jokingly.

144

"Concerned about my spear gun and tank, bro. Shit's expensive."

Jesse grinned, then took the speargun and rolled backward off the boat's gunwale. He gave a quick okay sign and raised his auto-inflator, pressing the purge button above his head.

Descending to thirty feet, Jesse still couldn't see any details of the bottom but knew it was no more than another fifty feet down. He slowed his breathing, wanting to conserve air. They'd spent thirty minutes drifting along the other side of the reef, but that had been at less depth, using less air.

Jesse looked all around, then up at the boat. He had no idea what they were doing, but he liked hanging in the open ocean that way. All he could see were shafts of light dancing through the water, disappearing into the murky darkness below. His depth of field had nothing to lock on, no reference point, except the boat.

Suddenly, something flashed behind him, going to his right, and he spun his head.

Whatever it was, it was gone.

Chapter Sixteen

———◆———◆———◆———◆———

Jesse felt abruptly vulnerable. He was hanging in the open, in deep water, not far from the warm waters of the Gulf Stream. He remembered Rusty saying he saw sharks just about every dive and Jesse knew great whites often frequented the Stream.

Whatever had sped past him, had disappeared through the shadow of the boat and was gone, just as quickly as it had appeared.

A game fish of some kind, Jesse thought, getting his speargun ready.

The speed with which the fish had moved both surprised and impressed Jesse. He'd seen some big gamefish while fishing with Pap, but he'd never seen one while underwater.

What Rusty had told him came back to his mind. If he took the shot, he had to be sure it was a kill shot. A marlin twice his size could easily drag him down or yank the tethered speargun from his grasp.

Jesse had no doubt in his mind what the outcome of a tug-of-war with a thousand-pound fish would be.

He kicked a few times toward the surface to reach the same depth the fish had been. It had moved past him so quickly, he couldn't even tell what it was, but the list of fish that were that fast was very short.

He purged just enough air from his BC to remain neutrally buoyant at the shallower twenty-five-foot depth. The water seemed clearer, but with no reference point other than the boat above him, there was no way to be sure.

Then suddenly, from about eighty or a hundred feet away, Jesse spotted movement—a darker blue shimmer heading straight for the shadow of the boat again, totally ignoring his presence.

The fish had nothing to fear. He had speed on his side and few animals in the sea would ever be able to catch it.

But Jesse didn't need to match its speed. He only needed to accurately judge it and compensate for it by leading the fish with the speargun.

It wasn't moving as fast now, circling to the right, probably confident that, having already made a reconnaissance pass, there was nothing to fear in the shadow of the boat.

But it might also be thinking about what sort of tasty morsel might be drawn to the shadow.

Its body was long and torpedo-shaped. Fixed pectoral fins stuck out almost horizontally, like airplane wings.

A bluefin tuna.

Probably five feet in length.

If nothing else, just seeing one so close underwater was a thrill.

Jesse held his breath half-full as he tracked the fish with his speargun. He made only small movements with his fins to turn and follow the tuna's trajectory.

The tether connecting the spear to the speargun was twenty feet long, so the fish had to come closer than that, which was something Jesse hadn't considered.

He kept the tip of the spear pointed just ahead of the big tuna and waited.

Has to be a kill shot.

It slowed suddenly, and Jesse moved his aim, his mind adjusting the lead he was giving the fish.

He pressed the trigger.

The spear caught the fish just behind the eye and it immediately began thrashing, moving in a clockwise circle.

It was a kill shot to the head.

The fish's brain was dead, but the muscle spasms were immensely powerful, propelling a body meant for speed.

Jesse took two turns in the tether around his right hand and hit the auto-inflator with his left, filling his BC and kicking toward the surface.

The fish tugged on the line, spiraling downward.

Jesse kept his eyes on his air bubbles, kicking hard toward the back of the boat, but ready to slow if he should start overtaking the bubbles.

He knew that surfacing too fast could cause an embolism. He also knew the fish was certainly big enough to drag him to the bottom if the spasms didn't stop soon.

He broke the surface, kicking hard toward the back of the boat with all his might, while the tuna tried to pull him back under with sudden tugs that threatened to dislocate Jesse's shoulder.

"What is it?" Rusty shouted, leaning over the transom.

"Tuna!" Jesse shouted around the mouthpiece of his second stage, not wanting to spit it out for fear of being pulled back under.

"Hot damn!" Rusty yelled, somersaulting into the water. He grabbed his BC, which he'd already put in the water, slipped one arm through the vest, and reached out with his other.

They'd done this before on some of the obstacles on the Confidence Course. The obstacles were designed to force teamwork on the recruits, and that training came in handy.

Jesse grabbed Rusty's outstretched wrist and Rusty locked onto his, and together they pulled and got Jesse close to the boarding ladder.

He thrust his right hand through the top rung, still holding the spear's tether, and held on tight as Rusty climbed aboard and turned around.

"Hand me the line!"

With his other hand, Jesse reached as deep as he could and looped the line around his left hand, then muscled the fish up, pressing the line over his head to his buddy.

"Got it!" Rusty shouted. "Get up here, quick! We're driftin' close to the reef!"

Jesse pulled his fins off and tossed them aboard while Rusty fought the fish.

"I told ya to make sure it was a kill shot," Rusty said. "Get the helm."

Jesse started the engine and put the shifter in forward, turning the wheel away from the reef.

"Hold it!" Rusty yelled. "He's gone under the boat!"

Jesse shifted to neutral instantly as Rusty moved forward, trying to pull the tether around the bow to the other side, so as not to foul the line in the prop.

When he finally got it around, Jesse put the boat in gear and idled away from the reef. When they were a hundred feet out, he killed the engine and joined Rusty, now at the stern on the opposite side.

"It was a kill shot," Jesse said, as they hauled on the line together. "This is just his nerves dancing. If he was alive, he'd have pulled us both down."

Jesse grunted as they hauled up together, gaining another two feet.

Rusty leaned over the side for a look. "Holy shit!"

"You got a gaff?" Jesse yelled, the thin line cutting his fingers as the fish continued to twitch, each muscle spasm sending it deeper.

"Yeah!" Rusty said. "You got him?"

Jesse nodded and Rusty crossed to the other side and removed a five-foot-long gaff from a rod holder under the gunwale.

Jesse reached down and got a lower grip, then hauled up another foot of line, his back muscles straining. The fish was thrashing less, but it was still almost more than one man could handle.

Finally, with another mighty pull, the end of the four-foot spear rose up out of the water, it and the tether vibrating excitedly.

Rusty reached out with the gaff, expertly hooked the giant fish through the back of the head, and added his strength to the pull.

Together, they wrestled the bluefin through the narrow opening in the transom, where it continued to flop on the deck, the shaft of the spear bouncing around wildly, and the tip cutting deep gouges in the deck.

Jesse grabbed the spear shaft and pushed it over, rolling the fish slightly. "See if you can get the tip off!"

Rusty dropped to all fours next to the tuna and managed to unscrew the tip. Then they pulled the spear shaft out as the last electrical impulses from the fish's dead brain reached its muscles and it flopped twice more, then grew still.

The two of them looked down at the fish, perspiration and seawater dripping from both their faces.

"This ain't fuckin' real," Rusty said, staring down at the bluefin.

"Damned real to me," Jesse said, holding out his hands and letting his blood drip from the cuts to mingle with that of the tuna.

"This thing's gotta be two hunnert pounds!" Rusty exclaimed, dancing around in what little room he had.

The fish, though technically not fully grown, lay across the fish box hatch on the deck, filling the cockpit diagonally. Rusty produced a long tape measure, and they measured the length from nose to fork.

"Seventy-four inches, CFL," Rusty said, breathing the words out softly. "Ain't nobody gonna believe this. It's gonna weigh in at two-fifty at least!"

"CFL?" Jesse asked.

"Curved fork length," Rusty replied. "Tuna are classed by size, and seventy-three to eighty-one inches is in the 'large medium' class, the most highly prized in Japan."

Rusty started the engine and Jesse went to the little swim platform and hauled their BCs and tanks back aboard.

"Ain't nobody gonna believe this," Rusty repeated.

"Got to," Jesse said. "We're bringing it in, right?"

"You know how long bluefins live?" Rusty said, as Jesse locked the second tank in the rack, BC and reg still attached. "I'll tell ya," he continued, putting the boat in gear. "This one here prolly ain't even seven years old yet, and they live to be forty and *never* stop growin'." He looked back at the tuna as Jesse joined him at the helm. "This thing ain't even a quarter grown in years, and likely an eighth in weight. They can reach a ton! We gotta get him back quick!"

"Why?" Jesse asked, as the boat gathered speed.

"*Why?*" Rusty repeated. "That's red gold back there, bro. Pop can get as much as fifteen a pound."

"Dollars?" Jesse asked, glancing back at the fish as Rusty got the boat up on plane.

"No, ya dumb jarhead. Fifteen jellybeans. 'Course, dollars. That fish is gonna make you at least two grand! Hot damn!"

Chapter Seventeen

◆━━━━◆━━━━◆━━━━◆

Jesse had caught a few bluefins with Pap—nothing the size of the one he'd speared—but he and Pap had never even thought of selling their catch. They were just ten and twenty-pounders, which they cleaned and put in the big chest freezer in the pantry.

Pap had told him about a giant he'd once caught while on a fishing expedition in Cuba when he was a young man. That bluefin had weighed nearly a thousand pounds.

"You're kidding?" Jesse said, truly surprised. "Fifteen bucks a pound for tuna?"

"I shit you not, bro!" Rusty said. "Depends on the quality of the meat. Turn on that radio in the overhead there and switch it to channel seventeen. Unlike most, you're gonna be leavin' the Keys with more money than ya came with."

Jesse turned on the radio and switched it from channel 16 to 17.

Rusty grabbed the microphone, pressed the button on the side, and spoke into it. "Pop, you got the radio on?"

There was silence for a second and Rusty repeated the question.

"I'm here, Jim," Shorty's voice came over the speaker. "What's going on?"

"Get your tuna man on the phone, Pop!" Rusty shouted. "We're coming in with a big bluefin!"

"How big?" Shorty asked, his voice sounding excited.

"My tackle box scale don't go that high," Rusty replied. "And I don't think the one on our dock will either, Pop. At least two hunnert pounds. Maybe three."

"I'll get him right out," Shorty replied. "Me and Mike will meet you over at Dockside."

Rusty turned the wheel and threaded the boat through the cut in the reef again, then pushed the throttle to the stop, heading almost due north.

"Mike's your dad's tuna man?" Jesse yelled over the noise.

"No, Mike's just a guide who spends more time at the bar than on the polin' platform."

"I take it this is some kind of big deal?" Jesse asked, hanging onto the bimini top support. "Big tuna?"

"Could be," Rusty said. "I've heard of really good bluefin selling in Japan for over forty bucks a pound, wholesale. The sooner ya can get it on ice the better."

Several minutes later, Rusty slowed as they approached a small island where construction was going on. Jesse didn't remember seeing it on the way out and said as much.

"That's East Sister Rock," Rusty explained. "Some rich guy bought it and is building a house there. We're going through Sister Creek into Boot Key Harbor. We ain't got no scale big enough at the bait shop to weigh that thing. Pop's gonna meet us at a place called Dockside, where we can use a friend's crane and scale."

Rusty kept the boat at high idle speed through the creek, homes on the right and mangroves on the left.

"How come there aren't any houses on that side?" Jesse asked, pointing toward the mangroves.

"A few," Rusty replied. "That's Boot Key. No electricity but there's a few old diehard fishermen still living there."

They entered the harbor and Rusty turned right, following a marked channel between an anchorage with at least a dozen boats and docks with five times that, wrapping all the way around the harbor.

"City dock's right over there," Rusty said, pointing directly across the anchorage.

There was a small crowd of people waiting when Rusty backed his boat into a slip, and there was no lack of hands to grab dock lines.

Shorty stepped down into the boat and knelt beside the fish as another man swung a small, hand-cranked crane out over the stern.

Shorty looked up at Rusty, surprise evident in his face. "You speared this fish, son?"

"Jesse did," Rusty replied. "Took both of us to get it aboard."

Shorty bent back over the fish, checking its mouth and eyes.

"Looks pelagic," Shorty said. "Probably swam up the Gulf Stream from the open ocean."

"That's good?" Jesse asked Rusty in a low voice.

"The best tuna comes from deep water," Rusty said, then pointed to an Asian man approaching with a silver briefcase. "Here comes Mr. Ono, Pop."

"Lower the cable, Mike," Shorty called up to the man at the crank.

A steel cable came down and Shorty held it over the fish's tail for a moment, then released it and looked up at Mike.

The Asian man joined Mike, who moved a small thumb dial on the control before nodding at Shorty. "It's on zero."

Shorty grabbed the cable again as Mike let out more, then he worked a large loop around one fork of the tail and then the other, snugging it to the base as Mike cranked the handle up again.

"C'mon," Rusty said, then stepped up onto the gunwale and over to the dock.

Jesse followed him as the tuna was slowly lifted out of the boat.

"Mr. Ono," Rusty said. "I'd like you to meet my friend, Jesse

McDermitt. He's the one who speared this fish."

The small man looked up at Jesse as if appraising him. "You *speared* it?" he asked, with no trace of an accent.

"Yes, sir," Jesse said.

"Then join me, Mr. McDermitt, and we will see what you have caught." Ono smiled brightly and turned toward the tuna coming up out of the boat. "It appears to be a very good, large-medium specimen." He looked over at Mike. "What is the weight?"

Mike looked down at the scale on the crane. "Two-sixty-seven-point six."

Rusty nudged Jesse with his elbow. "Wasn't far off, was I?"

Mr. Ono opened his briefcase and took out a neatly folded towel, then wiped a spot dry on the side of the fish. He put the towel away, took a marker out, and wrote 267.6 on the bluefin's side.

Shorty climbed out of the boat and went around Mike, helping him swing the crane arm over the dock. Then he placed a small step ladder into position next to the tuna.

Mr. Ono took two long, thin, tubular devices with wooden handles from his briefcase and handed them to Shorty. Then he stepped up onto the ladder, put his hands together and bowed toward the fish, saying something in Japanese. Afterward, he took one of the tools from Shorty.

"What's he doing?" Jesse whispered.

"Honoring the fish," Rusty replied. "Then he'll take two samples—one from near the base of the tail and one from behind the gills. The tool's called a *sashibo* and he'll use it to take a skinny little core sample. The redder the better."

Mr. Ono turned the handle back and forth as he pushed the tube into the dangling tuna's side a few inches ahead of the forked tail. Then he handed the *sashibo* tool to Shorty and climbed down.

Shorty put the tool on the towel, then handed the second one to

Ono, and the little man performed the same operation, taking a sample from the thickest part of the tuna, just behind its gills.

Ono went to his briefcase and took out a laminated card that had a pair of colored lines on it, one slightly paler than the other, ranging from brown to pink to cherry red. He removed the tail sample and placed the tube of tuna meat on the chart, then did the same with the body sample. Both were very close to the reddest end of the color charts.

Ono looked up at Jesse and shouted, "Sashimi!"

The onlookers cheered and several people patted Jesse on the back.

"What's that mean?" he asked the Japanese man.

"Sashimi is the highest-grade sushi," Ono replied. "I will offer you eleven-point-five."

Shorty stepped up beside Jesse and nodded at Mr. Ono. "Fifteen, please."

The Japanese man appraised the fish again, then glanced down at the samples. "Twelve-point-five," he countered.

"Thirteen and you have a deal," Jesse said, getting caught up in the excitement.

Ono smiled, then took a tiny filet knife out and cut four small pieces from the reddest end of the body sample. He picked up the first one and took a small bite, seeming to savor it. He offered the second piece to Jesse, grinning broadly as he chewed, his eyes mere slits with lines at the corners.

He was obviously enjoying it.

Not wanting to offend the man, Jesse took the raw piece of tuna and put it in his mouth. He'd never eaten raw fish before, but he found it wasn't that bad.

Rusty took the next bite and passed the last one to Shorty.

"It is done," Ono said and bowed toward Jesse.

Jesse bowed back, awkwardly mimicking what Ono had done with his hands on his thighs.

"Who should I make the check out to?"

Jesse shrugged and turned to Rusty. "You got a bank account?"

"Make it out to me, Mr. Ono," Shorty said, then turned to Jesse. "We can cash it at my bank right now if we hurry."

Ono opened a ledger-style checkbook, filled out a check and handed it to Jesse. "It is a pleasure to meet and do business, Mr. McDermitt. Congratulations on a fine catch."

Then he turned and summoned two men waiting beside a flatbed truck with a large freezer chest in the bed.

"Can I take your picture?" a young woman asked, stepping away from the crowd and approaching Jesse.

Jesse looked down at the check in his hands. It was in the amount of $3,478.80. His jaw dropped and he could feel his heart about to explode from his chest.

The woman moved closer, leaning sideways to get into Jesse's narrowed field of view. "Mr. McDermitt, is it?"

She wore a baggy, long-sleeved man's work shirt and loose-fitting khaki shorts with big pockets; shapely, dark-tanned legs were revealed below them. She was blond and pretty, which finally caught Jesse's attention.

"I'm with the local paper," she said. "Can I take your picture with the tuna?"

"Put that in your pocket and stand in front of the fish," Rusty ordered, shoving him gently. "Gina, meet Jesse. Bro, this is Gina. She's a photographer. Say hi."

She smiled up at Jesse. "How much did you sell this fish for, Mr. McDermitt?"

Jesse blinked and put the check in his shirt pocket. She looked about his age, maybe a little older, but probably not by much.

"Um... A little over three grand?" Jesse stuttered and pulled the check back out of his pocket, suddenly unsure of what he'd seen.

$3,478.80, just for his *one catch?*

No, he thought, looking at his friend. *His and* Rusty's *catch.*

"Half of this is yours," Jesse blurted out, as Gina took his picture.

"Let's try that again," she said. "Without any talking this time— this is a still camera, not a movie."

"Get over here," Jesse hissed at Rusty. "Half this is yours."

"No, no, no," Rusty said, waving two hands, palms out. "Catching fish is a solo thing, bro. You caught it."

Jesse smiled at Gina, then nodded toward the number written on the side of the fish.

"This fish outweighs me by more than fifty pounds," he said to the pretty, blue-eyed blonde. "And I was in *his* house. It took me and Rusty both to get it on the boat—even to get it *close* to the boat. If Rusty hadn't jumped in with me and grabbed my free arm..." He paused and looked up at the fish, then smiled at Gina. "I think this fish would've dragged me to Cuba. So, we should *split* it, don't you agree?"

Gina laughed. "Yes, I do. But I'm a little biased. I've known Jim since kindergarten."

"Get over here, Marine!" Jesse shouted, in a fair imitation of Sergeant Smith's strained vocal gymnastics.

Rusty moved up beside him and Gina took another photo.

"One of the two hundred people, huh?" Jesse asked, talking through his smile.

Chapter Eighteen

◆　◆　◆　◆

The storm arrived an hour before sunset, just as Shorty had predicted. Jesse and Rusty sat in the rum shack watching the rain move across the water in undulating sheets, as what sounded like machine gun fire peppered the rooftop. A gust of wind slashed rain against the glass, howling around the small shack.

"Feels really solid," Jesse said softly, sitting in one of the chairs facing the windows.

"The only time this shack's lost its roof was in Cat Three or bigger storms. It ain't goin' nowhere no time soon."

"The bait shop and your folks' house, too," Jesse said. "Solidly built."

"Yep," Rusty said. "Four direct landfalls here on Key Vaca and prolly two dozen near misses. Lost the roof of the house twice and the bait shop—well, it's been other things over the years—but the roof came off it three times. But that's goin' back to when Cap'n Augustus came here a hunnert and forty years ago."

They both looked through the window at the slashing rain and wind-swept waves crashing against the limestone outcrop offshore.

"Back then, folks didn't get no warnin'," Rusty said. "No radar, no tracking, no hurricane hunters. You only knew it was a landfall when the eye of the storm passed over. Then the wind changes a hunnert and eighty degrees with the same ferocity it left with."

Thunder rolled in over the water, sounding like a bowler's strike at slow speed.

"What're you going to do with your share?" Jesse asked, feeling the bulge of his wallet in his back pocket.

They'd reached Shorty's bank just before it closed and cashed the check from Mr. Ono. Jesse insisted that they split it evenly— $1,739.40 to each of them.

"Me and Jewels are savin' for a house," Rusty replied, his blank expression matching Jesse's as they stared at the whitecaps. "But there *is* a car up on the mainland I had my eye on."

"Yeah?"

Rusty turned to face him. "A '67 big-block Fairlane, bro. A guy up in Homestead who races super-stock came across it and don't have the time to build it out."

Jesse looked over and nodded. "You should get it."

Rusty turned back to the window as the howling of the wind subsided for a moment. The sky to the east was becoming lighter.

"The house is more important to Jewels, bro," he said, shaking his head. "As soon as we save up enough for a down payment, we're gettin' hitched. *Then* I can buy toys."

"What about the Bertram?"

"That ain't no toy," Rusty said, glancing over again. "Anyone who's lived here more'n a few months is a fisherman at some point. It's what we do down here. And the boat's just a tool, just like the rod and reel."

"Remember what Sergeant Smith told Couch when he found out he was married?"

Rusty shouted over the storm in a much better imitation than Jesse's. "If the Corps wanted you to have a wife..."

"We would have issued you one!" they finished together.

Their voices rang from the metal roof, echoing as the rain suddenly stopped, and they both started laughing.

162

"Okay, let's get ready," Rusty said, rising from his chair. "The churn out there will flatten out in less than an hour and Jewels'll be here in thirty minutes."

"How do you know?" Jesse asked. "You haven't even looked at that pocket watch of yours all afternoon."

"Island time, bro. The watch is great, but here, we mostly measure time by the sun, moon, and tide. Jewels don't like drivin' in the rain 'cause her windshield leaks around the frame. She lives just over on Big Pine, twenty minutes away."

"Island time, huh?" Jesse said. "Where's the other ten minutes?"

"Storm's movin' west... Big Pine's to the west... Won't stop rainin' at her place for a few more minutes."

"I should call Pap, then," Jesse said. "I haven't even told him I got here yet. Think your dad'd mind?"

"C'mon," Rusty said, leading the way. "He'd say ya shoulda done that when ya first got here."

They went up to the bait shop and Jesse couldn't help but notice that even on Sunday, there was no shortage of cars parked in the small lot and bar noises could be heard emanating from the other half of the building.

They went in the back way, only one light on at the counter to lead their way. The hum of water pumps for the live bait tanks was the only sound in the bait shop, but music and laughter could be heard through the closed door.

"You don't lock the door?" Jesse asked.

Rusty went behind the counter and lifted a sawed-off shotgun from behind it, placing it on the countertop. "'Round here, we don't call the cops. We call the shots, and we call friends. Pop can put together a small army in just a few minutes, but it could take the cops thirty minutes to an hour to get here. But we don't hardly ever get any trouble back up in here."

Jesse nodded. "Way faster response time."

Rusty put the shotgun away and took a desk phone from under the counter, turning it toward Jesse before setting it down.

Jesse picked up the receiver, listened for a dial tone, then dialed the number to his grandparents' house.

"Hello?" Pap said after just one ring.

He was in his den, where he had a second phone, right next to his recliner.

"Hey, Pap, sorry for not calling when I got here."

The old man chuckled. "We figured you'd be busy, son. Did your friend get you out on the water?"

It was Jesse's turn to laugh. "You're not going to believe it, Pap," he began, "but on the first dive, we speared a big black grouper, a cubera snapper, three hogfish, and two red snappers." Jesse paused and grinned at his buddy. "And on the second dive..." He paused again for dramatic effect. "I speared a 267-pound bluefin tuna!"

Jesse could hear the familiar whoosh of Pap's chair as he either sat down or stood up.

"You what?" Pap shouted. "Norma, come in here!"

Jesse could hear his grandmother enter Pap's den, then he said, "Okay, we're both listening. Tell her that last part again. I think I must have misunderstood you."

"I speared a 267-pound bluefin," Jesse said, picturing his grandparents holding the phone between their ears, faces close together.

"What?" Mam asked. "How?"

Jesse gave them a short recap of the dive, leaving out the meeting with Rusty's friends, and definitely leaving out the part about Rachel ambush-kissing him on the boat. Pap was amazed at the amount of money Jesse had sold the fish for and how quickly Rusty's dad had arranged it.

"Well, it sounds like you're already having the time of your life," Mam said. "You deserve it, Jesse. You've worked so hard to get where you are."

"Congratulations, son," Pap said. "That's a helluva catch."

Jesse winced slightly at the muffled sound of Mam punching Pap's shoulder for saying a curse word.

"Well, this long-distance call is eating up someone's dime," Pap said. "You don't have to call us every day. We know you're having fun and we know you're safe."

"How do you know that?"

"Always remember this," Pap said. "That new buddy of yours will always have your back. And you, his."

Jesse looked over at Rusty and grinned. "Ooh-rah, sir!"

Rusty leaned closer, having apparently heard Pap's words. "Don't you worry, Mam. Your boy's in good hands."

He said goodbye and they went back out into the cooler evening air, and, just as Rusty had predicted, the waves had diminished out in the bight and Juliet was pulling in, driving a beat-up old Toyota Corolla.

Jesse noticed that his car kind of stood out in the parking lot. It was the only one in the lot that didn't look like it was on its last mile with parts about to rust off.

"Why's everyone here drive old clunkers?" Jesse asked.

"That shiny hot rod of yours would be a rust bucket in two years if you lived here," Rusty replied, kissing his girlfriend.

"Glad you could come down," Juliet said. "It's good to see you again. The salt air coats everything. Even the morning dew is salty. So, we drive 'Keys cars.'" She smiled up at Jesse and held up a short, flat-head screwdriver. "And *my* Keys car doesn't even need *car keys*."

Jesse laughed. "My grandfather always bought older cars for the same reason, but I guess it's a lot worse here."

"Death, taxes, and rust," Rusty said, as they walked out to the dock. "We get *three* certainties in life down here."

Rusty stepped down into the Bertram, turned on the battery and lowered the outdrive into the water. Once he had the engine running, Juliet and Jesse untied the lines and pushed the boat's stern away from the dock first, to turn it around. A minute later they were idling out into a light chop, nothing but moonlight filtering through scattered high clouds to guide their way.

"Welcome to the Keys, bro," Rusty said, moving Juliet in between them to drive the boat.

"If you don't like the weather here," Juliet said, "just wait an hour."

She pushed the throttle forward, gently bringing the boat up on plane and following white poles set at fifty-yard intervals, barely visible by the light of the moon, which was now halfway up to its zenith. It wasn't quite full yet, but it was getting close.

Once clear of the poles, Juliet made a wide turn around the point of land to the south to be well offshore of East Sister Rock.

"That's our property line," Rusty shouted over the engine, pointing toward shore. "Our only neighbor is the school we all went to."

With the moon behind them, and Jesse's eyes growing accustomed to the diminished light, he could easily pick out landmarks and stars.

"That's the old Seven Mile Bridge," Rusty said, pointing to the north. "They started puttin' in pilin's last year for a new, higher bridge."

The water got rougher as they crossed the shipping channel that went under a wide swing section of the bridge. But it quickly calmed as they reached shallower water on the other side.

Jesse looked over the side of the boat but could see nothing.

"It's mostly five or six feet," Rusty shouted. "But there's a lot of shoals that are dry at low tide."

"What's the tide now?" Jesse asked, as Juliet turned the boat seaward and slowed.

"Dead low," Juliet replied. "This is the only sandbar we'll have to slow down for, though."

Jesse looked all around, seeing nothing but black water and the bridge in the distance. "What sandbar?"

"It's there, bro," Rusty said. "About a foot below the prop. Jewels knows these waters as well as any guide."

"What if we get stuck?"

Rusty chuckled. "Dead low means it'll rise soon. Relax, bro. After the day we had, time don't mean shit."

"Until the freezer gets low," Juliet added.

A few minutes later, Juliet brought the boat back up to speed and slowly turned west again. Then south for a few seconds, west, then north, and west once more, as if dodging unseen barriers.

The idea of simply living day-to-day, working when needed, was at odds with the values that Mam and Pap had instilled in Jesse from early on. He'd worked part-time jobs since he was fifteen and had saved money from mowing lawns before that since he was twelve.

Saving for the future.

But Rusty and Juliet had been born here in the Keys and the way they lived their lives was just different, not wrong. Jesse spent a lot of time on the water back home, but here, it was almost like land was a place they visited or where they went to sleep. And living the life they did, Jesse felt sure nobody who lived there would ever go hungry.

As they approached a small island with tall, thin trees growing on it, Juliet slowed. Jesse recognized the trees, even in the darkness, as Australian pine trees. He could see a number of small boats on the west side, pulled right up on the beach in the shallows.

A lone sailboat was anchored farther away, a single white light showing at the top of the mast.

"That's Rachel's boat," Juliet announced. "She said to come there, right?"

"Yeah," Rusty said, moving toward the bow as they got closer to the sailboat. "Yo, Rach!"

In the moonlight, Jesse saw blond hair pop up from the companionway hatch. "Hiya, Jim! Hey, JJ!" She climbed up, and Jesse could see she was wearing a yellow, halter-type dress. "And hello, Jesse McMyers."

"Is she just joking with that?" Jesse whispered.

"Oh, yeah," Rusty replied. "Woman's smart as she is crazy, with a weird sense of humor."

"Pull up and tie off," Rachel said, moving to the side deck. "We were just about to plunder the shoreline."

We? Jesse thought.

Juliet reversed the engine and spun the wheel to the left, stopping the boat and moving the stern closer to the other boat as another woman appeared on deck.

He and Rusty didn't have to throw the lines— the two women could just reach down and take them. In seconds, they were tied off snugly, with large, round fenders keeping the boats apart in the light chop.

"If it's not the generous fisherman," Gina said, cleating the stern and smiling at Jesse in the moonlight.

Chapter Nineteen

◆———◆———◆———◆———◆

A soft orange glow emanated from the companionway and the small windows along the side, above the deck. But it was a harsh light compared to the moon. Gina's hair and face looked alluring and innocent at the same time under the moon's soft glow. Though Jesse was confused by her being there, he smiled up at her.

Rachel hung a ladder over the side of the sloop's toe rail and the three of them climbed up to the side deck just as a large, bearded man stuck his head out of the companionway.

"Y'all coming in or what?" he asked in sort of a growl.

He looked vaguely familiar to Jesse, but it was hard to tell in the low light before he ducked back down inside.

"I didn't know my boyfriend was coming," Rachel whispered to Juliet, but said it loud enough for Jesse to hear, and she was looking right at him when she said it.

"You're with me," Gina whispered, taking Jesse's arm. "Big sister's loss is little sister's gain."

As the women headed down, Rusty pulled Jesse aside. "This guy's dangerous, bro. Just don't start no shit, okay? He prolly won't be here long."

"Why would I—"

"Just roll with whatever happens," Rusty whispered, an ominous tone in his voice. "Be polite and say, 'No, thanks.'"

Rusty started down the companionway and Jesse followed. The

bearded guy sat on a small sofa, Rachel beside him. There was a little table in front of them with a plastic bag lying on it, along with a lighter and a pack of cigarette papers.

Jesse could tell by the pungent smell that it wasn't tobacco in the plastic bag.

Gina slid to the end of a much longer couch, across the centerline passageway from the table.

Jesse had been around people who smoked it. He never had and had no intention of starting. But he also knew how to be courteous in someone's home, and looking around, the boat had all the trappings of a liveaboard.

He smiled at Gina and sat down beside her as Juliet and Rusty took up the rest of the couch.

"I hear you speared one big-ass tuna, man," the bearded guy said.

A leather vest hung over the back of the couch and Jesse saw the nametag embroidered on it. The synapses in his brain made the connection.

"A large-medium bluefin," Jesse said, reaching across the table. "We met earlier today. Name's Jesse McDermitt."

Bear leaned forward, eyes slightly bloodshot, and seeming to be a little confused.

Then Jesse saw the spark of recognition, though slightly dulled, as he took Jesse's offered hand.

"The Mustang!" Bear said. "Cool custom work on the hood and antennas."

He gripped Jesse's hand with firmness, a bit too much for a casual handshake.

A man used to having things his way due to his size, Jesse thought.

So he applied equal pressure. "Thanks. It gets me around. Your panhead? A fifty-two?"

Bear's eyes widened and the two ended their handshake. "It's a fifty-three," he replied. "Built it myself. That little pony got the original engine?"

Jesse grinned and shook his head. "Stroked 427 small-block."

He'd been around enough bikers—a couple lived in his neighborhood—to recognize the "one-percenters," and this guy was the real thing.

"We'll have a smoke to our rides," Bear said, as he reached for the baggie. "My pan and your sleeper."

"Thanks," Jesse replied, still holding the man's gaze. "But we can't. Jim and I could get popped on a piss test. We're Marines."

"Zat right?" Bear said. "I was Army before the war." He paused, studying Jesse. Then he grinned. "How about a beer then?"

Jesse nodded. "Thanks, I'd like that."

Bear nudged Rachel. "Get these jarheads a beer, hon."

She rose and glanced at Jesse, mouthing the word sorry.

He knew what Bear was trying to do. Interservice rivalry had probably started a lot of bar fights over the years. But Rachel's boat wasn't a bar.

If it came to a hand-to-hand fight, Jesse knew he could take the man. They were about the same weight, though more of Bear's was below the ribcage. He was older, mid-thirties at least, and obviously used to getting his way and not having to actually become physical. People feared him.

Bear started to light a joint and Gina held up a hand. "You know, I heard that even breathing the smoke could get these guys in trouble, Bear. Maybe we could go up on deck?"

"Y'all can if you want to," Bear said, indifferent. "Me and Rach are gonna spark this thing up and fumigate the boat. Then I gotta get goin'." He smiled, but there was no mirth. "Things to see and people to do, ya know."

"Let's go up," Gina said, rising and pulling Jesse's hand.

Rachel rose from the cooler and passed beer cans around. "Y'all go ahead. I'll be up there in a sec."

The four of them went up the companionway and Gina led the way to the foredeck.

"The bow's in the wind," she said, keeping her voice low. "We won't smell anything up here."

"You don't want to join them?" Jesse asked, realizing too late that his question might be taken as hostile. "Sorry. That sounded judgmental."

She smiled at him. "I don't smoke. Not even cigarettes. And the only thing that goes up my nose is salt air."

Jesse smiled at her as rock music and laughter could be heard through the deck hatch. He turned his face into the wind, looking up at the moon, then closed his eyes.

This boat, these people, Juliet, Rusty, his parents, and the bait shop... everything he'd seen since arriving seemed more real than how he'd felt in his own home—Mam and Pap's home.

It wasn't that things back home were different or that he had changed. It was just his past. The last three months had become a dividing line in Jesse's life. Everything before that was foreign, lost forever in the past. He knew his future would bring many trials and tests and he felt that he was up to the challenge. The past was the past and the future would be what he made it.

He looked down at Gina. "I'm glad you came with your sister."

"Ha! Be hard not to. This boat is *our* home."

The boat rocked and soon, Bear appeared at the companionway hatch, stepping up onto the deck. His vest made him look more imposing but was totally at odds with the surroundings.

"I'll see *you* next Saturday," he said, then kissed Rachel. "Don't disappoint me."

In the dim light, Jesse saw him grab Rachel's butt with his right hand as he waved with his left. "Pleasure meeting ya."

Then he stepped down into a small boat that was tied to the opposite side, pulled the starter cord a few times, then roared away, heading toward the west end of the Seven Mile Bridge.

"Tide's low, Jim," Rachel said, moving toward Rusty's boat. "I don't feel like swimming right now. You can beach your boat and when the tide comes up in a few hours, it'll be riding high."

"Fine by me," Rusty said, and started back along the starboard side. "Don't wanna get my watch wet, anyway."

"You and that watch," Juliet said, following behind him.

Jesse started to turn, but Gina caught his arm.

"I *do* feel like swimming," she said. "Stay and finish your beer."

Rusty looked back at him and grinned in the moonlight. "We'll catch up on shore, bro."

Then he jumped into the boat and started the engine as Rachel and Juliet untied the lines.

Gina looked up at Jesse in the moonlight. "I'm sorry about all this. But would you think me bad if I secretly wasn't all that sorry?"

"What do you mean?"

"There aren't a lot of single guys around here," she said with a smile. "Well, not many with ambition, or who can carry on a conversation."

"Why do you suppose that is?" Jesse asked, genuinely curious.

"There's nothing to become ambitious about here," she said, then glanced over her shoulder at a pair of beanbag chairs on the cabin roof. "Let's sit down."

"Is Rachel serious with that guy?" Jesse said, following Gina as she stepped up onto the roof.

"My sister's a little off," she replied. "And if you ask me, Bear's even farther off. I think he's cheating on her."

They sat and Jesse stretched his legs out as he took a long pull on the beer, relaxing into the cushion.

"She was married to a shrimper," Gina said. "He owned his own boat and everything. But he cheated on her, too. And when she confronted him, he ridiculed her in public. They divorced and it was pretty ugly."

"Sorry to hear that," Jesse said, and meant it. "People shouldn't get married unless they're really sure."

"You talk kind of old-fashioned," Gina said, looking up at the stars.

"Sorry. I was raised by grandparents, so I kind of skipped part of a generation."

"Don't be," she said. "I like old-fashioned."

"So, why do you live on a boat?"

"Have you ever tried to buy a house with just a thousand dollars?" she asked. "That was all we had when I moved out of our parents' house after Rach divorced Steve. And renting is even more expensive."

"Yeah, I guess buying a boat would be way cheaper," Jesse agreed. "But what about dock fees and stuff?"

"We tie up at Dockside every Monday for a couple of days," she replied. "The manager's a friend and he gives us a deal. Early in the week, he can barely fill half the slips anyway. We take care of laundry, stock up on groceries, and lug water and fuel cans to the dock. The rest of the time, we get back and forth from the anchorage by dinghy to go to work."

"As a newspaper photographer?"

"Oh, that's just freelance stuff. I sold your story and picture to the Citizen for fifty dollars. Rach and I both work at Dockside. I'm a waitress and she's a bartender."

He remembered what Rusty had said about how people in the

174

Keys hustled, doing whatever they needed to do to make a buck. He looked out toward the ocean, with the moon riding high above. "If it was easy living in paradise, I guess everyone would."

She laughed. "I wouldn't exactly call it paradise," she said. "But I don't have a lot to compare it to. I was born here, and I've only left the Keys a few times in my whole life."

"I've been around a little," Jesse said. "The Bahamas and Cuba, as well as South Carolina. But I think I could live in a place like this."

"If you come here, come correct," she said. "You need the right mindset and have to be able to add some value to the community to be able to survive."

"One day, I'd like to own a charter boat," he said, gazing up at the stars. "Spend my days on the water."

"That'd be hard to do while you're in the military," she said.

Jesse glanced over and grinned. "That's way in the future. After I retire from the Corps."

"Then you should," Gina said, studying him. "How tall are you?"

"Six-three in bare feet," Jesse replied, having fielded the question at least once a week since he was thirteen.

"That's a whole foot taller than me," Gina said, "and I don't consider myself to be short-short. Not like JJ."

"JJ?"

"Juliet Johnston," she replied. "Jim's girlfriend. She's only four-eleven."

"Is being a news reporter what you want for an end goal?"

"End goal?" she asked, turning her head to stare at the moon. "I wouldn't call it that, but yeah, I want to be a reporter for a big paper one day."

"And after that?"

She looked over at him again and smiled. "Become the editor, marry a nice guy, and have kids. But that's at least ten years down the road. What about you? What's your 'end goal'?"

"I've achieved it," he said honestly. "Being a Marine is all I ever wanted. Now I just want to be the best Marine I can."

"And after that? You can't be a Marine forever."

He let the inference slide. In his heart, Jesse knew that he *would* forever hold that title. "I plan to make it a career," he replied. "Thirty years."

"What about after that?" Gina asked. "You'll still be young. My uncle is retired from the Navy and his pension won't even cover his mortgage payment."

Jesse smiled at her. "Maybe he can come to work for me on my charter boat."

She laughed. "So you *do* have a plan."

"More like an outline," Jesse admitted. "I have thirty years to come up with a plan."

Chapter Twenty

———◆———◆———◆———◆———

Jesse lay in the bunk, awakened by the sound of a firetruck's siren out on the highway. The wail was barely audible, headed up the Overseas Highway, out of Marathon, growing fainter and fainter until it was gone.

It was still dark, but Jesse felt refreshed. He and Gina had sat in the beanbags for an hour, just talking. Then they'd swum ashore together and sat listening to one of her and Rusty's friends play guitar by a bonfire while they drank a second beer. At one point, they walked around the island together, the nearly full moon guiding their way from almost directly overhead.

She'd told him about her family, and the struggle of growing up in a place where throngs of outsiders invaded every weekend. The visiting tourists put food on the locals' tables, but it was unpredictable how many would visit, or where, so finding stable work was difficult.

He'd made no move on her, nor had she on him. It was like they'd just felt comfortable in each other's presence, and neither felt it necessary to move beyond the now. But as he, Rusty, and Juliet were about to leave, Gina had stood on her toes and pulled his head down for a kiss on the cheek.

Jesse rose and dropped silently to the floor of the old rum shack as Rusty continued snoring in the lower bunk. The windows were open a few inches, allowing the cool breeze to flow through the little building, and the sound of the tiny waves washing ashore drew him.

A faint light streamed in through the windows, and he looked out, expecting to see the first light of dawn. Instead, he saw only the rippling water reflecting the light of a billion stars above it. Jesse was no stranger to being on the water at night, but he'd never seen so many stars.

They glistened like tiny salt crystals spilled across a vast, black marble countertop that extended all the way to the horizon. Jesse knew he was looking to the east, where the sun would soon rise above the ocean, so he realized it was still very early.

He glanced back and, spotting Rusty's watch on his footlocker, picked it up and pressed the little button in the stem, flipping the cover open.

It was 0510, still two hours before sunrise. They'd stayed at the little island until after midnight, and by then, the moon had passed its zenith and was halfway down the western sky, so it had to have set hours ago.

The light shining through the windows was *starlight*, nothing else.

Inside the watch's cover was a picture. It had been trimmed into a round shape to fit in the pocket watch.

Jesse moved closer to the window, surprised that the starlight allowed him to see the photo so clearly. In it, Rusty and Juliet were standing on a dock at sunset, Shorty and Dreama stood beside Rusty, and another couple, who Jesse figured was Juliet's parents, were on her side. They were all smiling and seemed very happy. Jesse wondered what the occasion was.

Their high school graduation?

No, Rusty's hair was short in the picture, and Jesse remembered it being longer when they'd met on the bus. In the photo, he was wearing a high and tight, just like he was now.

Juliet was turned slightly toward him, her left hand resting on Rusty's chest. It was obvious they were in love.

Rusty stirred on his bunk and Jesse turned. He was about to close the watch when he noticed it. A little sparkle of light on Juliet's finger.

Well, I'll be, Jesse thought. *He proposed when he got home.*

Jesse closed and returned the watch, then quietly slipped out the door. It was a hike up to the bait shop and nobody was around, so he simply stepped over to the seawall and relieved his bladder.

As he walked back toward the shack, Jesse felt a mist of soft rain on his bare shoulders and looked up. He saw nothing but stars. No clouds.

Where was the rain coming from?

The chilly mist felt good. He paused at the door and turned toward the ocean, the light breeze full on his face.

As he stared out over the water, the stars above seemed to pulse with energy, and the vastness of the night sky began to make him a little dizzy.

He went back inside, feeling a little disoriented, and quietly sat down in one of the chairs. He stared out over the water again, wondering why Rusty hadn't told him about the engagement. Had he told so many people over the past week, he'd forgotten?

We're just not that close, Jesse decided, glancing over at the darkened shape on the bottom bunk.

They didn't really know each other at all. By chance, they'd ridden the same bus together from Jacksonville to Parris Island, had talked along the way, and they'd been in the same platoon. Outside of that, Jim Thurman was a total stranger. He liked the guy, they were brother Marines, and they had a lot in common that could eventually cement a friendship.

Jesse turned back toward the window, sinking into the leather chair as his eyes narrowed and his field of view became only what he could see through the two windows.

His mind drifted and for a moment, he felt as if he were on the bow of a large ship, watching more stars flicker on at the horizon and rise slowly into the sky.

"We're on a little blue ball," Rusty's voice whispered in the darkness. "Spinnin' and hurtlin' through space at over sixty-seven thousand miles an hour—almost twenty miles in the blink of your eyes."

Jesse hadn't expected Rusty to be awake, but he wasn't startled by his voice. Instead, it affirmed the visual sensation he was experiencing, and for a second, he felt like he was being pulled off the bow of the ship and into the heavens.

In his mind's eye, for that brief second, he was looking down on the Earth from a great height, like in pictures from the moon. In the vastness of the stars, it seemed so fragile and vulnerable.

The sensation made him feel extremely small and minutely insignificant. Just a speck on a little blue marble that was but a speck against a cosmos that was so vast that the light from the nearest star, traveling at over a hundred-and-eighty thousand miles per second, would take nearly four-and-a-half years to reach the eyes.

Jesse's mind was suddenly sucked back down into the little rum shack.

"Wow," was all he could say, gripping the armrests as he slowly exhaled the word.

Rusty chuckled from the dark cave that was the lower bunk.

"I remember my first time spendin' the night out here," Rusty whispered. "It's a special place, right on the sea. And I definitely recall the lure of the Siren. She don't just sing, ya know." He chuckled again, softly. "She done turned, bro," he said quietly, almost reverently. "And she's turned for you."

"Sorry if I woke you," Jesse said, as Rusty rose and went past him.

"Gotta take a leak."

The door opened and closed as Jesse continued to look at the stars, trying to recapture the sensation he'd felt.

Again, all that was visible through the window were the twinkling stars and the ocean. The sensation of near insignificance was gone.

Rusty came back in. "You up for the day? I don't think it's zero six hundred yet."

"A little after five," Jesse replied. "I looked at your watch a few minutes ago."

"Wanna get an early start, then?" Rusty asked. "I'm game. Me and Jewels only had one beer last night."

"I noticed that," Jesse said without thinking.

"You did?" Rusty replied, sitting back in the other chair. "Didn't look to me like you noticed anything but Gina."

"I got the feeling that she's very complex," Jesse said.

"Complex? What the hell's that supposed to mean?"

"I don't know," Jesse said with a slight shrug. "Like there's more to her than meets the eye, or even what you can learn talking for a few hours... Deep. You know?"

"You know you're kinda weird, right?" Rusty asked. "I don't mean that in an insultin' way, bro. But talk about *deep*. I watched you stare out that window for ten minutes, as layer after layer was bared to the universe. Don't know who you were in your past lives, but I'm bettin' one of 'em was a wanderer and a waterman—an ocean explorer."

"Past life?" Jesse asked, rhetorically. "You believe in all that?"

Rusty turned and looked at him and nodded toward the windows. "I seen you lookin' out past here. I done it too, and I don't

181

disbelieve nothin', bro."

They both stared out the window and soon, a thin, silver line began to take shape at the horizon.

"It'll be light in an hour," Rusty said. "Thought we'd take the boat up to the backcountry, do some explorin' and maybe catch some cobia. It's early in the season for 'em, but it's possible. Or we can go after snook or bonefish."

"Can't eat bonefish," Jesse said.

"See there, you're already thinkin' like a Conch." He paused and looked outside again. "Tourist anglers like to catch the gray ghosts, and their money puts food on the table for the guides. The guides spend some of that money locally and Pop gets some of it. They buy locally made lures from old-timers like Thorn up in Largo. Those guys have a beer or three on the weekend and Pop pockets a few more dollars. He buys fish from local fishermen and other local goods and services, and the cycle continues. That tourist dollar might stay here long after they leave, buyin' all sorts of stuff for dozens or hundreds of locals."

"You should be a tour guide," Jesse said.

Rusty looked over and grinned. "Done it and still wear the T-shirt. Look, I know a place we can snorkel and catch lobster if it ain't cleaned out already. Pops pays good money for lobster."

"You sell your catch to your dad?"

"Well, yeah," Rusty replied. "Most of the guides and fishermen buy bait here and Pops gives locals a discount. In return, we sell our catch to him, almost always above market rate. He supplies a lot of the restaurants with the catch of the day, and the guides all know he'll get a better price from them than they can get individually. Sort of like a co-op, but no contracts."

"If we can get our limit in lobster in a couple of dives," Jesse said, "we can bring them in and go spearfishing in the afternoon."

"Sure," Rusty replied, rising from the chair. "But rather'n go out spearfishing the reef again, how about we go on out to the Gulf Stream for some wahoo and dolphin action on the surface?"

"How far's the Gulf Stream?"

"Twelve or thirteen miles," Rusty replied. "Take us about half an hour."

Jesse sat forward. "Can we get some chow first, though?"

"I got just the thing," Rusty replied. "We need to get gas for the boat anyway, so we can swing into the harbor and while I gas up, you can run across Useless One and grab some go-bags from the 7 Mile Grill. Jewels'll be there by six. Best breakfast burritos anywhere."

"We stayed out that late, and she has to work this morning?" Jesse asked. "I feel bad about that."

"Hey, don't worry none 'bout that, bro. That whole time it was rainin' yesterday, I *gar-own-tee* she was sleepin'. Girl loves the sound of the rain."

"She sleeps in the afternoon?"

Rusty laughed as he opened his footlocker and pulled on a pair of cutoffs. "Things here are way different than on the mainland. Most folks here've been without a clock so long, they forgot how to tell time. And tryin' to constrain Mother Nature to a clock is just dumb. The sun rises, then it sets. The moon wanes and waxes. The tides follow the sun and moon, and we follow the tides and currents. Ever poled a boat?"

"You mean like a push pole?" Jesse asked, opening his own footlocker. "Sure. Inshore waters around Fort Myers are more for canoes and kayaks, but Billy and I spent a week poling a couple of flats boats in the Glades last year. And a friend of Pap's took us out to the Ten Thousand Islands dozens of times in his small powerboat that needed a push pole."

"Been there," Rusty said. "Cape Sable, too. That's real Florida."

"I need to get you and Billy together," Jesse said. "You two probably have more in common than different, skin color aside."

As soon as he mentioned it, Jesse realized that he'd never mentioned Billy was an Indian, and he had no idea about any biases his new friend might have. He hadn't displayed any in boot camp and less than half the platoon was white. He did say his third great-grandfather had helped the Seminoles, so there was that.

"Billy's a black fella?"

Jesse shook his head. "Calusa Indian and Seminole," he replied. "We've been blood brothers since we were like nine or ten. His dad's the chieftain of the Calusa."

"No shit," Rusty said, pulling on a T-shirt. "That's really cool. The Calusa been around here a lot longer than us Thurmans."

Jesse also pulled on a T-shirt, and then followed Rusty out into the darkness.

"We'll get the keys from the bait shop," Rusty said, trudging up the slight rise toward the building. "And there might be a half-eaten sandwich in the little fridge."

"I think I'll wait for the breakfast burritos."

They got the keys, then headed down to the dock. Though it was dark, and there were few lights on, Jesse found it was quite easy to see where he was going.

"How come there's no lights?" he asked.

"Ain't needed," Rusty replied. "We keep 'em off after midnight, when Pop closes up the bar, and the town rolls up the sidewalks for the night. Anyone wanderin' around in the dark sticks out like a sore thumb once your eyes adjust."

Idling out of the canal and into the channel, they again followed the poles sticking up out of the water every fifty yards or so until they reached deep water.

Rusty throttled the engine up and within minutes, they'd

rounded East Sister Rock, but Rusty continued west.

"Not going in the same way?" Jesse shouted over the engine and wind noise.

"There's a marina before the bridge on the west side," Rusty replied, as he steered wide around Boot Key. "It's idle speed in Sister Creek, so it's way faster to go around."

On the water, Jesse could see why the stars were so much more vivid. They had a lot less competition. On the water at night in Fort Myers, you could see a glow from the city to the east, as well as Cape Coral just across the river. Down here, the cities were constrained to little specks of land, stretching out into the ocean.

Jesse had done his share of boating, diving, and fishing, but in the Keys, the ocean was just a few steps away, no matter where you were.

A sensation of calmness came over him as Jesse looked up at the sky and then all around. The feeling of being out of place he'd had at home was gone. He felt more alive and in the present than ever.

Ten minutes later, they were tied up at a fuel dock and the sky to the east was beginning to lighten, the stars no longer visible in that direction.

After tying the stern line to a dock cleat, Jesse stood, and, using his height advantage, could look over the dock toward the marina office and well-lit parking lot.

"He didn't strike me as an early riser," Jesse said, nodding toward the big biker guy from the night before.

He was talking to a woman in business clothes with chestnut-colored hair, or maybe auburn. In the glow of the orange lights, it was hard to tell.

Rusty stepped up on the gunwale and looked over. "Bear? He's a building and remodeling contractor durin' the day. Some days, anyway. He must have some work today, though; that woman he's talkin' to is in real estate. Her name's Skylar Rizzi. She's from up in Largo, but has an office in Big Pine Key, too."

"Which way to the 7 Mile Grill?" Jesse asked, stepping up onto the dock as the marina guy approached.

"Just head up through the parkin' lot there to the street," Rusty replied, pointing past the biker and the woman. "It's about four hunnert yards north to Useless One, and you'll see 7 Mile just across the highway."

As Jesse walked toward the parking lot, Bear was walking away from him toward a Camaro. The woman he was with stopped by the door and he opened it for her as a gentleman would.

But then he leaned in and kissed her as he fondled her ass.

Rachel had said he was her boyfriend.

But then, Rachel *had* kissed *him* on Rusty's boat the previous day.

The real estate woman got in the car and Bear watched her take off, then turned around and saw Jesse approaching. His eyes were red and bloodshot.

Bear stopped beside the sidewalk and crossed his arms. "You didn't see shit, kid."

Jesse ignored him.

"You hear me, numbnuts?" Bear snarled as Jesse got closer, still not slowing his stride. "You didn't see nothin'!"

Jesse continued walking, passing Bear and ignoring his taunts.

The bearded man's arm shot out, grabbing Jesse's shirt. "I'm talkin' to you, mother—"

Jesse's reaction was instantaneous.

He grabbed the offending hand at the wrist with his left hand, twisted under it, and grabbed the back of Bear's beefy forearm with his right hand, forcing the elbow to either bend backward or the man to go forward and down, off-balance until he was on his knees.

Few would choose the first option.

Jesse levered Bear's arm up, forcing his shoulder into a very unnatural position with his face six inches from the concrete curb, in full and total control of the man.

"Look at that curb!" Jesse hissed. "See it!" He lowered his voice as he bent forward, applying more pressure, easily pushing the big man's face closer to the concrete abutment. "Do not trifle with me, Bear. I don't back down."

Bear's right arm began to tremble with the effort he was putting into holding his face away from the curb.

"I'm going to let you up," Jesse said. "When I do, you have a choice to make. There's nobody around to see what happens. Choose to walk away or choose to press me further."

Jesse released his hold and stepped back quickly, feet planted, hands up, ready for anything.

Bear rose slowly to his feet, his chest heaving. He looked at Jesse through strands of disheveled hair, a deep scowl on his face. "One of these days, kid."

"But not *this* day," Jesse retorted.

Bear looked all around. The two were completely alone.

"What if I have a knife?" Bear growled, his hand moving toward his belt.

Jesse took a crouching half step closer, bringing his hands higher. "You'll look real cute with the handle sticking out of your fucking ear. Now shut up and bring it!"

Suddenly, Jesse's fury spiked.

It had started building as soon as he saw Bear touch the woman in the Camaro, but he hadn't liked the guy last night either.

It wasn't any of his business, and he would have rather just walked past the man. But Bear had made it his business when he put hands on him.

Jesse knew the outcome was going to be the same whether the biker pulled a knife or a gun—an instant disarming and a disabling blow.

The only variable would be in what strike he'd use. And that depended on what Bear did.

He stared hard at Jesse through tangled hair, then slowly turned and walked away.

Chapter Twenty-One

Jesse straightened, letting his arms drop to his sides as he watched Bear disappear around a corner. He took a deep breath and slowly exhaled as the adrenaline began to subside. Then he continued up the sidewalk to the road and headed away from the water.

Jesse didn't want to hurt anyone and hoped he'd convinced the man that coming at him again would be foolish and painful.

He and Billy had both taken martial arts classes for many years, but never the same style. Often, they'd taught each other and sparred together, each explaining what they'd learned to the other. Eventually, they'd both achieved black belts in multiple disciplines. Due to his height, Jesse rarely had to employ the things he'd learned.

His self-defense skills were like Pap's fireplace—there when needed.

Jesse only glanced back once as he made his way up Eleventh Street; Bear wasn't following him. He only saw one other person—a man in his driveway, loading a cooler into a boat.

As he walked, Jesse wondered if he should tell Rachel what he'd seen. If it were him, he'd want to know. But it was none of his business. Also, he'd be gone in a few days and might never see her again. To tell her wouldn't change him, but it would change things for her and then he'd be gone.

Traffic was light when he reached the highway and he sprinted across, still undecided.

"Hey, Jesse," Juliet said, smiling brightly as he walked up to the counter. "You're going fishing and need food."

"Yeah," Jesse replied. "Rusty said to get some breakfast burritos and I'm starved. How big are they?"

"Jim... er, Rusty, usually eats three," Juliet replied. "But it'll be a few minutes. We had an early rush on eggs, and Benny had to go the store. It's just a block. Have a seat—he should be back any second. Coffee while you wait?"

"Yes, thanks." Jesse nodded and sat on a stool. "No hurry. Rusty's gassing up."

"You're going out to the backcountry?" she asked.

"For lobster," Jesse replied. "Maybe some snook fishing if we can't find them."

"He can find them," Juliet said, wiping down the countertop. "Few know fish the way he does."

Jesse noticed the ring and nodded his head toward her hand. "I'm surprised I didn't notice that last night. Looks like congratulations are in order."

She brought her left hand up so he could see the ring better. "He proposed the morning after we got home," she said, suddenly shy. "Most of our friends were there. I had to have it resized and my jeweler friend who did it, just dropped it off. It's his grandmother's engagement ring."

The ring was fairly simple—a single diamond set in a sturdy mount on a gold band. "It's beautiful."

She looked down at it, her face beaming. "This ring goes back in his family many generations, just like the one Dreama wears." She looked up at him, smiling. "They're identical, you know. They've both been handed down, leap-frogging from grandmother to granddaughter-in-law since the 1700s. He said it ensures a stronger bond between mother and daughter-in-law, both wearing the same ring. Did you have a good time last night?"

He nodded. "An odd assortment of people, but yeah, I had fun."

"Hard to tell by your face," Juliet said, putting the towel down behind the counter. "Is something troubling you?"

"I don't know if it's my place to say anything about it," Jesse replied. "It isn't any of my business."

"If it concerns Jim," she said, very serious, "it is your business. I don't know how—y'all were only together a short while—but he thinks quite highly of you, and he's not easily impressed. All last week, it was Jesse did this, and Jesse did that."

He'd felt it too, that instant fraternal bond, even before they arrived at Parris Island. He figured the two of them had simply gravitated toward one another because of where they were from. Out of their whole platoon, only he, Rusty, and Couch were from Florida, and Couch was from so far north in the state you might as well say Georgia.

The beginnings of a friendship were there, and the invitation to spend the week was an easy one to accept, but they were still somewhat strangers.

Jesse hoped the training they'd be going through would make them closer friends. He missed hanging out with Billy and doing guy things.

"He's a good man," Jesse said. "I'm proud to call him my friend."

"Is it something about him, then?" she asked. "I know he snores like a misfiring outboard, and in that tin-roofed shack, I bet it probably echoes."

Jesse laughed, then became serious. "It's not about him directly, but might affect him, and you, I guess."

"What is it?" she asked, genuinely concerned.

"How serious are Rachel and Bear?"

"Rach? Wait. You were with Gina all evening. And I can tell she likes you. Why would you want to get hung up on her nutty sister?"

"I'm not," Jesse replied. "I like Gina too. She's easy to talk to and smart. But I saw something on the way over here."

"What?"

Jesse went on to explain what he'd seen in the parking lot with the real estate lady, Skylar Rizzi, but left out the part about the scuffle with Bear.

A man came in carrying a bag and went straight back to the kitchen.

"Eight breakfast burritos, Benny," Juliet called after him, then turned back to Jesse. "I don't think she's in love with the guy, if that's what you're wondering. She smokes and he can get it. I know they've slept together once or twice, but I don't think it's serious."

"Do you think I should tell her?"

"No," Juliet quickly replied. "It shouldn't come from you, even if it's not serious between them. I'll get with Gina after work and we'll both talk to her. Now, tell me about Gina. How much do you like her?"

As Jesse dashed across the highway with the bag of burritos, there was a loud roar from the next street to his left and he turned to see Bear taking off on his Harley.

He had a pale-skinned, young-looking redhead on the back, wearing jeans and a blue, sleeveless shirt. Her long red hair was braided into a ponytail.

Jesse continued down Eleventh Street toward the marina, shaking his head. The biker apparently played the field, which was at odds with the way Jesse was raised.

He'd dated several girls all through high school, and even two different girls in the last two weeks—three, counting Suzie.

But never at the same time.

"I was fixin' to send out a search party," Rusty said, rising from the helm seat to take the bag.

Jesse handed it over, then stepped down into the boat. "They ran out of eggs and Benny had to run to the store."

"Met Benny, huh?" Rusty said, digging a tightly wrapped package out of the bag, then handing it back to Jesse. "He used to be a horse addict."

"Horse?" Jesse asked. "You mean like horse racing? A gambling addict?"

"Heroin," Rusty said, giving him an odd look. "Smack, China white, dope. Man's got old scars from tracks between his toes, bro."

Jesse looked up while unwrapping a burrito. "Tracks between his toes?"

"Come on, man," Rusty said. "Fort Misery ain't that small."

"I never hung out much with people who did drugs," Jesse said.

"Me neither, bro. But down here, it's impossible to ignore."

"How come?" Jesse asked, taking a bite.

Rusty opened the bag and took another package out. "Smug drugglers come and go in these islands every night."

Jesse laughed. "Smug drugglers, huh?"

"Just about everyone down here smokes or has moved the stuff," Rusty said. "Times get tough and it's easy money. Every tenth car headed up Useless One has a coupla keys of weed or coke stashed inside."

Jesse remembered the steady stream of cars he'd seen going both ways while driving down. They'd gone by at a rate of at least ten per minute. He knew "key" was slang for kilo or kilogram, nearly two-and-a-half pounds. Two kilos per minute, if Rusty's statement was to be believed, would be 265 pounds an hour.

"Juliet showed me your grandmother's ring," Jesse said, changing the subject before taking a bite.

Rusty chewed for a moment then swallowed. "Didn't I tell ya on the phone the other day? I took her up to the Contents the mornin' after we got home," he said, nodding. "That's where we're goin' in just a minute. We already knew we were gonna get hitched—knew it since the eighth grade—but I needed a job and steady income first, to qualify for a mortgage. Fishin' for a livin' is just too up and down."

"Set the date yet?"

"The year, at least," Rusty replied. "Not this comin' spring, but the one after. I should be able to make rank by then and will only have a coupla years left. I'll be twenty-five then and we'll start raisin' a family."

"Seems like a long engagement," Jesse said.

"I suppose it is," Rusty admitted, moving toward the bow to untie the line. "But we ain't in no hurry and we got a plan. Wanna start the Merc?"

Jesse went to the helm and turned the key. The engine started instantly and settled into a quiet burble.

Rusty went aft and quickly untied the stern line, then nodded at Jesse. "Take her out, bro."

Jesse grinned, then turned, nudging the selector forward as Rusty pushed the boat away from the dock. He steered down the middle of the narrow canal, noting that the banks on either side had another rise farther inland and what looked like the crumbling remains of a rock seawall.

"Was this basin once wider?" he asked Rusty, now standing beside him at the helm.

"Yep, it was deeper too. A marina for my great-grandpa Tolliver's boat, *Freyja*. She was the Norse goddess of fertility, luck, love, lust, the afterlife, and protection." He pointed toward the bridge. "See the X on those two pilings?"

Jesse nodded.

"Go through there. Once clear, point the bow straight to the far end of the long island you'll see on the left. That arch with the X is kept clear of debris and the current's cut a nice deep channel there."

"You're Norse?" Jesse asked, steering the boat into the visible current he could see flowing around the concrete pilings.

"On Pop's side, *way*, way back," Rusty said, then pointed toward the tip of an island in the distance. "There ya go, straight toward the tip there. Yeah, Captain Augustus settled here, but he was from Scandinavian stock in the Nantucket area for a coupla centuries before he settled here."

"How far back do you know your family history?" Jesse asked, impressed.

"It's written in the family Bible going back to the 1500s," he replied, then pointed again at the tip of the island. "You can hammer down for about ten minutes. Just keep heading toward the end of Big Pine and Barnes Keys. At this distance, ya can't tell there's two."

Jesse brought the boat up on plane, surprised at how light it felt after piloting mostly wooden boats. At a speed he felt comfortable, he pulled back on the throttle a little.

Rusty had to shout to be heard over the rushing wind. "The Thurman name goes back to a whaling family in Norway, but then it was *Thormund*, which means 'Thor's protection.'"

"That's a seriously long time," Jesse said, glancing over.

"That's just part of it," he replied "The introduction in the Bible, handwritten in 1502, describes the unrecorded oral history of my family's roots in Norway for a dozen generations before, maybe all the way back to the end of the Viking empire in the twelfth century."

"That's almost a thousand years," Jesse said, incredulously.

He leaned back against the seat, the rising sun feeling good on the back of his neck and bare head.

The tan line just above his ears was nearly gone.

He was glad he'd come to the Keys; he was eager to strike out on his own and make his own way. He and Rusty had another week before they had to report for duty, and if they had a couple more days like yesterday, it'd be a great adventure.

He wished Billy could be there with them. He knew he and Rusty would hit it off.

Rusty pointed ahead and to the right. "See that marker coming up on the horizon?"

Jesse looked in the direction Rusty was pointing, and at first didn't see it. What he was calling a marker was little more than a bump on the water where it met the sky.

"Got it!" Jesse shouted back.

"Turn that way for five minutes!"

Jesse turned, figuring the distance to the horizon in his head and matching it with the speed they were going and for how long Rusty said to maintain it.

They didn't add up.

"Slow her on down!" Rusty shouted without urgency when they were still at least a mile from the marker.

Jesse pulled back, slowly on the throttle, as Rusty pointed ahead. "It gets a bit tricky here," he said.

Jesse brought the boat slowly off plane to a high idle speed and looked all around. They were in calm, open water, miles from civilization, with just a few tiny islands visible.

"The cut's just ahead," Rusty said, pointing. "I'll go up on the bow and guide you through it. You just ignore everything else and try to keep my arm pointing forward. There's four turns, two of 'em pretty sharp. I'll let ya know which one's comin'."

With Rusty guiding, Jesse managed to steer the boat through what he could easily see was a winding cut through ankle-deep water just ten feet away on both sides. It opened into a wide channel that looked as if it was quite deep.

The low angle of the sun shining over the shallow bank hid the deeper bottom of the channel in shadow.

"Turn west by southwest," Rusty said. "This here's Harbor Channel. The light's on Upper Harbor Key and everything west of here is the Content Keys, then the backcountry."

Jesse turned the wheel and watched the compass. Then he picked a tree on an island about two miles away and steered toward it.

"Where's it go?" Jesse asked.

"The channel don't go nowhere," Rusty explained. "'Bout two miles ahead it spreads out into a series of smaller, natural channels through the backcountry. Harbor Channel was used by sailing ships as a safe harbor from storms. It's deep and surrounded by flats, except the dogleg at the east end, where it flows into the Gulf."

"Are any of these islands inhabited?" Jesse asked, reveling in the quiet, even with the engine at a burble. "I can see why they call them the Contents."

"Nope," Rusty replied. "Out here, the nearest road is on the north end of Big Pine Key, about five miles back the way we came.

"What's that island called?" Jesse asked, pointing to a mangrove- covered key with a coconut palm sticking out of the center of it.

"Remember I said yesterday how a lot of these little islands don't even have names," Rusty explained. "Most of these out here don't. That one behind us is Upper Harbor Key." He pointed at something near the island ahead of them. "Hey, what's that?"

Near the eastern shore of the lone palm island, Jesse could see something white sticking up out of the water.

"I don't know," he said.

"Head toward it," Rusty ordered. "Idle right up until the bow grounds in the sand."

He went forward, pulled an anchor out of the bow hatch, and placed it on the casting deck with a good twenty feet of line. Then he climbed up onto the bow and looked back.

"You'll know when you're startin' to ground when I jump off. Soon as I do, cut the engine, and come up here and hand me the anchor."

Jesse didn't even feel the hull on the sand when Rusty jumped, but the bow came up a few inches, then the boat gently came to a stop as soon as it came back down.

Jesse turned off the engine and hurried forward. Rusty was waiting in shin-deep water at the front of the boat, holding the bow rail.

"Tide's risin'," Rusty said, taking the anchor from Jesse. "Current'll flow from the north and east but won't be but a knot, if that. Pull another twenty feet out, just to be safe."

Instead of heading toward shore, Rusty carried the anchor to the right, following the edge of the drop off. Jesse realized he was anchoring so the boat would stay where it was instead of swinging around on an arc in the current when the rising tide freed it from the sand.

"C'mon!" Rusty shouted, after setting the anchor. "Looks like the stern of a wrecked boat."

Jesse climbed out and waded toward shore. It *was* the stern of a boat. But it wasn't sunk. It was literally just the back fourth of a powerboat, with the motor still attached.

"What do you think happened?" Jesse asked as the two

examined the find.

The deck and hull, just a few feet forward of the outboard, looked like a bomb had hit the boat. Still strapped to the transom was a five-gallon can.

"There was a boat fire up island back on July Fourth," Rusty said. "Pop wrote me about it. Happened in a marina on a waterway with a strong current, and several boats were fully engulfed. Some idiot thought cutting the lines on the burning boats would sweep 'em out into Florida Bay. It worked, but not before spreadin' the fire to two other marinas."

"Think this is one of those boats?" Jesse asked, looking around.

"Could be," Rusty said. "Looks like the gas tank under the deck exploded. The engine here looks in pretty good shape. Wind's been out of the east all summer. Mighta bounced on the bottom all the way from there. I can rebuild this engine and make a better profit than we will fishin'. Want to help me get it on the boat?"

Jesse scanned the island, thinking someone might be watching. But there was nobody around. There *was* something not right about the mangrove treeline on the shore, though.

"Yeah, sure," Jesse said, wading toward the island. "But I want to see something first."

When he reached the mangrove roots, it was obvious the interior of the island was cleared. He found a way through the roots and when he reached sand on shore, he looked out over the island's interior.

"Rusty!" Jesse shouted, without turning. "I think you need to come and see this."

Jesse heard splashing, then Rusty cursing as he came through the mangroves. "Where the hell are ya?"

He stopped next to Jesse as the two looked out over what appeared to be almost an acre of cleared interior, with raised, cultivated beds of marijuana plants.

"What in the—" Rusty started to say, taking a step forward. "It's a pot farm!"

"We have to destroy it," Jesse said.

"Are you nuts?" Rusty shouted, turning to face Jesse in obvious disbelief. "Anyone growin' shit on this scale is gonna be dangerous, bro, and these are people you don't wanna cross."

"What if some kid found this?" Jesse insisted. "What if your and Juliet's kid came out here in the future and found this?"

In Jesse's mind, there was only one right thing to do. Reporting it to the authorities would take time and they'd end up doing the same thing—burning it.

Rusty stared at Jesse for a moment, then looked back out over the field. "We'll need a lot of gas."

"There was a jerry can in that wreck," Jesse said. "If it's gas, we can set a fire near there. Maybe they'll think it was a boat explosion."

"They might," Rusty said, turning. "C'mon. Let's do it 'fore I change my mind. I just know this is gonna come back and bite me in the ass, though."

Chapter Twenty-Two

◆ ─ ◆ ─ ◆ ─ ◆

The boat idled slowly up the canal toward the bait shop, the sound of the engine muted, but still loud in the surrounding silence. Jesse and Rusty hadn't talked much since leaving the Content Keys. Fortunately, there hadn't been any other boats around until they reached the Seven Mile Bridge.

Likewise, there were no other boats tied up in the basin, and Jesse didn't see anyone around.

"Mid-mornin'," Rusty said, as if Jesse had actually asked the question. "All the guides and fishermen are out."

A screen door slammed, and Jesse looked over to see Shorty coming down toward the docks at a trot.

"Back so soon?" he shouted. "You just left a few hours ago."

Shorty helped tie the boat up, then stepped down into it, a concerned look on his face.

"What's wrong, son?" he asked Rusty.

"We found a uh..." Rusty began, then he looked his father straight in the eye. "We found a marijuana farm up in the Contents, Pop... And we burned it."

"You what?" Shorty exclaimed.

"It was my idea," Jesse said. "It seemed like the right thing to do."

Shorty looked up at Jesse, then back at his son. "It is what it is," he said. "Hopefully, nobody saw you. Any idea who it belonged to?"

Rusty shook his head, but Jesse sensed he knew more than he was letting on.

"I'll make a few calls," Shorty said, as he stepped back up to the dock. "See if anyone's heard anything."

"Who's he going to call?" Jesse asked, after Shorty left.

"Other bar owners and bartenders," Rusty replied. "We're the invisible sect of society, and folks talk too much." He sat down hard on the gunwale. "This could be bad."

"You know who owned it," Jesse stated.

Rusty looked up at him and nodded. "Best if you don't know, though."

"So I can walk blindly into something?" Jesse said. "No way, man. Who is it?"

"Bear," Rusty said. "He did the same thing on another island last summer."

Jesse sat down on the opposite gunwale and told Rusty about the altercation in the parking lot, what he'd seen before that, and his conversation with Juliet after.

"Lucky for you he didn't have a gun," Rusty said. "I told ya he was a dangerous guy."

"He's a bully," Jesse said, as if the word left a bad taste in his mouth. "I don't like bullies, and I don't like him."

"Who are you, bro?" Rusty asked, hanging his head. "Dudley fuckin' Do-Right or somethin'?"

"First to fight," Jesse said, standing tall and staring coldly at his new friend as he recited the chorus of the Marines' Hymn. "For *right* and freedom."

Rusty looked up, squinting into the sunlight. Then he stood and stuck out his hand. "And to keep our honor *clean*."

Jesse shook his hand firmly. "Semper fi."

"Ya know, I never really knew what that meant until today, bro.

I'm with ya, come rain, mud, shit, or blood."

"Hey," a voice shouted.

Jesse turned and saw Gina coming around the end of the canal from the path on the other side.

Just past her, he spotted Juliet's "no car keys Keys car" pulling in beyond her.

"Should we tell them?" Jesse asked, as he and Rusty stepped up onto the dock.

"Always, bro," Rusty replied. "I don't never keep nothin' from Jewels. Never."

"JJ saw you guys coming back in," Gina said. "She called me to see if you'd come to Dockside."

"She's just pullin' in," Rusty said. "We'll tell ya both together."

"Hey, Jesse," Gina said, smiling brightly. "Even if it's bad news, I'm glad I'm getting to see you again. Engine trouble?"

"Let's wait for JJ," Jesse said, sitting on a crumbling piece of the old seawall, hands on his knees and his feet planted. "You might change your mind when we tell you what happened."

She hopped up on the rock beside him, dangling her feet. "I'm a pretty good judge of character," she said. "Unless you're the one who kidnapped the girl this morning, then I doubt anything you did will bother me much."

"Kidnapped?" Jesse asked, as Juliet joined them.

"It's all over the radio," Juliet said, giving Rusty a quick kiss. "She was reported missing not long after you stopped in for breakfast."

"We burned somebody's pot farm," Rusty blurted.

The two girls looked at him, then at one another.

"It was a pretty big operation," Jesse said. "About two hundred plants I'd guess."

Gina smiled at Jesse. "Welcome to the dark side. You did the right thing, if you ask me. But my sister might be pissed, though."

"More'n ya think," Rusty said. "I'm pretty sure it was Bear's farm."

"That's all we don't need," Juliet said. "Hell's Angels coming in here and raising trouble."

"He's not with Hell's Angels," Rusty assured her. "I don't even think he's in any kinda biker club or anything."

"Yeah, well, you remember what he did to that guy last year?" Juliet said. "He put him in the hospital for a week."

Gina pulled Juliet down next to her. "Take it easy, JJ. These guys did the right thing."

"I know!" Juliet said, obviously distressed. "But it wasn't the *smart* thing."

"I talked Rusty into it," Jesse said. "He didn't want to."

Juliet looked up at Rusty standing in front of her, then took his hands. "He would have come up with the idea on his own after a few minutes of thinking."

Rusty nodded. "I don't want our kids to ever be exposed to stuff like that."

"Now that that's settled," Gina said, jumping off the rock and taking Jesse's hand, "want to take a walk down to the seawall?"

He grinned and stood up, then stepped up onto the higher ledge and helped her up. "After you."

She smiled and held his hand as they started to walk. "You talk like one of those actors from the black-and-white movie days, all serious and poised."

Jesse shrugged as they walked down the sloping yard. "I guess I am a little old-fashioned about some things, like you said last night. My grandparents tried to expose me to modern ideas, but I guess some of their older mentality rubbed off. What was this about a kidnapping?"

"Oh yeah," Gina said. "It happened this morning. Her friends said she was there one minute and gone the next."

"I didn't think the police called it a kidnapping until someone was gone for twenty-four hours. Was she a minor?"

"The news said she's my age, twenty-two." Gina paused and looked up at him as they walked. "How old are you? I don't think you told me."

"I'll be eighteen in the spring," Jesse said.

She stopped. "You're only..." She smiled at him. "That makes me an official cradle robber, then. I thought you were older than me."

"Is that a problem?"

She took his hand again and they continued walking. "Not for me. You're deeper than most of the older guys around here."

"So why are they calling it a kidnapping?" Jesse asked. "I mean, if she's just been reported missing."

"The police aren't. Apparently, she's down here from Ohio with a group of girlfriends and is supposed to be getting married next week."

"Cold feet?" Jesse asked, as they reached the seawall and turned left, following it.

"That's what the police say," Gina replied. "But her friends insist she's been taken."

"What's she look like?"

"The news report said she was last seen wearing jeans and a blue, sleeveless blouse."

Jesse stopped mid-stride and took Gina by both arms. "Red hair? Braided? Pale skin?"

"How do you know this?"

"I saw her!" Jesse replied, turning back toward where Rusty and Juliet sat under a shade tree. He grabbed Gina's hand and started pulling her along. "Come on!"

Chapter Twenty-Three

A thin line of gray-black smoke could be seen in the distance, rising into a clear blue sky, which was marred only by the smoke and a few puffy white clouds.

A mile to the south, a small boat was heading toward the smoke, slowly winding its way through a maze of narrow, unmarked channels and cuts.

As the boat drew closer, other smaller tendrils of smoke could be seen coming from the perimeter, curving inward to mix with the thicker plume in the center.

"This don't look good," the man driving the boat said. "Where you been all mornin'? Chuck said he left word everywhere before going back out there."

Bear stared ahead, his forehead creased with rage.

Under his beard on his left cheek were several straight scratch marks, already scabbed over and barely visible under his thick beard.

Bear had been pissed all morning, until he found someone to take it out on.

"Had things to see and people to do," he growled as the island came into view up ahead. "Whoever did this is gonna die."

The single coconut palm in the middle of the island still stood in stark contrast to the smoke curling around it and the devastation below. It didn't appear that the flames had reached its lofty fronds.

Another boat was anchored in the shallows just to the left of the little island, which Bear had gone to great expense to clear and set up.

"There's Chuck's boat," the driver said, turning toward it and accelerating in deeper water.

Like Bear, the boat driver also sported long hair and a scraggly beard, both unkempt. Unlike Bear, he was rail thin.

He drove his boat toward Chuck's, then slowed as they reached the shallows on the other side of the channel. Once he cut the engine, they drifted past the other boat. The driver went forward to drop the anchor, and they both climbed out into knee-deep water.

Chuck was coming toward them from the charred remains of the mangroves. "Total loss, man!" he shouted across the intervening water. "They put gas in the irrigation system, then started the little generator to run the pumps. Then they lit the whole fuckin' thing up! Pumps and everything, gone."

Bear sloshed toward shore in the shallow water, stopping when he met up with his partner. "Anything salvageable?"

"There ain't *nothin'* left," Chuck said, then nodded at the other man. "Thanks for runnin' him out here, Ansil."

He turned back to the burly biker. "Weird thing, though. There's part of a boat over on the east side, still has the motor on it. Looks like it caught fire and blew up."

"If it ain't kids stealin' plants," Bear growled, "it's the damned law burning my shit. I hope it took a couple of 'em with it when it blew."

"I don't think the wrecked boat had anything to do with this," Chuck said. "And I know it wasn't the law. I saw 'em leavin' as the fire grew."

"Huh?" Bear turned and faced the man.

"It was that Shorty Thurman's kid."

"You gotta be shittin' me," Bear snarled. "You sure?"

"I'd know that new Bertram anywhere," Chuck replied. "And the two in it had buzz cuts."

Bear remembered how easily the tall kid had taken him down that morning in the parking lot. He hadn't been prepared. He should have pulled his knife and carved him up then.

A mistake I'll soon fix, he thought.

"I'm gonna enjoy stomping the shit out of them two," Bear said, turning back toward the boats. "Come on, Ans. I got somethin' to do first and you're takin' me to Boot Key Harbor."

Chapter Twenty-Four

━━━━◆━━━━◆━━━━◆━━━━◆━━━━

Jesse knew without a doubt that it was Bear he'd seen taking off on his motorcycle a block away. He and the bike were easily recognizable, and the redhead he'd seen on the back fit the description of the missing woman to a T.

The trouble Jesse was having with the idea of it being an abduction was that it would be very difficult, if not impossible, to do it on a motorcycle—no way to control the abductee. And the woman hadn't seemed like she was in distress.

He, Rusty, and the girls had been sitting at a table under the trees near Rusty's parents' house, listening to the local radio station for an update. The redhead had been reported missing just after sunrise and it was mid-afternoon.

"How sure are ya that the woman you saw with Bear was the same one?" Rusty asked. "And are ya certain it was even him?"

"I know Harley Davidson quit making panheads a long time ago," Jesse replied. "A friend's dad had one. I doubt there are two like that in all of the Keys, much less on just those two blocks. And I'm certain it was him riding it. As for the woman? I've never met her, so can't say for certain. But the description fits."

"We should call the police," Juliet said.

"Let's think about that a second," Rusty said. "We just burned the guy's pot farm. If we go sendin' the cops after him, that's bound to come out. What if the redhead just went for a joyride with the guy? She might even be back with her friends, all safe and sound. We go sendin' the cops after him, and he finds out it was us and we also burned his pot, there's gonna be hell to pay."

"I think Juliet's right," Jesse said. "The woman I saw with Bear didn't look to me like she was being abducted, but she still might be in danger. Bear wasn't in the best mood when I saw him with the real estate lady this morning."

"What real estate lady?" Juliet asked.

"Skylar Rizzi," Rusty replied. "She met Bear at the marina this mornin'."

"What did *she* do to sour his mood?" Gina asked. "Back-charge him for being late on a job?"

Jesse explained to the girls what had happened in the parking lot when he'd gone to get breakfast at the 7 Mile Grill. This time, he included the encounter he'd had with the man.

"You've only been here twenty-four hours," Gina said. "And you've already caught a thirty-five-hundred-dollar fish, beat up the local biker bad guy, and burned his pot field. You're just a one-man wrecking ball."

Jesse looked up at her, somewhat ashamed of the accusation, but she was smiling.

"I would never intentionally hurt anyone," Jesse said. "Bear started it when he grabbed me."

"All badassery aside," Gina said, turning to Rusty, "I agree. We should call the police."

The music on the radio ended mid-song and a reporter's voice came on.

All four of them looked at the radio.

"Two tourist couples kayaking on the Gulf side of Long Key discovered the body of a woman just after noon today," the reporter said. *"It is believed that the body might be that of the woman who went missing earlier*

212

today in Marathon, but the police have not issued any statement."

He went on to give an account from one of the tourists, describing what the woman's clothes and hair looked like.

"Why don't the police say what's going on?" Juliet asked. "We have to tell them what we know."

"You mean what I *saw*," Jesse said. "We don't *know* anything. It's not for us to decide. And police never talk about an ongoing investigation."

"Is there a lot of this kind of thing in Fort Myers?" Gina asked.

"Not like a big city or anything," Jesse replied. "Once or twice a year, there's a shooting."

"So, are we gonna call?" Juliet asked.

Jesse looked over at Rusty. "What's Bear's real name?"

Rusty's eyes widened. "I dunno. Never heard him called anything else."

Jesse looked at the two girls and they both shrugged. "Rachel would probably know," Gina said.

"Where is she now?" Rusty asked. "We can't really turn someone in for murder if we don't know his name. That's what we're talkin' about here; accusin' a man who we know is dangerous of murder."

Gina looked at her watch. "She's probably on the boat by now. She got off work at two."

"We can take my car," Jesse said, jerking a thumb toward the Mustang. "It's right over there."

"That's yours?" Gina asked. "I saw it earlier. But we'll need to go by boat. Rach will have the dinghy at our boat."

"Oh, yeah," Jesse said, seeing Rusty's dad approaching.

"Tell 'em?" Shorty asked.

Rusty nodded.

Shorty sat down at the table. "Word is that Bear's been growing pot on a couple of islands," he said. "As well as in a couple of vacant houses for sale."

The real estate lady, Jesse thought. They were obviously more than just business acquaintances. Maybe their relationship extended to illegal activities. She hadn't looked the type, but who knew?

"The woman who was reported missing was found dead," Rusty said. "And Jesse says he saw her on the back of Bear's motorcycle this mornin'."

"A body fitting the description of the missing woman was found," Jesse corrected him. "And I saw a woman who also looked like that, riding north on the back of Bear's motorcycle from that same area about the same time."

Shorty rubbed the back of his neck. "A lot of conjecture," he finally said. "But it looks like the dots all lead to Bear. You want my two cents? You should call the law. It doesn't involve any locals."

"We were about to do that," Rusty said. "We just now heard the news report about the body. But we don't know Bear's real name."

"Bert something," Shorty said. "He's from up on the mainland somewhere and been comin' down here for years."

"We were gonna head out to the harbor and see if Rach knows his last name," Rusty said.

"Nothin' can be done for the dead woman," Shorty replied, rising from the table. "Yeah, go do that. But come back here before you call the cops. I want to be around when they come."

They rose together and Shorty headed back to the bait shop while the others went to the dock and boarded Rusty's Bertram. In minutes, they were idling out the barely marked channel, then bouncing across the chop toward East Sister Rock.

Rusty turned toward Sister Creek and dropped the speed, finally slowing to an idle as they entered the waterway.

"Where're y'all anchored?" he asked Gina.

"Past Dockside a little ways," she replied. "Near the shallows."

When they entered the protected harbor, Rusty turned right and followed the line of docked boats. He passed the slip where they'd weighed the tuna, then an open deck area. Then he turned left, heading toward Rachel and Gina's sailboat.

"Rach!" Gina called out, as Rusty carefully guided the Bertram toward the stern and shifted to reverse to stop the boat.

There was no answer. The dinghy was tied to the stern of the sailboat, so Rachel was obviously there.

"She might be taking a nap," Gina said, moving forward.

"My bow's about the same as the side deck on your boat," Rusty said. "Climb on up there with the bowline and I'll put you right on it."

Jesse went with her and held her hand while she steadied herself on the foredeck.

Rusty nudged the Bertram alongside, then reversed and turned the wheel, causing the bow to swing toward the sailboat.

Gina stepped over and then took the line Jesse handed her back to the stern and tied it off to a cleat. The current pushed the boat back and Gina held it beside the little swim platform.

Rusty killed the engine, then he and Juliet joined Jesse and climbed over to the sailboat.

"She must be a heavy sleeper," Rusty remarked.

Jesse heard a low moan and went quickly up the steps in the sugar scoop transom. The companionway hatch was open.

"Rach?" Gina shouted, moving past him in the cockpit and climbing quickly down the steps.

Jesse went right after her, sensing trouble. When his feet hit the deck in the salon, he was ready for anything.

Or so he thought

Rachel lay on the deck, groaning, barely conscious. There was blood on her shirt, as well as on the deck, and even some on the

Gina ran to her sister and knelt beside her. "Rachel? It's me. Can you hear me?"

Rusty and Juliet came down, and Jesse spotted a first-aid kit mounted on a wall in the galley. He pulled it down and rushed to where Rachel lay on the deck. Rusty grabbed a towel and wet it, then joined him.

"Let us in, Gina," Jesse said, trying to nudge her aside. "Rusty and I have this."

She began to push back, but Jesse took her shoulders in his hands and looked into her eyes. "We're trained for this, Gina."

She moved back, clinging to Juliet as Jesse and Rusty went to work, carefully turning Rachel flat onto her back and putting a pillow under her knees. Rusty bent and listened to her breathing as Jesse checked her pulse by placing two fingers along the side of her neck, as they'd been taught at Ellis Island, just off of Parris Island.

"Pulse is regular but weak," Jesse said, taking the damp towel and wiping some of the blood from Rachel's battered face. "Deep laceration on her left cheek."

"Respiration sounds clear but fast," Rusty said, looking up at Jesse, then glancing at her face. "Jesus... what kind of animal—"

"A bear," Jesse growled quietly, feeling the heat rise at the back of his neck. "She has a split lip and a couple more facial cuts, but the one on her cheek is pretty bad."

Rusty quickly opened three butterfly bandages, sticking one end of each to the table beside her. Then he opened a bottle of anti-bacterial ointment and used a cotton ball to better clean the largest of the cuts on Rachel's left cheek. Her cheekbone was visible. Using the butterfly bandages, he pulled the skin together.

While Rusty was closing the worst of the wounds, Jesse prepared a large bandage to cover it and her left eye. "Looks like there might be orbital damage," he whispered.

"What?" Gina said, moving closer again. "What's that mean?"

"Give us a minute," Jesse said, a bit too harshly. He looked up at Gina. She had tears running down her cheeks. "She's going to be okay," he said in a softer tone, trying to reassure her. "I promise."

Rachel coughed, then moaned, her eyelids beginning to flutter.

"Get me some water," Rusty said, as the two continued to work on cleaning and bandaging the smaller cuts. He bent closer to her face. "Rach? Can ya hear me? It's Jim. We're gonna get ya over to Fishermen's as soon as me and Jesse get you stabilized."

Juliet turned to the small cooler and opened it. Not seeing anything but a few floating beer cans, she grabbed a plastic cup from the cupboard and dipped some of the melted ice water into it.

"Do you hurt anywhere else?" Jesse asked. "Back? Ribs?"

"No," Rachel croaked softly through a split lower lip. She started to cry. "He hit me... in the face."

"Here," Juliet said, kneeling beside Rusty with the cup.

"Think you can sit up if we help ya?" Rusty asked, holding one hand under Rachel's head.

She nodded, slightly.

Jesse and Rusty clasped hands at the back of her neck and each took a shirtsleeve with the other, raising her slowly to a sitting position.

"Drink this," Rusty said, holding the cup for her. "But be careful, your bottom lip's swollen."

"I'll be... okay," Rachel said, looking up at Gina. "It was..." She sobbed. "It was Bear."

I should've smashed his face into the curb, Jesse thought, his anger ratcheting up, *The animal outweighed her by a hundred pounds.*

"What's his *real* name?" Jesse asked, his voice as cold as Arctic ice.

Suddenly, there was a loud explosion, though it sounded as if it were some distance away.

"That was near the bait shop!" Rusty shouted.

Gina knelt down by her sister. "Go, if you need to," she said urgently. "Take the dinghy to Dockside. JJ and I will take Rach to Fishermen's in your boat."

"C'mon!" Rusty said, stepping up the companionway steps. "I see smoke! And it's definitely coming from our property!"

Chapter Twenty-Five

◆ ◆ ◆ ◆

Rusty got the little dinghy's motor started on the second pull as Jesse jumped into the front and untied the line. Rusty twisted the throttle and Jesse leaned forward in the bow until it came back down, then he dropped to one knee, bracing himself with his hands on the sponsons.

It only took a minute to reach Dockside, where there was a small dock with several dinghies tied up. Smoke could be seen rising over the trees to the east.

Jesse quickly tied the line to a deck cleat and they both climbed out and sprinted toward the foot of the dock.

"This way!" Rusty shouted, running through a gate and turning left in loose gravel next to a paved road.

Jesse tore after him, his long legs catching the shorter man in just a few strides.

"Pace yourself," Rusty said, running at a steady, double-time pace. "It's a half mile and the last part's through the woods."

They fell into step without realizing, their footfalls sounding as one as they ran shoulder to shoulder on the road, passing a long line of docks, then a condo.

The road ended at an intersection, and they crossed it, Rusty leading the way behind a split-rail fence and then under some overhanging tree branches.

Jesse followed right behind him, dreading what they might find as they disappeared under the high branches of the overhanging foliage.

The trail was barely above the water on either side, and it twisted one way, then the other.

They ran in single file, but still their feet fell in perfect unison.

Ahead, Jesse heard the roar of a Harley engine, then it faded for a second, then rose up and down as the rider accelerated and slowed on the winding driveway to Rusty's house.

Jesse was right on Rusty's heels when his friend broke out of the trees into the parking area, and he almost ran him over when Rusty stopped suddenly.

Ahead, black smoke and orange flames curled out of the blown-out rear and side windows of the Mustang.

Jesse froze.

Then his blood began to boil as his fists clenched in rage.

Shorty came running out of the bait shop with a large silver cylinder, spraying foam as soon as he got close enough. In seconds, the flames receded as he covered the car in dripping white foam.

Rusty and Jesse sprinted around the end of the canal as Shorty put the fire extinguisher down.

"It was Bear!" he shouted in anger. "Must've coasted partway in and walked the rest. Saw him as he was running back toward the driveway. Then the car blew up."

"You okay, Pop?" Rusty asked. "He beat up Rachel."

"Aw, now why'd he go and fuck with a local?" Shorty said. "Is she okay?"

"She will be," Jesse said, his tone even colder as he stared at the car his best friend had built. "Can't say the same for Bear when I get my hands on him." He turned toward Shorty. "You said he was growing pot in some vacant houses. Where are they?"

Shorty looked up at Jesse, then turned toward his son. "Jim, go get the guns." Without a word, Rusty ran toward the bar side of the building as Shorty looked again at Jesse. "You come with me, son."

Jesse followed Shorty into the bar after Rusty.

"I knew he was trouble first time he came in my bar, twenty years ago," Shorty muttered, moving quickly behind a heavy-looking, dark-stained wooden bar. He put both hands on the bar and leaned against it.

"You need to know something," he said, pausing to look up at the younger man. "Around here, we don't call the law. We call family and call friends."

It was the same thing Rusty had said.

Two older men were sitting at the bar, but Rusty was nowhere in sight. Shorty picked up a telephone and a box of business cards from behind the bar, placing them on it, and started thumbing through the cards until he found the one he wanted.

The two old men looked over at Jesse, both of them hunched over beer mugs as quiet country music played on a jukebox. They nodded and Jesse nodded back.

Shorty dialed a number and waited. "Is Sky in?" he asked, then listened for a moment, and said, "Tell her it's Shorty Thurman and she needs to interrupt her meeting. She'll take the call."

Jesse took a step closer. "Who are you call—"

Shorty held up a finger, silencing him. "Sky, I need you to meet me at the house on Big Pine where you and Bear are growing pot. Don't deny it; the whole town knows. Don't debate me, and don't ask any questions. Just get in your convertible and drive. I'll see you there in twenty minutes."

He hung up the phone just as Rusty came out of the back room carrying three handguns and an old, bolt-action rifle. When he placed them on the bar, the two old men had no reaction. It was as if guns on the bar were a normal occurrence.

Maybe they were.

Rusty handed Jesse a Colt 1911, just like they'd fired on the pistol range at Parris Island. "Seven in the mag," he calmly advised. "One in the pipe. Safety's on."

Jesse press-checked the slide anyway, seeing the round in the chamber, and checked the safety before tucking the gun backward in his pants on his left side.

"Let's go," Shorty said. "The bait's dangling and the little fish will draw in the big one."

Chapter Twenty-Six

◆ ◆ ◆ ◆

The three of them climbed into a rusty old Chevy pickup that, if looks were the deciding factor, wouldn't make it out of the parking lot. But the engine started easily, and Shorty backed out from under the tree.

The Mustang lay smoldering on flat tires on the other side of the tree.

"How bad was she beat up?" Shorty asked, as he drove fast through the dense jungle.

"Her left cheek was cut bad," Jesse replied, looking straight ahead. "It'll need stitches, and she might lose that eye."

"A man who puts hands on a woman..." Shorty said, shaking his head as they approached the highway.

A VHF radio mounted under the dash squawked, a static-covered voice saying something unintelligible. Shorty reached over and turned it down.

There was nothing coming in either direction, so Shorty jammed the truck into low gear and floored it, driving through the grassy median and turning left. The front tires protested loudly when they caught pavement on the other side.

"Give me just five minutes," Jesse said, his anger not dissipating in the least.

"Because of what he did to your—"

"You didn't see her!" Jesse exclaimed, snapping his head to the left, the anger overflowing. "He could have killed her."

"Just checking your mindset, son," Shorty said, as he shifted up through the gears, reaching fourth just as they got onto the bridge.

For the first two miles, Shorty kept his foot on the floor, reaching eighty miles per hour. Then they came up behind a car pulling a camper, and a long line of oncoming traffic blocked the other lane.

Finally, when the other lane was clear, Shorty downshifted and pulled out to pass the camper. The bridge was narrow, and the driver of the car, clearly annoyed at Shorty's tailgating, flipped them a finger as the old Chevy roared past.

When they passed a sign welcoming them to Big Pine Key and advising them to slow down for Key deer, Shorty downshifted, took a sweeping left curve, then turned off on a residential street on the right.

"There's no way she's here yet," Shorty said, driving slowly. "That means he probably isn't either, unless he's here tending the plants."

"That would be just fine with me," Jesse said.

"We're not going to kill the man," Shorty said. "Not in cold blood, anyway. If he draws, shoot to kill, boys."

Jesse looked over at Shorty and Rusty. Both had their jaws firmly set, and defiance blazed in their eyes.

Their family had been on this island before Florida was a state and it was likely they had settled differences and disputes in their own way before now.

Shorty made several turns, finally stopping just before a large house on a canal on the right, set way back from the road.

"How sure are you that they're growin' there?" Rusty asked.

"Ab-so-posi-lutely," Shorty replied, studying the house. "Doesn't look like anyone's here."

He put the truck in gear and then drove slowly into the long driveway. It ended in a circle, which surrounded a small fountain. Shorty went all the way around, so the truck was pointed back down the driveway, just as a Camaro pulled in.

Jesse recognized the car immediately. "That's her."

The real estate lady parked on the other side of the circle and got out of her car.

"Stay here," Shorty said. "I want to have a word with Miss Rizzi alone."

He got out and met her in front of the truck. They said a few words, then Shorty motioned for Rusty and Jesse to get out.

Jesse strode straight toward the woman. She wore the same business clothes he'd seen her wearing earlier. She was slim, attractive, and older, about Shorty's age.

Only two hundred people in a six-year age span, he thought.

"I've seen you," she said. "You were at the marina this morning."

"When you were meeting your boyfriend," Jesse said. "Did you know he was also dating a younger woman named Rachel?" He could tell by her reaction that she knew. "He beat her up a little while ago."

She turned her head slightly, raising a hand to her left cheek.

"He hit you, too?" Shorty asked her.

"No! He'd never—"

"We think he kidnapped and murdered another woman," Rusty added. "Right after you left the marina this morning."

"That's just ridiculous," she protested, but without much conviction.

Jesse sensed that she knew about Bear's cheating and thought that Shorty was right. He'd hit her, too.

"Rachel didn't die," Jesse said, taking a step toward her. "And neither did you. She said it was Bear who beat her. Where is he?"

She took a step toward Jesse. "Now you just—"

"Easy, Sky," Shorty said, inserting himself between them. "We know what's inside this house. You'll go down for a long time when the cops figure out that you're involved. And there's no way what's going on in there could happen without your direct knowledge and approval. You know me—I don't judge. This is *your own listing*, Sky. I've known you since we were kids. You never made a bad business move until now."

She turned and stomped a fashionable heel. "I never should have let him—"

"But you did," Shorty said. "What's done is done. Where's Bear, Sky?"

She turned back to face him. "Can you help get me out of this?"

"You called him before coming here, didn't you?" Jesse asked, figuring out what Shorty had meant by dangling the bait.

"He's on his way here now," she said, trembling slightly.

Shorty pointed toward the house. "Sky, inside, now! Jim, you take one corner, and Jesse you take the other."

He took Sky by the elbow, and though he was half a head shorter, he forced her up the steps as Jesse sprinted to one corner of the house and Rusty went to the other.

Sky got the door unlocked, and Shorty pushed her inside. "Stay in there," he told her.

"What are you going to do?" Jesse heard her ask in a frightened voice.

"I want to talk to the man," Shorty replied. "Try to get him to turn himself in."

"He carries a gun," she said.

"So do we," Shorty replied, then closed the door. "Jim! Jesse! I'm going to talk to him first. Try to get him to turn himself in. You boys be ready."

They waited.

Then they waited some more.

An hour passed. Shorty continued to pace back and forth on the porch. Sky watched through the window.

"He's not coming," Shorty finally announced.

Jesse had already come to that realization himself. Bear's pot farm had been discovered and destroyed, a second one was on the verge of being lost, and he was on the run after killing one woman and beating up another. When the girls got Rachel to the hospital and she made a statement, the police would be looking for Bear, and they were probably expecting Jesse to come and make a statement or something too.

He and Rusty both stepped out of concealment, the angled rays of the setting sun shining fully on the porch as they approached the steps.

The door opened and Sky came out onto the porch. "He was at Josh's when I called him. He should have been here long ago."

The two came down the steps, and Jesse and Rusty met them at the bottom.

"What now?" Rusty asked.

Jesse looked at Sky's face and could see where she'd carefully hidden a bruise on her left check with makeup. "Where does he sleep?"

"His boat!" Shorty exclaimed. "Gulf side of Bahia Honda."

"He could be long gone, Pop!" Rusty shouted.

Shorty turned toward Sky. "Get some people. Get this house cleared out before morning. This is all gonna unravel before then and you're neck deep."

"But—"

"No buts, Sky!" Shorty shouted. "Bail and cut your losses. Get this place cleaned out. Now!"

They ran back out to the truck and got in.

"If his trawler's still there," Shorty said as he turned back onto the road, "and that little jon boat he uses for a dinghy is there, then we got him."

"And then what?" Jesse asked.

"If he's not there," Shorty began, "we tell the cops what we know. If he is, we wait for the cops."

"What if he's there, but leaving?" Rusty asked.

Shorty turned and looked at both of them. "Then we stop him."

Chapter Twenty-Seven

———◆———◆———◆———◆———

Before they even arrived on Bahia Honda, Shorty pointed out the boat, a small trawler with a high transom and a swim platform. There were a few other boats in the anchorage, some closer to shore than others.

"He's there," Shorty said. "At least the jon boat is."

Jesse studied the trawler carefully in the gathering dusk. The sun was almost to the horizon, highlighting the old railroad bridge that was once part of the Overseas Railroad.

Bear's boat wasn't very well kept, which was obvious by the messy metal jerry cans and propane tanks he had strapped to the swim platform. There were stains running down the sides of the hull and clutter everywhere on the decks. It had a small salon sticking up from the middle and high aft freeboard and transom, which meant it probably had a cabin there with the engine below the salon.

"It ain't gonna be easy even talkin' to him," Rusty said, looking back over his shoulder. "He's a good three hunnert yards from shore."

Jesse's eyes cut to the hunting rifle Rusty was holding between their knees, then to the marine VHF mounted under the dash. "That's an older boat, right?"

Shorty nodded as he downshifted for the stop sign. "Yeah, probably built in the late fifties. Why?"

"Runs on gas?"

"I think so," he replied, taking a right.

"I saw a couple of propane tanks on the swim platform," Jesse replied. "Some jerry cans, too. Could be gas."

Shorty looked over at him, then at the rifle. "Oh, no. I told you we aren't going to kill him."

"Stop there!" Jesse shouted, pointing to a phone booth.

Shorty pulled over. "We can't call him."

"Sure we can," Jesse said, turning the VHF back up. "But first, we call the cops and report a boat on fire. When they're on the way, we get him on the radio and tell him he has ten seconds to jump overboard."

"He'll be listening on channel 68," Rusty said. "That's how he sells his pot."

"I'm not gonna ask how you know that, son."

"And I won't ask how you know Skylar Rizzi," Rusty replied.

"Make the call," Shorty said, then switched the channel on the radio.

Jesse opened the door and got out, Rusty climbing out behind him.

"Get back in the truck, bro," he said, then pointed to where the high bridge span met the island. "You're gonna need a head start to get up there. Pop'll drive ya over and I'll come runnin' as soon as I call the cops."

"Get in, Jesse," Shorty ordered.

He did, and Shorty took off. "You sure you can hit a propane tank at that distance, if need be?"

"Yes, sir," Jesse replied.

"Open the glove box. There's a handheld radio in there. Take it up there with you, but just listen."

"Up where?"

Shorty pointed ahead. "The railroad trestle."

Jesse opened the glove box and took out what looked like a brick with an antenna as Shorty pulled to a stop.

"Start on sixty-seven," Shorty said, switching the radio under the dash again. "Once you're in position, let me know, then we'll switch to sixty-eight."

Jesse nodded and got out with the rifle in one hand and the radio in the other. He sprinted to the massive, man-made hill that kept the old railroad bed elevated as high as the bridges.

It was steep, and he took his time, so he wouldn't get winded. Once he reached the top, he looked out over the anchorage. Then he moved out to the edge of the old bridge.

When he found a spot, he sat down, noting that the sun was almost at the horizon. He turned on the radio, put it on the right channel, and pressed the button. "I'm in position."

"Go up one," Shorty replied. "Don't say anything."

Jesse changed the channel, then laid the radio beside him as he checked over the rifle. He removed the magazine, noting the .30-30 Winchester cartridges, and reinserted it. Then, he moved the bolt up and slid it back slightly. There was a round in the chamber. The safety was on and in easy reach of his thumb.

He would have preferred an M-16—it'd be more accurate at that range, or a more high-powered rifle, like a .30-06. But he was at least familiar with the .30-30. Billy had one.

Shorty's voice came over the radio speaker, partially distorted by static. "Bear, do you copy?"

Jesse double-checked the radio. It was on the right channel. He looked down to where Shorty was parked a few hundred yards away and could see him through the open driver's side window.

"Bear, do you copy?"

"Who's this?" a man answered, his voice loud and clear.

"Switch to low power," Shorty said.

231

There was silence as Jesse viewed the boat over the rifle's sights. He was at a slight angle to the stern, but the nearest tank was an easy shot, if he had to take it. A part of his insides still raged, though that rage had turned somewhat cold.

Can I take a man's life? he wondered.

"Been listening to the local radio?" Shorty asked.

There was silence, but Jesse knew if he'd heard Shorty the first time, he could still hear him. A curtain parted on the starboard side of the boat.

Jesse moved his sights to the window.

Bear is an animal, not a man, he decided. *Yes, I can.*

"What?" Bear asked, his voice slightly distorted.

Jesse looked around the anchorage, triangulating the distances he was from Shorty's truck and Bear's boat, and expanding that to include any other nearby boats.

Only two would be within the same distance and, like Bear's, they were both dark.

"Just heard a news report a minute ago," Shorty said, "the police are looking for you. They have evidence you killed that redhead."

The silence was shorter this time.

"Who is this?"

In the distance, the sound of a siren could be heard, echoing over the water from seven miles away—the other side of the bridge.

"Hear that, Bear? They're coming."

"Who the fuck is this?"

"Look astern," Shorty said. "Up on the high ground, where the bridge joins land."

A curtain in a rear window opened.

Jesse rolled onto one elbow and lifted the rifle high, waving it back and forth. Then he pulled it back down into a firing position.

Though he couldn't see him, he knew Bear's face was in the window.

"Now look down on the beach," Shorty said. "The Chevy."

Jesse turned his head and looked down. Shorty had the door open and was standing beside the truck, waving his pistol, bathed in light from the interior and the setting sun.

Beyond him, Rusty was standing beside a palm tree, also waving his weapon over his head.

"In ten seconds," Shorty said, his tone even, "That man up there with the rifle is going to blow a hole in one of those cans on the back of your boat."

"Who is this?"

"Eight... seven."

Jesse reached over and picked up the radio. "A boat for a Mustang."

"Jump if you want to live," Shorty said. "Five... four..."

Jesse saw movement at the main hatch. Bear stepped out, raised a handgun, and began firing in his direction, the rounds falling uselessly on the rocks below.

The vision of Rachel's battered face appeared in Jesse's mind.

"One," he said, and put the radio down.

He welded the stock against his cheek, aimed at center mass, knowing that if the rifle was sighted for a hundred yards more or less, it wouldn't make any difference at that range.

He breathed in, exhaled, felt the beat of his heart as he took the slack out of the trigger, and when the next beat came, the rifle roared.

Chapter Twenty-Eight

---◆---◆---◆---◆---

Twenty-four hours later...

Jesse stared absently out the window at the scenery going by, thinking back on the past few days and what he might have done differently. He wondered if the time ever did come when he had to, would he really be able to kill?

Across the aisle. Rusty also seemed distracted by what was outside the window on his side.

They'd planned to drive to North Carolina for infantry training, but the Mustang was totally demolished, so that plan was gone.

Jesse turned from his friend and looked out the window again.

If a man ever needed killing, it was Norbert "Bear" Bering. As it turned out, the cops really *did* have evidence in the murder of the red-haired woman. And they'd never asked how the boat had caught fire.

If it came down to it, Jesse *could* claim self-defense—the man *was* firing on him.

Unless there was just one person on the jury who knew anything about guns. A handgun was useless at three hundred yards. Even with the rifle, it wasn't an easy shot.

He could have killed Bear. He wanted to, after what he'd seen of Rachel's injuries and the rumors they'd all heard about how he'd killed the redhead.

Bering deserved to be dead.

Instead, Jesse had moved his sights from Bear's chest to the propane can, and the boat had exploded, knocking the drug dealer into the water.

By the time the police arrived, all the guns had been stashed, the boat was fully engulfed, and Shorty had even pulled some fishing rods from the bed of the truck, to augment their story that they were fishing. The cops had thanked them for calling in the fire, and as they converged on the big biker coming out of the water, Shorty had slowly and quietly driven away.

No, Jesse decided, *I'd do the same thing again if given the same situation.*

"All evil needs to get a foothold," he remembered Mam telling him on several occasions, "is for good people to stand by and do nothing."

Earlier that morning, they'd heard on the news that Bear had been arraigned and charged with two counts of assault and battery, one count of kidnapping, and one count of first-degree murder. Nothing was said about the pot farm on the island or what they were growing in the house.

Shorty had suggested that Rusty and Jesse might spend the rest of their leave somewhere else, so they changed their travel plan.

"I can never get used to flying," Gina said from the seat next to Jesse.

"Same as diving," he offered. "Just equalize the same way."

"It's not that," she said. "It's the fact that we'll be hundreds of miles away in less than an hour."

"It ain't but about two hunnert miles," Rusty said, leaning across Juliet. "The Bahamas are even in the same time zone."

"I know what you mean," Jesse said. "I'd rather travel slower, but Rusty and I only have a week of leave left."

Gina squeezed his hand. "You haven't done enough in the first week?"

"I'm just glad your sister's going to be okay," he said, giving her hand a return squeeze. "I really don't like bullies."

She laughed. "Really? I couldn't tell." She leaned on his shoulder. "I feel safe with you. And you're right, Rach seemed her normal self when they released her this morning. She insisted I go with you, by the way. The doctor said she might not even have a scar, thanks to you and Jim and your first aid."

"That's *Rusty*," Juliet said. "And one day, hopefully a long time from now, Shorty's Bar and Bait Shop will be the Rusty Anchor Bar and Grill."

"I always wanted to be a restaurant owner," Rusty added.

"I like it," Jesse agreed. "It sings."

"Haha," Rusty chuckled. "Like Provo's Privy?"

"Never mind them," Juliet said, leaning closer to Gina. "Probably some macho movie reference. Anyway, we're going to get some of those huge, rusty anchors from pirate boats or something to decorate the yard."

Gina leaned over Jesse and peered out the window. "What's that down there? It looks like a desert."

"The Bahama Banks," Jesse replied. "You're actually looking at the sandy bottom under six to ten feet of water. Lean over a little more and you can see Andros Island, where we'll be staying."

She did, pressing her body close to his to see better. Even through both their clothes, she felt warm against him.

Then she sat back and looked at him. "This whole thing must have been pretty expensive—plane tickets and a week in the Bahamas."

Jesse smiled at her. "It only cost about a quarter of a fish."

They'd booked the flight and a week's stay through friends of

Shorty's, who was a travel agent in Nassau and had a vacation home on Andros.

The man really did know just about everyone.

Shorty had also taken care of the Mustang, the thought of which left Jesse devastated. He'd had to call both Pap and Billy to tell them what had happened. One had wanted to know if Jesse had hit back, and the other reiterated that the Mustang, like all things, could either return to the ground or be resurrected like a Phoenix by someone else.

Gina kissed his cheek. "Well, thanks for asking me. I didn't want to leave Rach, but she was really insistent. Seriously, though. How much is all this costing? I want to pay my fair share,"

Jesse laughed. "Oh you will," he said. "The owner of the house traded our stay for some maintenance work."

Juliet leaned over, looking from Rusty to Jesse. "What kind of maintenance work?"

"He's got an old wooden boat that needs some minor repairs," Jesse replied. "And a wooden fence that needs to be replaced."

Afterword

———◆———◆———◆———◆———

A huge influencer of mine passed away yesterday, September 1, 2023, at the age of 76.

If you're a fan, I'm sure you've caught the occasional references I've made in my stories to Jimmy Buffett's music—even a lyric or two. His music and lifestyle are reflected in not just my writing, but many others as well.

Thank you, Jimmy, for adding the sound track to my life for the past *fifty* years. Sail on, *Incommunicado*....

It isn't often that a man gets to relearn the lessons from his youth, and that's what this story is partly about. Jesse's first car was my first car; his drill instructors and platoon were also mine. As I've said before, I'm Rusty, not Jesse. It was Private Couch with my assistance, who pretended to be Lieutenant Holstein. It was me telling my dad that the car he was about to pass was an unmarked police car. Pap's car was the car I owned when I left the Marine Corps. Reliving those times was a whole lot of fun and I learned a lot about myself.

The lessons Jesse learned from Pap were based on how he grew up during the Depression years and World War II and had taught Jesse's father before him. They were lessons hard-learned and were similar to what my dad taught me about work and life, and how to be a man others could count on.

I wrote this story alongside two others, *Liable Charity* and *Weigh*

Anchor. I worked on it in my spare time, so it didn't interfere with those stories. I found ways to weave the stories together, even though they were set more than forty years apart. It was the summer of 1979 in this story, and Charity Styles won't even be born until the following winter.

If you've been following the *small* details in my stories closely, you might have guessed who the two little blond girls were, who were standing outside the gate at Parris Island, waving American flags as the recruits left.

I enjoyed the challenge of entwining stories that span decades.

In the last weeks of writing this story, July 15, to be exact, I suffered a very debilitating injury. I ruptured the Achilles tendon in my right ankle, which required surgery to repair. I'll be in a boot, using crutches to get around, for a few months. It's not easy for someone used to doing things independently to have to accept help in doing them. Even little things, like carrying a mug of coffee from the kitchen to the game room where I've been working, is completely impossible when you're on crutches.

My wife has been my rock for over two decades, the one person I always knew I could lean on. These last few weeks have shown me just how much. This same injury, just a few thousand years ago, would have meant that the victim was nothing more than meat crawling around on the forest floor, waiting for some predator to come along. Greta helped calm my anxiety before the surgery, catered to my needs since coming home, and she never complained, though we both know that I'm not a good patient. I love her with all that I am.

On any ship, there are a lot of sheets that need trimming, and while I've been down, our daughter Jordan has stepped up. She's in the summer before her senior year of college, working toward a bachelor's degree in business marketing, and I know there are a million and one things she'd rather be doing. She's been managing part of my business for several years, and during my convalescence, she's taken on even more, to the point where I no longer follow up to check her work. She understands that what's "inside the fence" is more important than what is outside, and that knowledge will help carry and sustain her through the rest of her life.

Our kids, grandkids, and now great-grandkid, are the reason I work, and they are now working to support me emotionally, cheer me up, and push me to want to be better.

My core reader group never gets to see this afterword. They get the rough manuscript right after I type *The End*, and this time, even before I went through and reviewed it. I want knee jerk-reactions to the story from them, and many of them have far greater knowledge than me in many areas. They give me those reactions and more, which helps make the story better. On this one, special thanks go to Alan Fader, Dana Vilhen, Debbie Kocol, Douglas Pennock, Glenn Hibbert, Jason Hebert, Katy McKnight, Kim DeWitt, and Mike Ramsey.

Once finished, the manuscript goes to my wonderful editor, friend, and now honorary Tropical Author, Marsha Zinberg, then my final proofreader, Donna Rich, both of whom have far more knowledge of the English language, as it pertains to writing, than anyone I know. And they freely share that knowledge, which only makes their clients better writers.

When this manuscript finally gets to Nick Sullivan's sound studio for the audiobook recording, it's been cleaned and polished almost to perfection. It's only when he puts voice to my characters that a few small flaws are found and corrected before the final manuscript can go to Aurora Publicity for formatting and final cover design. I personally listen to his recording as I read along, to find any mistakes he might have made, and my listening to the life he breathes into my characters helps me to write them better.

As you can see, it's a big ship with lots of specialists doing many tasks. Without all the help from my crew, this ship would have foundered while the captain was laid up. Yet, she sails on, her course true and unimpeded by shoal waters. This is a testament to the strength of numbers. My dad told me that a man didn't need to be smart to succeed, but it helped. He only needed to surround himself with smart people.

And that includes you, my readers. I hope you've enjoyed this story and the glimpse into Jesse's past. I really enjoyed writing it, and am anxious to get started on volume two, *Bad Blood*, which will come out in the spring.

If this is the first book of mine you've read, there's a whole, very long series after it, that starts when Jesse retires from the Marine Corps.

In the meantime, I have two chapters left to write in *Weigh Anchor* before it's finished, and then I'll be on to the twenty-seventh book in the original series, *Swift and Silent*, which will be released this coming winter.

Wayne

Also by Wayne Stinnett

The Jerry Snyder Caribbean Mystery Series

Wayward Sons   Voudoo Child

The Charity Styles Caribbean Thriller Series

Merciless Charity   Vigilant Charity
Ruthless Charity   Lost Charity
Reckless Charity   Elusive Charity
Enduring Charity   Liable Charity

The Jesse McDermitt Caribbean Adventure Series

Fallen Out   Rising Storm   Steady As She Goes
Fallen Palm   Rising Fury   All Ahead Full
Fallen Hunter   Rising Force   Man Overboard
Fallen Pride   Rising Charity   Cast Off
Fallen Mangrove   Rising Water   Fish On!
Fallen King   Rising Spirit
Fallen Honor   Rising Thunder
Fallen Tide   Rising Warrior
Fallen Angel   Rising Moon
Fallen Hero   Rising Tide

The Young Jesse McDermitt Tropical Adventure Series

A Seller's Market

Non Fiction

Blue Collar to No Collar   No Collar to Tank Top

The Gaspar's Revenge Ship's Store is open.

There, you can purchase all kinds of swag
related to my books. You can find it at

WWW.GASPARS-REVENGE.COM

Made in the USA
Columbia, SC
20 November 2023

26838042R00139